The Heart Stone

The Rites of Passage
Book 2

Curtis Sagwete

Printed in the United States of America

Chapter 1

Ido

Smoke blew hazily from Masekela's pipe as he watched his great-grandchildren tend to the livestock in his family's cattle enclosure. He loved the sound of hooves digging at the earth, and the natural smell of the dung. It reminded him of his youth, when it was his and his siblings' duties. They would jest, sing songs, and play fight as they led cattle back to their enclosure as the amber sunset blazed behind them. This was easily the best part of his day. In his old age, he couldn't do much but try to impart his wisdom upon the new generation, like he had done the generation after him—the numerous children he had sired and theirs. "Careful, *Gotwe*," he harkened. The boy was the youngest of his great-grandchildren. It wasn't uncommon for cow herders to be trampled, but the boys had to learn. It was their livelihood, the cradle of their civilization.

Masekela had sparse hair that trailed around his bald head. A long snowy beard ran down well over his chest, a beard so thick one could only see his lips when he spoke, which was often enough, for he was old, and feared he did not have much time left. There was so much Ido history, custom and lore he had yet to impart.

Ido, one of the many constellations of villages that formed the Piripiri Kingdom, used to be a prosperous community. Once upon a time, a tannery that treated hides before distributing them throughout the kingdom and beyond flourished. There was also a textile company that prepared cotton for export, but these operations were now either run down or working at a quarter of their former output.

As a child, his favorite of these establishments was the tannery, where he would visit his uncle to satisfy his appetite for stories about Pyyros. He would listen starry eyed, mouth agape, as the tanners described the royal city and all the heroic deeds of King Nuru, who ruled before A'hi, King Maghedzi's father. He had meant to immigrate to Pyyros. There he could fulfill his passion for the arts amongst the notable artisans of the day. However, when his older brother died at his inauguration ceremony, Masekela had to forsake his dreams and take the Ido seat. *I was never meant to be chief*, he wrestled with himself. *Why did you take on the bull?* He had advised his brother against it, but Mulinzi was a hardheaded one, a peerless hunter, with red-hot blood that ran through his veins.

That often got Mulinzi into precarious situations. One such incident was when he started a minor war with a neighboring village after eloping with the chief's son's wife. Masekela had been too young to fight, but was relieved when the quarrel was solved by the offering of many cows and grazing lands, something Ido still suffered for today, and one could see it by the run-down tannery and textile operations.

"Chief," a voice hollered. Masekela turned his head after the third cry. "It's time, father," notified Dada.

"Send the women and children to their huts."

Dada whistled and went about the chief's instruction. He walked up to his father and tried to help the old man up, but Masekela was defiant. He had been all his life. After all these seasons, Masekela finally realized that he and Mulinzi were more similar than he thought. "I can raise myself up," he defied, using his staff to hoist himself up, his old bones creaking as he erected himself and tried to look chiefly. "Has the child arrived safely?"

Dada, also fair of beard, but full with hair, nodded his head. As heir to the Ido chieftaincy, it seemed as though he had been waiting two lifetimes to take the reins of the humble village.

"And the others?"

"They have now left."

"Good." Masekela strained a smile and refocused his vision toward the dusty pathway. His eyes had now betrayed him, but he could see a menacing blur march toward the village, their long-burnished spears dancing above them as they moved closer. It brought great fear in his heart, but he had made a promise. "That girl will be instrumental against the coming Evil that once reigned over our realm! She has a role to play more important than mine . . . than ours!" *She has to . . . the oracle saw it!* He had put everything on the line, his village and all the people in it, their history, customs and lore. He looked up toward the ancestors and asked for strength. "Grant it to me so what needs to be done, is done!" Even though he was a chief, elevated over his subjects in life, he now saw that he was only a man, with all of man's weakness and frailty. He had made a pledge and meant to keep it. When his time came, he would return to his ancestors as honest as a babe unborn.

"But father, what if the oracles are wrong? The Evil was defeated and sealed in days long past!"

He put a paternal palm on Dada's arm. "Do not be afraid, my son. What have I taught you?"

"That the only thing I should fear is the ancestors."

Masekela rubbed Dada's rugged cheek. "You are a good son. Now do it!"

Dada hesitated ambivalently for some moments before turning, and then ordered the gates to be opened.

Soon afterwards, the visitors marched in. First through was a robust young man with a bow firmly clasped in his palm. He wore a crocodile skin loincloth studded with yellow, red and violet stones. A crocodile skull sat at the base of his stomach and jutted over his crotch. Larger skulls sat over his shoulders, held together by a golden chain, and behind him, a long heavy crocodile skin cape that made him look like a perched ground hornbill anticipating death.

"Atakachi, the king's son, I presume?" greeted Masekela.

He had a cocky smile and fiery asymmetrical eyes, which he set upon Dada like there was something amusing about his face. After a quick smirk, Atakachi turned back to his men and whistled.

A tunnel formed and through it, thundered down a short package of a man, slightly shorter than Atakachi, but more robust—regal and everything kingly with a bright ruby red Heart Stone the size of a fist sat between the crack of his broad chest. His crocodile skin loincloth flapped over his massive thighs. His strides were purposeful, and with each giant step, Masekela's breast thumped. *The Raging Inferno*, he gasped. After all the winters he had seen, Masekela thought he had nothing more to fear, not even death, but here he was, barely able to hold his staff. He remembered his ancestors, his brother and his father, the chief before him, Yamikami, and found resolve—a surge of energy he hadn't experienced since he first scooped Dada from his mother's bosom and over his head declared, "The heir of Ido!"

When the king was a few paces away, Masekela struggled to his knees and rather clumsily, fell onto his face. Maghedzi stood above the old chief, his chest heaving back and forth as his large nostrils took in the dung tinted air and exhaled minor gusts of wind. The red-beaded flame toe-bars on his heavy-soled sandals sent a chill through Masekela's withered chassis. They seemed to be alive, radiating. He could see the fires of the underworld and feel its voracious heat beat upon his furrowed forehead. "What brings you to our humble village, King Maghedzi of the Piripiri Kingdom, our Eternal Flame?" He welcomed, looking up momentarily.

"Get up, old man. There is no need, for that is not what I come seeking."

Masekela rose and then responded, "You must have heard of my wives' cooking!" He soon learnt that the king had no sense of humor by the wrinkling of his nose, but he already knew that.

"Will you come into my hut and eat? You and your fireflies must be famished, having travelled such a long way from the capital." Masekela did not give him time to answer. "Wife," he beckoned with all the force a frail old man could summon. "What are you waiting for? Do you not see what a special occasion this is? Our king has come to visit us! Not since King Agni the Flamebearer has such occurred! As is our way, we shall eat, and then we can commence our business with one another, my king."

Maghedzi looked at Masekela incredibly long, as his jaw, as wide as the savannah with a cleft scooped like Mount Pyyros' crater, rippled. The king too was a man of custom, even to the point of self-sabotage. "As you say, Chief Masekela."

The chief bowed and ushered Maghedzi toward his private chambers. "It is truly a blessing that you have come to visit us."

"Is it?"

"Indeed, my king. Our oracle predicted this occasion generations ago, in my youth, but I feared because of my old age, I would never live to see it."

The king craved the adulation and absolute loyalty of his people—his reign had earned it, expanding the Piripiri kingdom and reclaiming villages his predecessors had lost, however, flattery was something he always endured with slit-eyed suspicion.

It was a modest chamber. Maghedzi liked it, but only the ancestors could have known that. It reminded him of his compartments back at Pyre Fortress, minus the barp of skulls he kept next to his throne. After his feet and hands had been washed, and the food-taster had confirmed there was no poison, his thick fingers dug into the clay bowl with amber and red flames painted over the black exterior. He ate the sorghum pap, amaranth, goat bones and intestines with his customary haste, lapping up the soup like a stray dog. When he was done, he cast aside the bowl and continued gnashing on a bone. "You are an old man, Masekela. You must be well versed in our proverbs."

The chief nodded his head as he jammed a thicket of camphor leaves into his pipe. "A wise man learns until his dying breath. And even in death, a wisdom is discovered."

"My kingdom is vast and for it to flourish trust is the mortar that holds it all together, is it not?"

"Yes, our ancestors teach us that without trust, the bond between the herdsman and the herd is shattered."

"Yes, so you can imagine how I felt when I returned home from a campaign to find some of my possessions gone."

The chief remained silent as he lit the tip of his pipe and exhaled a mushroom-shaped cloud toward the thatched roof. After taking a few more sips of it, he offered it to the king who gruffed, so Masekela took another sip and continued, "It takes two to perform the dance of fidelity—each must play their role."

"That is true, old man, but is there not always a lead, the one that sets the pace, the variation of movement?"

Masekela let that digest and then set his pipe down and shifted closer to the king, until Maghedzi could see the sickly patches on his face and iris' that burnt a mild fire, the true sign of Volcan lineage. "Let me tell you a story, young man. One day, a chief wanted to marry a farmer's daughter. He tells the daughter that if she doesn't marry him, he will evict her father from the farm. She begs for mercy, so the chief gives her one chance to save their farm. He picks up two stones and places them in a bag. 'Reach into the bag and pull out one stone,' he tells her. 'If you pull out the black stone you will agree to marry me. If you pull out the white stone I shall not bother you or your father anymore.' The thing is, Maghedzi, the girl knows that the chief picked up two black stones, so no matter which stone she selects, she will be forced to marry him. What is this girl to do?"

The king just stared at him as the fire flared. He casually threw the bone he had been gnawing on into the fire and then rose. "Will you join me outside, Chief Masekela?" Soon he had his hands around the old man's arm. He hauled him up roughly and dragged the squirming chief outside. Masekela's stomach fell as soon as his sight refocused. "Son," he cried. Dada had a spear by his neck, a long black shiny thing, as did other members of his court. "So, Chief Masekela, now that we have performed the pleasantries, are we going to conclude our business?"

"What do you mean?"

"Are we still playing games? Where is my queen? Where is my daughter, Nia?"

"Your queen? Your daughter? Why, my king, what would they be doing here?"

"Do you know how many cows I paid to gain my queen's hand in marriage?" Even a man residing under a rock knew this one, the story of how Prince Maghedzi offered Chief Lume of the Moto so many cows the chief dishonored his prior agreement with King Kubulani of the Akuwa. "You have been hiding my property and I have come to claim it back!" The chief did not reply. "You still insist on playing games, well I have one. Atakachi!" he bellowed.

The heir to the Piripiri throne put on a blindfold. After that, he pulled out his bow and released an arrow. It missed Dada's shaggy grey hair by inches. "Atakachi is my best archer. He rarely misses. Are you ready to stop playing games, old man? No? Son!" The Coming Flame released another arrow hitting Dada by the thigh. "Again!" This time it creased his side.

The king seemed exhilarated as blood flowed from Dada and into the soil. His head wondered into the vastness of his past, when he was much younger, treading through the northern desert. The same sands he had plucked the Desert Snake from his family's life's blood. He had thought of giving the child the mercy of death, but as he raised his spear ready to strike, something in the boy made him stop, opting instead to scoop him up and raise him amongst his flock. "My son has one more arrow. Where do you think it's going to hit?

"Take me instead," pled Masekela.

"Take me instead," Maghedzi mocked. "Do you know the amount of times I have heard that line, 'take me instead,' but never, 'I made the wrong choices?'"

An assemblage of the king's men returned to the village center. "Father, we have searched the whole village from top to bottom," informed Mukina, the king's second eldest son. Unlike Atakachi, he was tall for his age and his face, not as smug. He wore the same assemble as his brother, but rather than a crocodile skull, a wildebeest skull painted blood red sat over the waistline of his loincloth. "We couldn't find them, but we found this . . ." He presented a scarf.

It felt soft to the king's asperous fingers as he raised it to his face and sniffed it like it contained life-enhancing properties. He finally exhaled like he had been underwater for eternity, before casting it to the side. "They were here." He turned back to Chief Masekela. "Where did they go?"

"I don't know."

Maghedzi lifted his spear and placed it under the chief's chin. It was wider than the others, longer, sharper, and gleamed brighter in the sun. "This is the last time I will ask."

Masekela turned his eyes toward the Raging Inferno and grinned. "They are far away. Far away from you!"

The king let him go. "Where?"

The chief chuckled sardonically, spitting out a tooth as blood sailed down his neck after another of the king's savage backhands. "Many said you were cruel, but purification? You would maim your own daughter with some foolish old custom? Marry a woman that does not love you? Against her own will? You are not MY king, Maghedzi!"

Shortly after, Masekela fell to the floor as Maghedzi slipped his spear out of his chest. "The scent of her is still fresh," shouted the king as he wiped his spear clean with the scarf. "Find them!"

Atakachi put a fist on his chest, nodded his head and darted off with a handful of men and dogs.

"Capture all the unmarried women, so they may be purified. Set the boys to the excavation site on Mount Pyyros, and then, burn this whole village down!"

"But father," stuttered Mukina.

"You heard what I said, boy. Leave no hut un-charred!" Maghedzi walked out through the village gates as the screams of men, women and children gave him great satisfaction. He turned and cross-armed, relished, as one by one, roof after another caught aflame, and in no time, Ido was engulfed in a cloud of smoke.

Chapter 2

The Snake Pit

The scent of fish and the crunch of the ocean colliding with the rocky shore tickled the Desert Snake's senses as he waded through the Snake Pit thoroughfare, hopping from one stall to the next in search of Queen Zandile and Princess Nia of the Piripiri Kingdom.

"Bring them back to me," King Maghedzi had commanded, in the dimness of his chambers as he fiddled with a skull.

The Desert Snake was an obedient son, so he set off the morning after on a journey that had taken him across kingdoms. Now he was at the Snake Pit, the capital of the Boaboa Kingdom, travel-worn and growing desperate, wondering if he was pursuing a lost cause.

The Snake Pit markets were bustling with a plethora of merchants, peddlers and purchasers, united in the song of commerce. On his travels he had discovered that fashions in material, design, and color varied from city-to-city, and within them, even from clan-to-clan. Some regions had a preference for muted and somber colors. Other regions preferred bright and saturated dyes, dazzling whites and extravagant pastels. In this wen there was a combination of all, like a melting pot of cultures.

"Heed my wordsss," screamed a sore riddled man, stood atop a looming statue of a coiled serpent, his dirty and threadbare cloths flowing behind him. He spoke with a lisp, as did the majority of the people at the Snake Pit—S' long and where they ought not to be. "The end is near!" His mouth twisted between a course mangle of beard, and spittle splashed over his cracked lips. "Sssoon this civilization will fall, and all who do not repent will be devoured whole, one by one until we are no more! Make right with the Great Ophidian, then we will be free from this oppression, and when the old is cut down, in ssshall come the new!"

Not long after, a group of guards marched toward the soothsayer, pulled him down in the middle of his harsh, truth telling diatribe, and hit their *sjamboks* about him mercilessly as the crowd that had gathered to hear the man speak jeered. As swiftly as they came, the guards took the riddle speaking prophet away. The congregation murmured and hurled stones, rotten fruit, and in a united hymn kyoodled, "Gaya, Gaya, Gaya," on and on, louder and louder every time they belted the name. This carried on until the crowd's cries became murmurs, and then awestruck whispers. When the guards were out of sight, the happenings were now seemingly out of mind, as the thoroughfare returned to the normalcy of bustling and bartering.

The Desert Snake turned to a whistle. "Hey, you," a tout hollered at him, pulling out a tangle of snakes, hissing and coiling. "How about a sssouvenir? For your children?"

He didn't have any, only his sword and flame shaped *mbira*, all of which his adopted father, King Maghedzi had bestowed upon him. He politely declined and moved along to the next stall.

Dead fisheyes looked at him from their display and crabs clawed at each other in their bowls, latching at the desperate crustacean that dared make the impossible climb away from the cook's cauldron. "I am looking for a woman with eyes that burn fire, olive skinned, almost like mine, and with her, a girl, scruffy looking, with shortly cropped hair."

Next was the weapon and utility store. Metal sang as Tuku the Weaponsmith's hammer connected with a half molten blade. He turned it using a tong and repeated the sequence, his veiny forearms lined with sweat. He set his equipment down, wiped his forehead with a towel and replied, "I'm afraid I haven't, but I wouldn't mind buying that sssword of yours." He pointed. "I haven't seen a blade like that in ages. Can cut a man in half with one ssstroke."

Such was the quality of *masimbi* steel, the Desert Snake reflected. "Not for sale." He let his thumb caress his sword hilt, moving along to the pommel, a golden cobra's head with tanzanite eyes that shone like two eerie blue flames.

"I can let you have that one for half itsss price. Your shotel does look lonely."

The Desert Snake continued to admire the fine detail of the products on display before he answered, "I don't do teamwork well."

"And ssshe?"

"Takes good care of me."

"And you?"

The Desert Snake was adamant.

"Swords," Tuku praised with such great reverence. "Sssuch an insatiable appetite they have."

The Desert Snake knew all too well. His shotel had tasted a few. Most warriors gave their weapons names—names like Blood Letter, Flaming Comet, Lion's Tooth, or Snake's Spite. He had heard of blades called Night's Bane, like the night was something to fear—for him, it was his solace. He had heard of blades called Shadowsteel and The Void, Lightening, even Last Rites. The Desert Snake's had none. A sword was not a pet. It was an illiberal instrument, which in the right hands, was deadly.

He took some moments to admire Tuku's work. On one wall hung a spear made of a long wooden sheath imported from the enchanted woodlands of Domboshawa. Next to it was a bow and several shields made from animal hide, pounded wet onto wooden forms, dried and removed. Another shield hung on the northern wall, distinctively in the Tsavo style, a convex, elliptical shield composed of buffalo hide sewn onto a wooden frame. The handle was attached at the center back of the shield and wrapped with snakeskin leather strips.

The Desert Snake thanked him for his time and moved along to the footsmith's stall, but that proved as fruitless as the last. He inquired at several lodges and probed the different inns and eateries, tanners, butchers and utility stores, but no one had seen such a couple.

He sighed as he turned from a torrent of abuse from a group of rogues that were jesting and basking in the warm morning sun with conspicuous smoke blowing from their pipes. One of them fiddled with a harp with luminous snakeskins laved over its soundboard, a color that matched the gang's wrist and leg bands.

"Calm down boysss," ordered a casual but authoritative voice approaching from behind. "The foreign man wants no trouble, isssn't that right . . ."

"Asha," the Northman answered, "But I am mostly known as the Desert Snake." He looked the man up and down, as well as the other two that stood behind him on each side.

They were dressed in warriors' attire and by the air they carried themselves, armed. Their swords, kaskara, were a yard long, straight, double-edged with a spatulate tip. Two wore the instruments horizontally across their backs in belts made from snakeskin-leather with elaborate patterns and geometric designs. The one in the middle, older than the others and evidently, the most arrogant, distinguished himself with a sour countenance, a headdress made of large ostrich plumes and a kaskara worn between his upper arm and thorax. The sword looked formidable as weapon, but he was not called the Desert Snake for nothing. He was beyond peradventure that his sickle-shaped shotel could quell any trouble at a moment's notice. "Whom am I speaking to," inquired the Northman.

"I am Sssheriff Punda," he introduced, displaying a coiled copper amulet. Unlike the majority of the people Asha had come across in the Snake Pit with stretched limbs, long slender necks and torsos, this man was short, and plump. "That means I am the law. These two," he gesticulated toward his adjutants with feathers too, but fewer and less grand. " . . . Are my lieutenants. Lieutenant Kwaza and Lieutenant Tizwa."

They erected themselves and saluted. One was taller than the other, but both had similar dumb faces that begged to be slapped, considerably so. The Desert Snake felt his fingers twitching whenever he got a glimpse of them.

"Well good day sheriff, I am looking for a woman of about seven fists, with eyes that burn fire and her hair, a reddish tint. The girl . . ."

"Look, Asha, or whatever else you call yourself. The people you are looking for aren't here."

"How do you know that?"

"Thisss isss my city. It is my business to know who comes in and who goes."

"Surely, as big as this city is, and all the people, coming in and out, even the most vigilant city guard wouldn't manage to regulate all the movement."

"Are you sssaying I am bad at my job," catechized the sheriff, plucking at his knife-belt.

"I'm not saying anything at all. I'm just looking for some people."

"Then do it quickly and leave. Those boys there, are dangerousss, and we won't be able to help you once they've stopped drinking and get bored."

"Those boys should watch out for me." With those stinging words, the Desert Snake turned and moved to the next stall.

When the sun had descended, and the markets had closed, he thought to unwind and fill his belly at an inn. Perhaps with a stomach full of food he could gain enough energy to plot his next move—think of something that had thus far eluded him.

A man sat at a table adjacent to him, peering his way every chance he could. Finally, after a few refills of his large calabash, the man found enough courage to holler, "You're a man of the north," he called.

"Was," replied the Desert Snake stiffly. He was now of the Piripiri, even though he wore long dark hair and the crisp white kanzu of his ancestors.

"I always wanted to go there, but that's impossible now, after the Great Divide formed. Will you tell me what it was like?"

The Desert Snake went back in time, back when he was just a little viper—the horrors, the lifeless men, children and women with blazing violet eyes overrunning villages, eating the living in their wake. "Look," he finally responded, when he snapped himself out of his trance, "You seem like a nice man. I just want to have my drink quietly, if that's okay with you."

Tears began to form around the man's ducts.

The Desert Snake gasped inside. "Sorry. I have to go now. I forgot I had an appointment. Enjoy the remainder of your evening." He bowed, paid his bill and left the eatery.

His door was barred when he arrived back at his lodgings, so he walked over to the keeper's hut and knocked. "The door to my lodgings won't open."

"No ssspace. Room's full."

The Desert Snake peeked around. It didn't seem that way. "Is it money? You want more?"

"No room," the lodge keeper reiterated and then shut the door in the Desert Snake's face.

He tried the next lodge, but he found no luck there either. It took half an hour in the dark, navigating through the dark stoned circuitous passageways where women of the night lurked and flashed their skirts. He passed starkly grand towers that hid the illicit transactions of contraband, through domestic dwelling and public squares where the destitute huddled around fires, all the way to the other end of the city, only to hear solid thuds as doors shut.

Goose bumps now lined the Northman's forearms. He found himself a patch of frosted grass and laid a thin mat over it. He felt his back dampen and could hear a brusque wet wind swirl through the alleyways. He decided to think about something else, anything to take his mind away from the cold.

He gazed into the heavens. The moon shone full and bright, and the stars twinkled worlds away, far away from his earthly sorrow to a time where the shifting sands of the Great Divide hadn't swallowed animals, people and entire cities. It pained him, all that was lost, and likely to never be seen again, large marauding armies of camel riding, shotel wielding Northmen thundering over the boundless sun-beaten plains, and his father at the front. He gave each star the names of his family members—his father, Moza, Zuri, his mother, Zara and Fe'yi, his sisters. The final star was himself, but much younger with a wide smile, rather than the perpetual scowl he now frayed. Sadness gripped him when he realized the other stars were faceless, one of many victims of time. "Farakaii," he muttered, as he did every night as he struggled to sleep. He would get his vengeance against the Akuwa king, and as the night became day, and winter became the rainy summer with the optimism of new life, he grew impatiently impatient.

His sleep was interrupted in the wee hours of the morning when two men abruptly hoisted him up and set him on his feet. In front of him stood Sheriff Punda. "Asha, you are under arressst."

"For what?"

"Breaking the law."

"What? This is ludicrous. I was just taking a nap. I didn't do anything wrong. I didn't have anywhere to stay for the night."

"Vagrancy, foreigner. I don't know where you are from, but here, it is against the law. That is the foundation of our glorious society. We cannot have people like you changing that, squatting where you like. Scaring honest citizens. My job is to make sure our city remains lawful."

"I haven't caused any trouble."

"Yet."

"Excuse me, but do you have a problem with me, sheriff?"

"Yesss, I do."

"What is it then? Is it the lightness of my skin, or the thinness of my hair? Is it my long-hooked nose? Or is it the clothes that I wear? The cloths of my ancestors?"

"It's all the above, foreigner, but mostly, your eyes. I don't like them. I don't like them one bit. You are trouble. I can sssee it."

The Desert Snake did not resist. He quietly surrendered his sword and allowed them to bind his wrists together and lead him away like livestock. When they got outside the gaol, they stripped him naked and cast a pail of water over him. He could feel his body being hit by an avalanche of eyes as passersby watched. Some women and men produced noises from their throats. Some went further, laying their hands over his bottom, and others, even his manhood. "Sand man," one man pointed, apparently amused by the Northman's hairy legs and heavily coarse midsection. "He's more beast than man, that one!"

"Vampire ssspawn," another yelled, with monkey chants following his words.

"Cast him into a hole!" hissed another.

The Desert Snake covered his manhood with his hands as he was ushered to his cell. Waiting for him was a large man with blade in hand. "Please! Don't," he finally begged, but the man's heart remained obdurate as he grabbed a good batch of his black hair and then only then, Asha wept.

Chapter 3

The Royal Entry

When Prince Themba of the Akuwa Kingdom finally awoke from his slumber, slumped atop his great equine, he looked up, and there it was in the distance, the chain of mountains that cupped the heart of the Piripiri kingdom. In the center the volcanic Mount Pyyros menaced above Pyyros like a winged phantom gliding over a hamlet. "We've finally made it," he smiled, but that soon evaporated when the volcano rumbled and spat out a puff of smoke into the clouds.

"Calm down, Themba," chuckled his uncle, Munyaradzi, who shared a father but different mother with King Farakaii of the Akuwa. As a famed womanizer, Munyaradzi had been selected to aid the young prince in his pursuit of Princess Nia's heart. "Pyyros is welcoming us."

Not long after, a Piripiri contingent of welcomers arrived. Themba quickly clapped his hands alerting Pikoro whom he had made his page. The boy from Shambamuto placed a cheetah skin cape over the prince's shoulders and helped secure his necklace of hippopotamus teeth—jewelry that announced his prowess as a hunter over the entangle of gold and silver that hung over his chest. With that, his retinue broke into dance as drums thundered and gigantic horns and trumpets made out of elephant tusks heralded the prince's arrival with a stormy, heroic tonality. The Pyyros welcoming committee arrived to the showcase as the Akuwa contingent performed acrobatics and showered jacaranda leaves around the prince and in the air until they landed softly on the red Pyyros earth.

Munyaradzi slipped off his equine and greeted the bare-chested Fireflies. Themba had a hard time deciphering their strange dialect, but he still managed to interpret most words. Soon there was a spear under Munyaradzi's chin, prompting the Akuwa to unsheathe theirs. Pikoro fumbled his stick before he mimicked a Hippo Stance, though one could tell, the boy had yet to fully learn a true warrior's grip.

What looked like the leader of the unit pointed his shiny black spear at them. "What is an Akuwa prince doing in the land of the Piripiri unannounced?"

Themba flipped off his equine and struck his spear into the earth, creating a cloud of dust that had the welcome committee coughing and sneezing. When the dust had settled, the prince answered expressively with his hand held tightly by his breast. "I come seeking the hand of Pyyros' most beautiful woman."

"Then you have come a long way for nothing. The last time I checked, Queen Zandile was married to our lord and protector, the Raging Inferno, the Eternal Flame, the Bush Fire, King Maghedzi of the Piripiri Kingdom." His eyebrow rose. "Or do you mean to make our sire cuckold? If that is the case, I assure you, prince . . .?"

"Themba."

"Wars have been fought for less."

The Akuwa prince stayed calm. He had encountered such temerity before, and the saying, 'the spider does not bother a hippopotamus,' resonated to him more than ever, and the guard's roughcast features made it hard for Themba to take him quite as seriously as he might. "Are you going to present yourself?" he demanded with princely condescension.

"My name is Wasike, First Guard of the king."

"Well Wa ... t'ever, spare me the wit. It has been a long and tiresome journey filled with obstacles that were only overcome by love. I seek the hand of the lovely Princess Nia."

"But you have never seen her, have you? What if she were hard to look upon? What makes you so sure she is lovely?" Themba was about to say something, but Wasike had continued. "What makes you think she would marry you?"

"Well . . ." the prince looked around, amused by the question. "What is there not to like and in time, love? I am a prince of the Akuwa Kingdom and I'm sure you can see me. Besides, it is her father I mean to speak to. It's of little consequence if she likes me or not."

"Yes, prince, I see you very well and can hear you loud and clear." Wasike pursed his large and long lips and scrutinized the prince for a few moments, and then commanded his men to let go of Munyaradzi. After the Piripiri men had unburdened the esteemed guests, Wasike announced, "Welcome to Pyyros, Prince Themba."

Chapter 4

The Crime Lord

The Desert Snake shivered as naked as his born day, curled tightly in his gaol's corner. All he had in his confinement was what was left of his hair on the stone floor, an old bucket where he could relieve himself, and a frowzy mat in the corner that was draped in fleas. He sat cross-legged in the middle of the compartment and brooded about King Farakaii, of how he would finally get his vengeance. He thought about his adopted father, Maghedzi, who had scooped him from his family's life's blood and how the king had fed him, clothed him, and taught him the way of the warrior.

The next morning, Sheriff Punda walked in and announced he was free to go. The Northman picked up his now dirty and creased garment and quietly slid into it with little fuss. He was on a mission. All his life he had been a dutiful son, and he also knew how Maghedzi dealt with failure. He meant to find him his wife and daughter and return them to him as bade. "What about my sword," he implored the sheriff.

"What sssword?"

That was my father's. The only thing I have left of him. "It is very dear to me." And *masimbi* steel was hard to come by. To forge it, a special kind of metal only found on the peaks of the most perilous mountains and caves was required. Furthermore, because of the characteristics of the metal, only the most superior mystics had the knowledge and power to forge such volatile and unexplained steel.

In his youth, he had been summoned to King Maghedzi's chamber, and sitting on the king's lap, rather than a newly acquired skull, was the shotel. The bared fangs of the pommel hissed as Maghedzi lifted the sword as the young viper bowed before him. Down the king came with the blade, next to one ear, and then the other. "This was your father's," the king had informed matter-of-factly, laying the instrument into a young Desert Snake's palms. "Learn it well." Hence he did, far surpassing many of the notable blade-bearers of the age.

"Well, what about my gold," Asha demanded. The sheriff's answer was the same, a wide smiled question that left the Northman seething inside, but he was far outnumbered and his shotel had been taken from him. He was loath to return to the confinements of his dark cell, so he left it at that.

He scratched his head as he stood in the midst of the thoroughfare traffic. He needed gold to help complete his mission. He went back to where he first met the sheriff and his goons and approached the group of louts he had encountered when he had first arrived in *the damned vile city*.

"What do you want, foreigner?" spat the leader of the group, a big headed one, so big, the diameter of his head sat parallel to his bare shoulders. The Desert Snake had heard his associates refer to him as M'gazi.

"I'm looking for work," replied Asha.

Similarly to the first time the Northman had met him, M'gazi had his fingers over his harp's numerous strings, but this time, plucking a flurry of big, lush and sustaining notes. He played it skillfully despite looking worse for wear and seemed to be dozing off, but with sudden movement, he quickly sprung up, slowed down the tune to a more sinister, looming melody, and set his pink-tinted eyes upon the Northman, his khat stick jerking in his mouth, up and down, left and right matching the beat he played. His eyes were curious, with a hint of childish humor, like there was something stuck unawares on the Desert Snake's face. "Follow me," he finally responded.

M'gazi led the way, snaking through the city streets as his luscious notes followed behind him like a tail, until they reached the back ends of the Snake Pit with no shiny paved paths, but mud and destitution. Two men stood in front of a tent with weapons in full view and ready to bite. M'gazi twisted his fingers into a sign the Desert Snake assumed was a secret greeting. When the guards were satisfied, after patting them down, they were ushered into the hut.

Inside, lying on a luxurious mat with three women coiled around him eating wild plum and other luxurious fruit was a man. He paid them no mind, giggling as one girl stuck her tongue down his ear, whilst the other fondled about his belly. "How can I help you, M'gazi?" he finally greeted, pulling away from his female companions.

"Thisss isss the man I told you about. The one with the big nose."

"I can see that." The man clapped his hands and on cue, the women got up and crept out of the tent, leaving their sweet vanilla scents lingering in the room. The man got up, put on a gown and poured himself a cup of ale from a shiny bronze jug that sat on a short table. After he had washed it down, he poured another cup and then sat himself on a stool. "Please sssit," he offered courteously. "My name isss . . ."

"I know who you are. You are Kwelo," finished the Desert Snake.

The crime-lord was of medium height with long lean muscular limbs. A gold-laced kanga patched with various shades of snakeskins covered him from his waist downward. He had no jewelry either on his wrists or around his waist—Just a gold necklace of the Great Ophidian hanging over his chest and down to his nave. He looked at the sandman rather amused with eyes one pale brown, and the other an elliptical peru. "Very well, how can I help you?"

"I am looking for work."

"Why? Did you gamble away your money?"

"It was taken from me."

"Hopefully not by one of my men?"

"By your reputation, it probably was."

Kwelo laughed. "What have you heard about me?"

"Nothing really," the Desert Snake shrugged. "Just that you are the man to see if one needs some work."

Kwelo chortled even harder this time. "I like thisss one." The others in the tent joined in the heedful laughter. "There is sssomething about you. You look like you can handle yourself. What's your purpose in the city?"

"I'm looking for a woman and with her, her daughter. The mother is fiery eyed with rose tinted hair. The daughter, scruffy, bony, with a mischievousness about her."

"Why Desert Sssnake, you could be describing a dozen sssuch people in this glorious city," replied Kwelo with a hint of sarcasm.

"Trust me, if you had seen them, you would know."

"Well then, Northman, I haven't." The crime-lord looked at him closer and read him for some moments and then explained, "I'm expecting some ivory from Hippo Valley in a couple of daysss. Hippopotamus ivory to be exact. I need men I can rely upon to retrieve it and then get it to where it's supposed to go—quietly, with little fussss."

"That doesn't sound too complicated."

"You'd be surprised. Hippopotamus ivory is a very sought-after product and illegal in the Akuwa Kingdom. Their king has outlawed its poaching. He even has a militia called the Green Rangers, tasked to protect his 'holy' creaturesss. I hear he thinks when he dies he will reincarnate as a big ol' hippo." He chuckled. "I say, when you are dead you are dead, but who am I to judge? Anyway, hippopotamus ivory is well sought after, and I intend to be rich."

"You look well enough." Despite the grimy area they were in, rare ornaments, pricy furniture and exotic fruit filled Kwelo's tent.

"I say, why have a hundred cows when you can have a thousand?"

"Most men who are content with a hundred cows live long lives. They die on a warm mat surrounded by wives."

"I used to think like you. I always said to myself, once I have a hundred cowsss I will retire from my life of crime, move to the country and tend to my livestock. When I made a hundred cows, I thought, two hundred will suffice. Do you know how many I have now?"

"Three hundred?"

Kwelo sighed. "Two hundred and fifty."

"So, this job will get you three hundred?"

"Five hundred, Desert Sssnake," he laughed. "Then I retire."

"I just need enough to complete my mission."

"You see, we are more sssimilar than you think. I am glad the Great Ophidian led you to me."

"I thought you didn't believe in any of that?"

There was a long silence until Kwelo laughed aloud and then M'gazi and the rest. "Desert Sssnake, I like you. One day I might even love you! You are such a breath of fresh air," he exhaled. "Unlike all these men that work for me, you don't flatter me." The men in the room pulled their heads down in shame. "You shall stay with me tonight. We shall enjoy life's wonders and then you shall help me sssecure that ivory." Kwelo clapped his hands and not long after, his feminine company plus more slid back through the tent slit and onto his welcoming lap.

Chapter 5

Kwa'Jivu

The sun's merciless rays beat down hard as Queen Zandile of the Piripiri Kingdom and her daughter, Nia, staggered toward the ancestral village of the Moto dominion, Kwa'Jivu. Ginger trailed a few paces behind, no longer a pup, but a battle worn terrier as large as a lioness. It was a while since Zandile had visited, but the large conically thatched roof that sat higher than any other in the palace grounds was unmistakable. "Open the gate," she commanded truculently, startling the watchman by her authoritative delivery.

"We do not answer to beggars," he replied with a twig in his mouth.

"Not even to your queen?"

The guard squinted his eyes, which later bulged in surprise. "My queen. I, I, I . . ."

"Just open the gate."

"Yes, of course, Queen Zandile." The barrier parted and mother, daughter and the dog, strode in. The watchman quickly took their baggage and followed behind as they made their way toward the chief's palace center.

It was a grand village of well-fortified walls, which once upon an age housed kings. Now it was one of the many satellite dominions bound to the Piripiri throne by conquest, and in present times, marriage.

Her father, Chief Lume, sat under the coral tree Zandile used to watch her long lost brother Neo climb, where she used to sit, knit and sing songs with her friend, Sekai. When the chief saw the attenuated pair limp toward him, he immediately rose from his chiefly ottoman laced with animal hide and carvings of flames. He smiled and waited for them to arrive. He was a short and stout man, the kind with loose flesh about him. His chest protruded not unlike a woman's, so his teats danced around in agog upon seeing his daughter. "My sweet Zandile," he greeted, helping her up to her feet as the queen bowed and clapped her hands. "You are home." He looked her up and down as his triple chins flopped. Her garments were mangy and threadbare, and her jaws, lean. She wore no jewelry that distinguished her as a queen and her perky lips were dry and lined with cracks.

Her mother, Tarisai, having heard the commotion was next on the scene. Her walk became a jog when she realized her daughter had returned. "You know, the ancestors work in mysterious ways. I was just talking to them about you." She smiled widely, the same smile Zandile once had, and though creases had settled around Tarisai's eyes, they gleamed with the ferocity the queen was renowned for. "Come into my hut, daughter, and we will put something into your stomach." She clapped her hands, alerting one of the chief's youngest wives. "Start the fire and bring me a chicken."

After they had broken fast, Zandile looked somewhat recognizable in a black turban embellished with little red flames. She wore a similarly patterned sleeveless cotton wraparound dress and modest jewelry that covered her arms and legs.

Nia on the other hand was the opposite of her usual self, now in a beautiful dress of green, yellow and red beads Zandile used to wear in her youth, with little amber flames embroidered all around. "Do I have to wear this?" sulked the princess.

Zandile bridged her eyebrows. Their trials and tribulations, the interminable savannah, the searing heat of the day, and the cold chill of the night had eroded anything resembling patience. "You will wear what you are given, and you will say thank you, is that understood?"

"I hate it," Nia expostulated.

Zandile stopped what she was doing, turned and stared down the princess momentarily before her brow began to tremble, ushering in a torrent of tears.

"Mother," Nia whimpered, now ashamed of herself.

Zandile turned away and covered her eyes. During their flight, she had been a rock throughout, but now as it seemed, she had reached her melting point.

The princess sighed, hung her head in shame and crept out of the hut.

There was silence at supper. They ate voraciously and asked for more. When their bellies were satisfied, the questions began. "So, Zandile, what brings you here," queried Tarisai. "Alone, just the two of you with no men? It is a long and dangerous journey from the capital."

Zandile saw no reason to lie so she bluntly declared, "I have left my husband."

Tarisai dropped her knits. "You what?"

The Moto chief uttered the same words when Tarisai related the story. The chief looked graver and graver, greyer and greyer as the story wove along.

Zandile told them about the Sangoma and how his pernicious effect had bound the king to his will. She told them about the purification they had planned for Nia and how she killed the guard Masuku as they escaped. That night had replayed over and over again in her sleep—his salacious grin, vile hog grunts and his course undergrowth. She was often awoken by the strange sound he had made after she had put a knife through his neck, and often found herself peeling skin off her fingers as she scrubbed her hands manically with a stone.

"This is bad. This is really bad," Chief Lume finally ceded when she revealed what had happened to Ido.

"Father, I would have never come here if I had a choice. Lelakabe, Ilangabi and Ashu all turned me down. The Huni chief said he was willing to help me if I let him . . ." She didn't want to say it in front of Nia, but recent history had made her no longer a child. " . . . Lie with him, for just one night he said. He even offered to maim his little finger. Such, he admitted, was his desire for me. We have suffered getting here. When we figured that all the lords of the Piripiri Kingdom were craven, we sought refuge at the Snake Pit, the capital city of the Boaboa Kingdom." The king had offered marriage as a condition, but Zandile's pride wouldn't allow her to become the king's twentieth wife—a few notches above a concubine, so she decided it was time to return home, to Kwa'Jivu.

"Of course, they refused to take you," trembled the chief finally. "Do you know what King Maghedzi would do if he knew they were hosting you? Of course you do, you saw what happened to Ido." He shook his head and contemplated for a while, scratching his greyish black beard, a course batch of hair that tickled his breasts. He was well respected by his people and beyond as a wise and just ruler who did not try to obtain the wives of his subjects by force or finagle, or by relying on his immunity as chief. He was renowned as a ruler who had overseen one of the Moto tribe's most prosperous eras. He was recognized as a ruler who always gave clear and decisive judgments, when cases were brought before him, however, tonight, he was dumbfounded. "You have to return! Immediately! Maghedzi paid an unprecedented number of cows to marry you. He will come here and burn our village down." Chief Lume was by Maghedzi's side, in times long past, when he smote the village of Molora. He could still remember the screams, the smoke, the smell of burnt flesh, and the heads of the leadership displayed on pikes outside the charred remnants of the village.

"Never," Zandile replied incontrovertibly. "I would rather die than return to him."

"If it is death you are looking for, then you have done well, my dear daughter." He looked at Nia who had been silent throughout and shook his head in sympathy for the girl, and for Chief

Masekela, who had travelled all the way from Ido in the long ago, to celebrate the birth of his first-born son, Neo. "Leave."

Zandile and Nia rose, performed the customary courtesies, and crawled out of the hut opening.

"What should we do," asked Lume, when he and his wife were alone as the night's fire sent sweet, scented smoke into the thatched roof.

"We are stuck between a pride of lions and a pack of hyenas. You are the chief. It is up to you, but I implore you to remember that she is our daughter. Who knows what Maghedzi would do if she returned to him. I don't know if I could forgive myself . . . not after Neo."

Neo had been the pride of his clan. The future of the Moto people, whom oracles had prophesied upon his birth, would grow to be the greatest son the Moto had ever produced. He had disappeared on a hunting expedition many seasons prior. Tarisai could often be found on the village perimeter, peering into the wild, willing, hoping to see her beloved son appear in the distance.

"But he is my king." Kwa'Jivu and the surrounding villages bound to the Moto clan had been autonomous before King Gai'tan the Fire Breather took King Iri of the Moto's mystical spear, Flame, for his own in the age of old. The spear had been in the Moto household for countless generations but was now a legend only spoken of hunched over campfires. Chief Lume shook his head. "Leave me be, wife. I must ask the ancestors for the way."

Zandile and Nia woke up in the queen's old room. She had spent the best part of her juvenescence in this chamber with Sekai and the memories of her childhood gave her some solace, back when they were just girls, playing and dreaming about their futures, Sekai dreaming about Neo, and she, about Prince Farakaii of the Akuwa Kingdom, the heir to the Stone Houses of Hippo Valley.

After breakfast, they were ushered to the chief's chambers. "My daughter, I haven't slept a wink. I have been praying all night.

Zandile felt she had been praying all her life. The ancestors often enough granted her wishes, but always at a cost. "And what did the ancestors say, father?"

Chapter 6

The Ivory Trail

The Desert Snake, Kwelo, and his group of thugs set out the next morning before dawn. They passed through the hilly somber-grey dry season landscape, with misty blue hilltops rising here and there and beyond like pale blue smoke. They marched down a hill's spiraled stoned pathway, always wary of snakes that were abound in the Boaboa Kingdom, until a slit appeared which they entered, emerging out of the passageway with savannah before them once again. Just before sunset, they arrived at a compound next to a copse. An old woman sat outside one of the several huts that made up the complex, seemingly speaking to no one in particular, but when she discerned her approaching visitors, defying her age, she lifted the python that rested on her shoulders, set it down, and then began to skip merrily.

Kwelo beamed from ear to ear as he rushed toward her. "Grandmother, look at you. You haven't aged one bit since I last saw you. How is thisss possible? Have you found the fountain of youth? Please tell me you have, grandmother, then we will be rich!"

"Now, now my sssweet Kwelo. You already are!" She felt his arms and shoulders and looked him up and down with her pale brown eyes. "You are not eating enough pap. Come in. Bring your friends."

When supper was ready, before they could sink their fingers into the food, Kwelo's grandmother, Penina, held her hands out. The Desert Snake wearily met her little fingers, dry and hard, with the crinkle of age. When the human chain that consisted of

M'gazi, the local hoodlum and his cohorts, Radebe, Nkrumah, Mongezi, Jabo, Sisilu and Kiri, the old woman began. "Oh Great Ophidian! Protect usss in the coming seasons and forevermore. Blessss this food that my grandson has provided. Provide him with power. I pray for wealth and influence over all those that oppress usss. Curse them all. Curse those that killed my husband and my son. I pray for revenge. Control usss, oh Great Ophidian, and use us in the way you want. Let us be your instrument, forevermore!" Without hesitation, fingers were in the bowls. "So, Kwelo. Why have you come to visit your grandmother?"

He answered after he stopped chewing. "I am expecting some friends here, any time sssoon. They have a package for me."

Penina shook her head. "Another one of your packages? This one," she pointed, as she looked at the Desert Snake. "He is just like his father, my sssweet boy. That is how he died. All these deals he makesss, with strange bad men."

In Kwelo's company was the Desert Snake, a man oft regarded amongst his Pyyrisian peers as soulless. Also, in Kwelo's company was a man with one eye and another with a short shank fashioned onto his amputated hand. One man wore a mask hiding a nose-less face and another had the side of his head burnt off, leaving a gash where the ear used to be. Resting on the curved hut walls lay an array of weapons, ranging from short and long swords, spears, bows, clubs and other exotic tools of violence. Though many of the swords were sheathed, Kwelo's were not, as he considered his enemies' bodies the only appropriate scabbard.

"Your father left you with a nice compound," Penina continued, "And many cowsss, did he not? Yet you pursue this line of business." She turned toward the Desert Snake. "When we lived in the Sssnake Pit, his father's compound was in a nice quiet neighborhood, but he always used to run off to the bad parts and play with bad kids, stealing, fighting and bothering girls. That is why I sold that home and built this compound here in the middle of nowhere, to get him away from all of that nonsense. I would be a rich woman if I collected a snake-fang each time I had to look for him and bring him home by the ear."

As a petty crime graduate, Kwelo began by stealing fruit and vegetables from peddlers when he was little enough to squeeze through cracks, crawl through windows and hide in baskets. He had the uncanny ability of looking so innocent when caught that most times, his victims would let him go with a small scold, or none at all. When he was older, he and his friends began robbing foreigners, merchants and anyone who caught their lustful eyes on the busy Snake Pit streets, all in the name of acquiring fanciful loincloths, or the latest footwear to impress each other and the girls they were now suddenly attracted to. At around three fists of age, he was recruited into a gang, stealing, transporting and selling contraband. By five fists, he owned a gang.

Penina shook her head. "When will you return home? I get lonely here. I need help with the hut work, the crops and the livessstock."

"I always send someone to help with the maintenance here, but she always sends them back," Kwelo reassured the listening crowd, in case they thought he was a neglectful grandchild.

"They are never good enough. They destroy my pottery and crops. They ssssteal!"

"No, they do not. You are just paranoid. You probably misplaced those things yourself. My workers would never steal from me. Of that I am sure. Besssides, no one is good enough for you grandmother."

"Only you. That is why you should return. You need to stop that life of yoursss and settle down with some wives and children. You are only going to get you and your men killed."

"Thisss is my last job, grandmother."

"That is what you said the last time you came to visit. Or should I say, do your strange business dealsss." She got up, took one of his ears and squeezed hard.

Kwelo squirmed as laughter filled the room. Even the typically silent Desert Snake couldn't help but be amused as he did when he was a child, before his family was slaughtered in the desert.

When she finally let go, she shuffled to the pot and scooped out another portion of vegetables. She slammed them into Kwelo's plate, then the Desert Snake's and sat herself down.

"Who is your friend, might I asssk? I know the others, but this one I do not."

"This is Asha. He isss . . ."

"A Northman. Yesss. Like your grandfather. I met your grandfather when I was travelling. He was so smitten by my beauty he chose to leave his home and move to the Snake Pit with me." She shook her head. "We should have never done that. He would still be alive." Tears began to form.

"Now, now, now, grandmother," Kwelo interceded. Before he could continue his sentence, there was a knock on the door. Kwelo grabbed his weapon, as did the Desert Snake and the others in the hut, including Penina, who held her large wooden spoon she used to whip sorghum tightly. Kwelo put a finger on his lips instructing the room to fall silent, then crept up to the door, peeking before he opened it.

A thick golden moustache curling upwards at the ends like wildebeest horns shone in the darkness, as did the golden cow-tails he wore around his arms and legs. They matched his tanned vest and rare quagga skin loincloth, an outfit that did well to camouflage him during the long days he spent in the bush searching for his prey. "Isiqu, you bastard," greeted Kwelo, as his mismatched eyes lit up. "I didn't believe you had what it took, but here you are! With the merchandise, I presssume?"

"Come and see for yourself," answered the poacher extraordinaire, his lion claw necklace gleaming in the night, as did the rhino horns that stuck from each side of his head dress. "I have white rhino horns, black rhino horns, elephant tusks, hippo tusks, warthog tusks, and listen to this . . . grootslang tusks and even dragon horns."

"Enough with the manure, Isiqu, you do not have dragon horns, or grootslang tusksss for that matter."

"Not presently, true, but I can find them." His gold tooth gleamed as he smiled.

"Good luck with that. Finding them, if they still exist, is like finding an honest man in the Sssnake Pit."

"I found you, didn't I, Kwelo?"

That made the crime-lord chuckle before he jammed some fingers into his mouth and produced a whistle, beckoning his crew. Several beasts of burden waited outside with large baskets on top of them. Some dragged the heavy baskets atop wooden planks. With the help of one of the other men, Isiqu had a basket down. He reached into it and pulled out a tusk. He caressed it like one does a lover and then handed it to Kwelo. After a good rub of the product, Kwelo's eyes widened, as did his smile. "How did you manage all these hippo tusks with all these Green Rangersss abound?"

"If I told you, what use would you have of me?"

"Yesss, you are right, poacher. I would probably have to kill you."

Isiqu afforded himself a slight chuckle before he rubbed his hands together. "And the gold?"

Kwelo whistled. M'gazi and Radebe ran behind the hut, into the shed amongst some livestock and returned with baskets full of the yellow stuff. It landed by Isiqu's foot with a solid thud. "It's all there. Measure it if you want."

Isiqu knelt and brought his torch over the gold. He brushed a finger over it, rose and declared, "It's not enough."

"It is as your agent and I agreed."

"We brought you more ivory than we had agreed, enough to fill every shelf in every shop in your city with pendants, sword hilts and statues. You can keep it if you like, otherwise, there are always other buyers."

Kwelo walked a few paces to his grandmother and whispered into her ear. He lent his and nodded as she whispered. When she was done, Kwelo whistled again and bade M'gazi and Radebe to bring the remainder of the gold. When they returned, Isiqu was satisfied. "You know Isiqu, one day you are going to get trampled by one of these hipposss, or impaled by a rhino."

"Until that day, as long as there is demand, then someone will supply."

"Will you stay for supper, now that our businessss is concluded?"

"Of course! You can't stop talking about your grandmother's cooking and I'd sooner have your mouth shut!"

The Desert Snake felt a sense of triumph, as banterous laughter faded into his background. The day's business wasn't quite the revenge he longed for, but stealing the Akuwa king's precious ivory was a good start. As he relished in his small victory, and followed Kwelo toward Penina's kitchen, an arrow flew past him and into Nkrumah's shoulder. His face was already ghastly from the horrible burns on the side of his head, but his agony made him infinitely more grotesque.

Kwelo's eyes broadened with panic. "You were followed? Great Ophidian," he cursed, as now, one of his men was face flat on the ground. He performed a short prayer and produced his twin golden swords. "I told you there might be trouble, Desert Snssake!"

Chapter 7

Yananayii's Desire

The women of Boroa, one of Pyyros' several districts, loved to hate Yananayii Kukongola. Those that didn't, flocked to her side, perhaps so they could somewhat bathe in the glory of her sprawling shade. She looked like a woman, but still glowed with the frolic exuberance of youth. Her walk exuded confidence and much more, something onlookers attributed to her flawless bone structure and smooth unblemished skin. Her wooly thick jet-black hair bounced about her shoulders as idle grandmothers swore they once had hips and breasts just like hers.

It wasn't always so. As a young girl her face was riddled with spots, she was way too skinny, and her teeth always seemed too many for her mouth. Now she was the cynosure of the thoroughfare, unable to walk Boroa without turning heads. She seemed to have everything she wanted, but alas her greatest desire had so far eluded her.

She and a group of other girls were coming back from fetching water when Khamukelo, a girl who lived next to the compound she shared with her father, came running toward them. "It's done," she screamed, as her fist punched the air triumphantly. "My father has accepted Kambarange's proposal!"

"Gyiku'o!" the girls cried with one voice, invoking their oldest and most powerful ancestor. "Praise be to him!"

"I never thought this day would happen," Khamukelo confessed, beaming from ear to ear.

In Yananayii's estimation, Khamukelo's forehead was way too wide and her teeth too crooked to win such a betrothal. Kambarange was a well-admired young prospect in the district, earning a name for himself in the stick fighting circuits. He also came from a notable house. "Prayer is the key," she chimed. "The ancestors do listen."

The other girls cheered, tapping their mouths as high-pitched ovations bedecked the clear blue sun-drenched sky.

Flattered by the applause, Khamukelo curtsied in appreciation and then excused herself. "I have to go and prepare for the ceremony."

"We will be praying for your success."

When Khamukelo was gone, the girls turned to Yananayii. "What about you," inquired Batsirai, the youngest of the bunch, and also the most garrulous. "When are you going to be married? We need that to happen so that the boys can look at us for a change."

"That is all they do," replied Yananayii matter-of-factly, but inside she was sighing. "They just look, but only from afar. No boy dares ever approach me."

Over the seasons, Yananayii had seen several of her friends and relatives marry, many even younger than she was. Some who shared her age now had several children, and here she was, still living at home with her father. She tried her best to be happy for Khamukelo, but she couldn't help but have the crunching feel of jealousy swell in her belly. Why were her peers' wishes being granted and not hers, she oft prayed to Oya'un, Gyiku'o's principle wife.

"*Baba,*" she began, later that evening, as she served her father supper, a combination of amaranth, horned cucumber and chicken she had boiled with a variation of herbs and spices. "I am not getting any younger. I long to be married."

Matibiri, who was a prominent landowner and merchant, dropped the bone he was gnawing. He stuttered for a few moments, and then cried, "My only daughter! What are you saying? You are my gem. There is no man in the district that is worthy of your beauty."

Yananayii had anticipated her father's reaction, so had equipped herself with an old adage. "Do the elders not say that there is no man good enough for any man's daughter?"

Matibiri pondered for some moments as he stroked his luscious beard, recalling his now deceased father-in-law's face the day he approached him for Yananayii's mother's hand in marriage. "That is true," he finally yielded. "I shall grant you your desire. We begin our search at once. However," Matibiri informed, "This marriage of yours can only happen after the purification ceremony during the Water Plea in a full moon's time. As our king has decreed, all women that are purified shall require a higher fee." He rubbed his palms with glee as Yananayii leapt into the air with her arms spread out wide.

It is actually going to happen. I am finally going to be married. "Thank you, father, I love you, so very much!"

"Don't thank me yet. The man we choose must be very rich, and very handsome."

She smiled. "I wouldn't have it any other way."

With haste, word had got around the district that Matibiri Kukongola's daughter was looking to marry—and also, the conditions her father, Matibiri had imposed. In spite of this, some of the men in the village still thought they might have a chance. Therefore, some of them would call on the Kukongola compound bearing gifts. One of them was so unsuitable that Matibiri, with a cane propped at his elbow, chastised, "You fool! You think I would allow an old and unsuccessful man with no titles to marry my precious daughter? The most beautiful girl in all the district? Get out of my face!" So when people heard about this episode, the suitors stopped trickling in, afraid of getting a similar tongue-lashing.

A full moon had passed, and they still hadn't found a suitable husband for Yananayii. The poor girl had even fallen to bouts of sadness, some which lasted well into the hour of the owl and disrupted her appetite. "What shall we do, father?" She was weary, resigned to the life of a spinster, laughed at by her neighbors and branded a witch only good for spells. The process had proved harder than they had anticipated. Sure, there were prominent men in the district with cows to spare, but handsome and rich? This was going to be tricky.

Matibiri looked down at his daughter. She looked just as her mother did the first time he laid his eyes upon her as she carried a pot of water on her head with effortless grace. A tear broke down his eye. He missed her so much. "Do not worry, my sweet princess. We will find you a husband. The Water Plea is soon upon us. All the district's most eligible bachelors will be in attendance. On that day you are going to be perfect!"

Chapter 8

A Prince's Claim

A couple of moon cycles had come and gone and Prince Themba of the Akuwa was still at pains to control his ineffable yearning for his future bride, Princess Nia. He had been patient, but that was becoming as scarce as the rains. He had entertained himself through regular visits to the Pyyros taverns, gambling and hunting. When he wasn't, his mind was plagued by paradisal visions of his household, his wives and daughters whipping sorghum, presenting food and beer as his dozens of sons sat leisurely, hanging onto his every word as he bestowed wisdom upon them.

Themba and his entourage had been given their own compound. His compartments, he had to admit, was a sumptuous room with an extravagant décor of splashed dark browns, shiny maroons and sparkly silvers. Plush drapes shielded the room from unwanted light, and exotic animals embellished the walls. The floors, ceilings, beams and rafters were gilt with gold, as were the chairs, tables and benches. The torch holders and branches were made of ivory inlaid with gold, and hung from the ceiling by silver chains. Despite the princely extravagance, Themba was not satisfied. "It's not spacious enough," he caviled. Sometimes he liked to practice in the privacy of his quarters. Comrade Chengetaii's brutal training regime had seen him master the first form of the Hippo Stance; however, there was a plethora of other techniques he meant to learn that would help him become the greatest warrior of them all.

One afternoon as he soaked in the morning sun after a chilly night, eating breakfast made up of Pyyros' choicest dried game and sour milk, he turned to that look of distaste he had become accustomed to. "The king summons you," grunted Wasike.

Finally, the prince boasted. *I knew this fire king would come to his senses!* "Tell him we will be there as soon as we finish our meal."

Wasike walked up to the table, grabbed Themba's plate and turned it upside down.

Not long after, Themba was bowing before the king who was clad in his customary greyish-green crocodile skin loincloth fidgeting with the eerie Heart Stone that hang over his chest, seemingly in his own world, far away from the dignified throng that had convened. Though Maghedzi had heavy shadows under his eyes, and deep wrinkles that dug into his forehead, his chest was tight and stomach, flat. The prince exuded an air of confidence, but in reality, he felt like he was walking into an abattoir. The grim shades of the room, skulls and statues that lurked in the chamber's shadows didn't help. Nor did the king's cold domineering stare.

"Who comes into our vicinity?" The king preferred to talk at the skull, rather than the prince. It couldn't have been more than a few moon cycles old, with sparse hair around the melted patches of skin, and under the agape mouth, the remnants of a once snowy glorious beard. To his left sat his youngest son, Alinafe, who had obviously taken more of his mother's features, and to his right, his second oldest, Mukina, who was every bit his father, freakishly wide-jawed and pale.

The elegant chief-treasurer, Mutasa, charged with the mission's brinkmanship, rose to his feet. He was easily the finest dressed man in the room, with arms covered in gold, and a body wrapped in the finest animal hides. "That young man there," he pointed, "is Prince Themba, son of the great conqueror, the

Mighty Hippo, King Farakaii, Lord and Commander of the Akuwa Kingdom. He comes bearing gifts."

The entrance to the audience chamber parted and in came Akuwa men carrying sacks and baskets and set them in front of the king. Inside were an assortment of goods, buckets of shea butter, salt, and faggots of dried meat seasoned the Akuwa way. Lastly a large wooden box was carried in and set before the king.

"*Mambo*," continued Mutasa, we have heard about your admiration of the crocodile. Behold!"

The hinges of the box were unfastened revealing what seemed like a baby croc. However, this reptile's legs lay under its body, rather than on its side. Like the king before it, the creature was built for war, with an armored snout for ramming, and three sets of dagger-shaped fangs for slicing that resembled a boar's.

"This is a very rare species," continued the treasurer. "One of the last of its kind. In Hippo Valley we call this boar-croc, ngiri'mamba. It represents protection and is seen by our people as a spiritual being who wards off evil." The hatchling snapped at the crowd, sending the congregation into a wild frenzy, which only ended once a cloth was placed over its confinement. If the king was pleased, no one could have known. "*Mambo* and distinguished men of great title, of all the kingdoms the Creator presides over, there are none more glorious than the Kingdom of the Piripiri and Akuwa. However, Eternal Flame, our glory has been tarnished by the conflict between our tribes that was created not by our doing, but our ancestors. In Hippo Valley, we have a saying, when two hippopotamuses fight, it is the grass that suffers."

Prince Machupa, the king's brother, cut in, "Here, in Pyyros, we say when two elephants are at peace, the trees suffer."

"Only if the elephants are greedy," Mutasa intercepted. "And our ancestors, as I am sure yours, have warned of the perils of gluttony. The Mighty Hippo means to extend his hand in solidarity so that we may prosper in light of the coming dry oracles have unanimously predicted. That is why he has sent his son, Prince Themba, to form an alliance between the Piripiri and the Akuwa and what better way is there than by marriage?"

There was silence in the room for a while, whilst the king's nose became smaller, larger, smaller again and tighter. "Is it you, a glorified messenger that means to bed my daughter, or is it this Themba? Do Akuwa princes not have tongues?" His voice was raw and oppressive.

Themba rose confidently, brushed his smooth cheetah skins he had hunted himself and accosted, "Yes, your majesty. I intend to marry your sweet, sweet daughter."

"He talks!" Laughter filled the room. Maghedzi waited for the noise to subside. "I thought you were just a pretty face, but as it seems, you are more than that . . . barely." The king paused and then continued. "You have an older brother do you not? Unmarried?"

"Erm, yes, no. We are twins," Themba replied tentatively.

"Twins?" The king looked disgusted. In some tribes' beliefs and customs, twins were considered a bad omen, supernatural beings that could bring devastation to entire communities. As a consequence, many had been given to the Forest of Abominations or used by dark magic practitioners for abominable ends. "But twins come out one at a time, do they not?"

"Your majesty, Simba and I came into the world hand in hand."

"Prince Themba, of Akuwa . . ." The king uttered the last word with scorn. "Whose head popped out of . . . what is that queen's name," he asked whomever cared to answer the question.

"Queen Sibongile," Prince Machupa answered, before shaking his calabash and taking a swipe of his *whawha*.

"Yes, young man, who popped out of Queen Sibongile's womb first?"

Themba looked down and muttered. "Simba."

"Speak up young man."

"Simba," Themba shouted in a sudden stentorian manner.

"That's more like it." Maghedzi studied the prince in silence as his eyes twitched and blinked frantically. After a few moments, he waved Themba away.

"But . . ."

Chief-Treasurer Mutasa held him by the shoulder. "Let's go, Themba."

"But, he just waved us away. He won't even listen to my offer."

"Exercise patience young prince," the treasurer cajoled. "Without it one cannot make beer, is that not so? This is not the end. This is just the beginning."

Chapter 9

Slaver's Cove

Kwelo was waiting inside his tent when the Desert Snake arrived back at the crime-lord's headquarters. "Here's your reward for your services." He tossed a heavy bag at the Northman. "You don't have to weigh it. Asssk around. I am a man of my word. That is how I became rich."

The Desert Snake opened the bag anyway and felt its contents.

"I like what you did out there," continued the crime-lord. "We would have all been dead if it wasn't for your aid."

Thanks to the Desert Snake's intervention, Kwelo and his men had managed to keep the hippopotamus ivory and gold after they had been ambushed at Kwelo's grandmother's compound. The crime-lord said nothing on their journey back to the Snake Pit. Someone had betrayed him. How else would the Green Rangers have known when and where to find them with the ivory and gold? Now Radebe, Sisulu and Jabo were dead, and trusty men were hard to find at the Snake Pit. There would be an inquest and Asha meant to be far away from the crime-lord's ensuing wrath, hopefully with Queen Zandile and Princess Nia secured.

"I have another job for you if you like. Less dangerousss, but you'll get well compensated."

"Thank you, Kwelo, but no thank you. I have to resume my mission."

"Very well. Good luck to you, Desert Sssnake. I mean it." Kwelo gave him a steady handshake and a wink. "If you ever need more work, you know where my tent is."

Now that he had managed to earn some well-needed gold, after exchanging some of it into the local currency, snake-fangs, Asha found a kind lodge keeper to take him in for the night lest he be arrested again for vagrancy. To his luck, the innkeeper had seen a pair in the western side of the city that fit Queen Zandile and Princess Nia's description. With a new sense of optimism, the next day he set out.

Just when he was about to give up, a rose tint haired woman appeared in the crowd. "Zandile," he yelled. "Nia!" There was too much noise.

One man was shouting out different prices of his products, amaranth, jute-mallow and nightshade. The second boasted of the best catch his fishing line had ever plucked, whilst another bellowed the best prices in the city for his snakeskin-leather products—vests, belts, loincloths, sandals, slippers and other apparel.

The last shouted prices for the slaves he had lined up on a wooden display. "Healthy young adult male for sssale," the slaver shouted. "Adult woman with proven fertility."

Asha shook his head and pushed through the crowd until he had a hand on the woman's shoulder. "Zandile!"

The woman turned and smiled. "Do we know each other?"

Asha looked down at the girl beside the woman and froze. He felt like he knew them . . . the shape of their noses and the kindness of their eyes. "Sorry, I thought you were someone else." He turned around and walked back to the slave market.

"Good afternoon," welcomed the slaver courteously.

The Desert Snake didn't reply. He looked at the slaves on display, with metal chains tied around their necks, wrists and ankles. "Who are these people?"

"This ssstrapping young lad was taken from the savage tribes of the eastern jungles." He looked well fed and healthy, but his back was lined with tracks. "He is trained in the arts of violence by our very own Rovambira Household. He has won some fighting competitions and is also good for manual labor, though that would be a great waste of such a fine ssspecimen." The slaver said the last sentence as he admired his product, brushing his fingers over the slave's pectorals and well-defined arms. "Every bit worth the fangsss."

The slave had been captured during King Sukukuyiri of the Boaboa Kingdom's failed incursion into the Muimba Peninsular in the Bird Lands south of the Boaboa Kingdom. During war, rather than killing their enemies, the snake-peoples preferred to capture their foes alive. It was a revered skill that helped the kingdom gain labor for the crop fields and mines.

The slaver shuffled to the next slave, grabbed her by the mouth and forced it open. "As you can sssee," he displayed, "She would be a fine addition to your labor . . . or pleasure," he winked. "For her young age, she hasss already produced three offspring. For the price I am offering, you'd be a thief to have her."

Next was a little girl with a long face and tightly braided hair. She stared up at the Northman with her large lugubrious eyes. "How much?"

"For this little snakelet?"

"No, for all three." Asha didn't give him time to answer, placing a pouch into the slaver's hand. The merchant handed over the title deeds and delivered the slaves into the Desert Snake's care. Soon thereafter the slaves' chains were unbuckled. "I hereby free you," he declared. The slaves looked at each other bemused, mystified by the day's occurrence. "It means that you are free to do whatever you like." He reached into his bag and produced heavy pouches, handing them over to the emancipated bunch. "This should be enough to help you start your new lives as free people."

They were apprehensive at first, but once one of them snatched at a pouch, the others joined in and darted off into the crowd.

Next Asha found himself at a stall, and in it, sat a man maniacally peeling at a wooden block. Before him was a mock village with a main hut adorned by smaller satellite rondavels connected by tunnels around it. "That's impressive. What is that," Asha inquired.

The man looked the Desert Snake up and down for some moments, twisted his neck about, and then put a finger on his lip and lisped, "Just between you and me, General Chinotimba of Domboshawa is searching for the finest builder in all the kingdoms to construct him the grandest palace man has ever ssseen. I intend to win that contract worth five hundred cows."

"Is that so?" The Desert Snake surveyed the model and reached out for a piece.

"Don't you dare," hissed the man.

"Apologies. What is your name?"

"Mariga, Mariga the Carver. You might have heard about my grandfather, Mariga the Sssculptor?"

"You are Mariga's grandchild?"

"In the flesh."

Mariga had a massive forearm with thick fingers. His left hand was bigger than his right. His eyes were close-set and fastidious like a hawk. He momentarily took off his hat that was patched together with a dark blend of snakeskins, and scratched the top of his short crop of greying hair. It had a wide brim with cowries hanging all around, which rattled as he placed the hat back on his head. He was bare-chested and in good shape for a man his age, though the clouds under his eyes showed a man who barely slept. A crimson cloth tied around his waist spilled over his snakeskin kanga, in the front and in the back.

"My father was a merchant. On one of his journeys, he returned home with a little wooden carving your father made."

"And here we meet, all the way across the world. I assume you are not from these partsss?"

"You are correct. You know what, Mariga, for all the happy times your grandfather gave me in my youth, playing with his miniature sculptures, I ought to buy you supper and you can tell me all about your work."

The carver studied the Northman for some moments and finally offered, "How about you join me and my wife at my house for supper?"

"It would be my pleasure."

"No, no, no, my friend. The pleasure is all mine and my wife'sss. It is not often we have a chance to dine with a Northman. My house is on the upper west side, overlooking the ocean. You will know it is my home by the sssuperior architecture. Now let me be, I have much work to do."

Chapter 10

The Water Plea

The Boroa district of Pyyros' thoroughfare was alive with anticipation on the day of the Water Plea, for the famed Chief-Witchdoctor of the Piripiri Kingdom, the Sangoma, had been scheduled to oversee the purification ceremony that was to take place.

"What do you make of this purification business," Tauya Mundu, a young man of about four fists of age with a personable and wholesome face quizzed, as he and his friend Rafiki sluggishly moved toward the district center.

Rafiki didn't quite know. "My mother once told me that some clans in the northern parts of the kingdom still practiced the ritual when she was a child, but that most tribes around the kingdom had abandoned the practice altogether. It sounds pretty gruesome to me, but hey, if the Eternal Flame has decreed it, who am I to question the will of kings?"

"I say anything to get the rains flowing again, right?"

"Right. I could do with some rains, I don't think we can sustain another rainless season for much longer."

"What do you think he's like?"

"Who? This Sangoma? I hear he is as tall as a tree, and built like a bull!"

"That's nonsense, Rafiki. When have you ever seen such a tall and strapping witchdoctor?"

"Well, when have you ever heard about a witchdoctor that can resurrect the dead?"

Tauya had no answer to that. "Do you think he can resurrect my mother?"

"Your mother is now a pile of bones, dear friend. Let the dead rest."

After an antelope, which the Pyyrisians saw as a symbol of good harvest was sacrificed, a loud trumpet interrupted their conversation. They looked up from where they sat, front row seats at the district square, and in skipped the district's young maidens in little colorful beaded skirts, a combination of whites, yellows and red. When the drum rang, in sync, their mouths opened with a high pitch intro as they reached for the sky and wriggled their fingers before bringing them down as though they were welcoming a guest. They bade the rains return in heartfelt harmonies, and asked the ancestors to forgive them solemnly. They lifted their legs, and then swung them back and forth as their arms, fluid like liquid, moved in sync with their leg movement. When the chorus was sung, a solemn plea to the clouds, they fell to the ground as though they had fainted. When they rose, they began kicking and squatting at the same time, and then as they had begun, reached their arms out to the heavens and beckoned the rain.

"Wait," stuttered Rafiki with a curious eyebrow raised.

The lead dashed forward from the line of dancers, and skipped around in an effortless saunter, and performed a haughty strut. The clicking of her heels added rhythm to the drums that now thundered without pause at a frantic pace. Her eyes seemed to survey the area with determination, and all the while, a toothy smile that reached Tauya and Rafiki in the deepest parts of their souls when she momentarily met eyes with them. Rafiki almost fell off his stool when she began wriggling her belly, and he began to salivate like a thirsty dog when her hips thrust sideways, exposing the upper part of her thick thighs. When she curtsied and skipped back to the rest of the girls as her skirt lifted and fell exposing her buttocks, the crowd roared, so loud the neighboring Pyyros districts must have heard it.

Tauya sat there in silence, stupefied, his mouth ajar and his eyes, like he had transformed into a bushbaby.

"Mundu," Rafiki hollered. There was no response. It took a nudge on Tauya's shoulder for him to come out of his trans. "Look," Rafiki pointed. "He's here!"

The dancers parted, and in through the human tunnel emerged the Sangoma in a cloud of smoke. "See," pointed out Tauya. "He's tiny."

"And so skinny. Look at those arms!"

If they were not impressed, now they were when the Sangoma performed a cartwheel and then two forward somersaults before landing deftly with his staff firmly clasped by his side. When the mist had subsided, next to him stood Reza, giggling wildly. The hyena snarled at the crowd and bared her teeth for all to see, sending the crowd into a deep panic that had many flee. The Sangoma brushed the spikes on Reza's back with the tips of his fingers and then raised his staff into the air, a long gnarled stick with the head of a fanged serpent. He put a finger to his mask and when the crowd had silenced, he began. "The ancestors are very angry."

The crowd looked at each other. One could see their fright by the faces they bore as they displaced their guilt amongst each other.

"It is plain for us to see, the lackluster rains, the dry rivers and lakes—the hungry, the sick and the destitute. The ancestors have ordered us to change our ways, and these girls have been chosen to be the sacrifice, the heroes that shall right all our wrongs! Behold them in their imperfectness for one last time." The crowd clapped and cheered. "Let us not waste time, the fate of our kingdom is in peril." The Sangoma's bright red eyes began flaring more viciously when he snatched the knife that was waiting between Reza's carnassials and moved toward the first girl waiting by the stone podium. "What is your name?" he lisped as he helped her onto the dais.

"Yananayii," she replied confidently. "Yananayii Kukongola."

"May the flame guide you, sweet child."

When Yananayii was on her back and fastened, the mage dipped his blade into the flame nearby and raised it into the sky for the throng to see. The crowd shrilled awestruck as though Gyiku'o had descended Pyre Mountain carrying bountiful harvest. He set his mask by the girl's face and hissed. He was proud of her. He saw no fear in her eyes, unlike many others he had purified. *They know not what service this is to their people*, he lamented. *To the world! To our existence!* "You are a shining example to all of us," he encouraged, as two priestesses, one a crone, the other a lass, held the sacrifice tight by her wrists and ankles. The Sangoma shuffled toward her legs and when he was at a good distance, he slashed.

Later in the afternoon as the sun began to wane and Boroa feasted, Tauya looked up into the sky to find a red comet zipping past. A thought crossed his mind. He stood up, wobbly from the afternoon's *umqombothi* and dragged Rafiki to his feet. They whizzed past the district gates and into the dry bush where they could hear the sound of laughing hyenas in the distance, as well as an orchestra of trumpeting elephants. It took what seemed an eternity, but finally Tauya's eyes lit up as he reached down, gently caressed a fire lily and plucked it from its root.

"You brought me out here to look for a fire lily in the middle of the festival?" Rafiki was incensed, but Tauya didn't care. His gaze was firmly placed on the flame shaped plant.

"What luck we have finding these in these times." Tauya split the plant and handed Rafiki a leaf. He reached into his bag and brought out a log with a v-shaped notch and a spindle. He rubbed the spindle between his palms as fast as he could, moving his hands up and down the spindle rapidly. When the log began to smoke, he used a tinder nest to catch the glowing spark he had produced.

"What are you doing? Not here! Remember what the king decreed? No fires in the bush! It's so dry, any spark can ignite a bushfire," harkened Rafiki.

"Don't worry, we'll be quick." Tauya pulled out his fire lily leaf, exhaled, and set it aflame. "My mother once told me, if you see a blood red comet in the sky, light up a fire lily, make a wish, and it will come true." He looked up into the sky and followed its smoke toward the ancestors. He closed his eyes and mumbled something. "Now it's your turn."

Rafiki looked confused, but nonetheless he shook his head, lifted his leaf to the flame and made a wish.

"Where have you been," asked Tauya's father, Lumambo, when Tauya arrived home. It was a small household. Tauya was Lumambo's only child, despite Lumambo having taken four wives. "The Water Plea ended a long time ago."

"I was with Rafiki. We took a walk."

"Where to?" It was clear that he had drunk several calabashes of *doro*.

"Oh, nowhere really."

"Nowhere, huh? I hope you were trying to find a wife. You are almost two fists of age and unwed. Sometimes I question whether you are my son," Lumambo chuckled. "Your mother must be upset in the afterlife, I tell you."

Tauya often slept with his mother's urn cradled in his arms and weep. He would do this for a long time, often until the break of dawn and often woke up in the morning with dry crusts that flowed down his neck and chest. "Don't worry about that, father. I am waiting for the right one."

"The right one?" Lumambo laughed. "How hard can it be, with all these beautiful young girls around the district? Just this afternoon during the Water Plea, I saw a couple of unmarried girls I would inquire upon their fathers, if not for my old age and dwindling kraal. As my only child it is your duty to me, to the ancestors, to your king!"

"It would be easier for me if I didn't have to be drenched in pigeon poop and cow urine at work all day. Do you know how bad that smells?"

"Oh, we can smell you all right," Lumambo laughed. "Stay strong, son. Once these rains return to us, we can commence to our farming ways and you can stop this tannery business of yours."

"I was going to keep it a secret until I was sure, but I have been working on producing a bride for you."

"Have you now?" Lumambo rubbed his hands in glee.

"Indeed. I don't want to say too much right now, but don't be surprised to hear some news some time soon."

"I'll hold you to that, son."

"Oh please do." He reached into his cloths and rubbed the fire lily leaf gently. As he did, little patters came from the roof, and then thunder roared announcing a torrent of rains. Water began to leak from the ceiling.

"Tauya, I thought you had fixed the roof," chided Lumambo.

"I did," the boy lamented.

Tauya was sure he was about to get a thorough reprimand and even perhaps a good smack at the side of his head, but instead Lumambo rose to his feet, lifted his hands into the air and smiled. "This Sangoma is good!"

Chapter 11

The Carver

Mariga the Carver's compound was a wondrous abode of architectural elegance with snakeskin padded window seats and arching windows that brought in the salty smell of the sea. An elegant woman with flowers woven in her hair strolled in as Asha and Mariga laughed and drank a sweet drink made from marula fruit in the well-lit room with torches hanging around the apartment on terracotta holders. She was about the most elegant woman the Desert Snake had ever seen, bar Queen Zandile, with a style that merged apparel, cosmetics, and coiffure perfectly. She combined those qualities with the grace of a peacock that seemed to subdue time as she glided in, her wrap dress hugging every detail of her marvelously molded contours, her jewels glittering with every delicate, yet deliberate movement. "Good evening, husband," her sultry lips that were made to kiss greeted, as she brushed a finger over Mariga's shoulder. "What have you brought us today? Another one of your architectural masterpiecesss'?"

"This is Asha."

"Is he dangerousss?"

"He is a Northman."

"Then I would do well to tread carefully," she smiled, placing herself onto an ivory footstool—casually but seductively. "Ssso, tell us about yourself, Northman. By the look of you, there isss plenty."

"There isn't much to tell. My family was murdered when I was a child. I was scooped up from their lifeblood and raised by my adopted father."

Mariga and Adina looked at each other, visibly startled by the Northman's frankness that made the carver almost spill his drink.

"Now, I am looking for my wife and daughter. Perhaps you might have seen them?"

"All business this one," she laughed tremulously as she snapped her fingers.

A servant was soon on the scene, pouring Adina a cup of freshly squeezed mobola plum juice. The maid was shortly driven off with a sharp word.

"As I am sure you have figured by now, this is my beloved wife, Adina," introduced Mariga, mildly embarrassed by her sassy introduction.

"The cause of all his misery, he likes to tell me."

Mariga nodded in agreement and then finished, "And the cause of my ecstasy," he chortled back, leaning over and giving her thigh a good rub. Soon he was cupping her breast and had his tongue wriggling at the back of her neck like an elephant trunk navigating a thorn tree. A series of coughs interrupted the couple in the midst of their passions. "Oh, forgive us. My wife has been away, visiting family. I have missed her ssso dearly."

"So, have you seen them? A woman of seven fists, with eyes the color of almond, bright like fire and a girl," he paused. Time had flown by. He realized Nia was now no longer a child. "…Just a woman grown?"

"I'm afraid I haven't. I am so engrossed with my work I barely lift my eyes to see what's happening around me. Have they left you," Mariga asked, cautiously.

"Yes."

"Why?"

The Desert Snake took some moments to reflect and then produced an answer. "I have been a neglectful husband. I gained my wife's hand in marriage at great pains, and when I had her, I favored warring. Rather than spending time with my family I preferred to pray, waste days obsessing over a stone and excavating a volcano for its hidden secrets."

"That is a shame, Asha. When you find them . . ." The Desert Snake could see the doubt in her eyes. " . . . What if they don't want to go back with you?"

"That is out of the question."

"Will you drag them back to your hut against their will?"

He had never failed his adopted father. He wasn't going to do it now. "If I have to, yes."

There were some moments of uneasy silence before Adina erupted into a hearty laughter until first Mariga joined, and then the Desert Snake, mirthlessly. "Then they must surely be special."

"They are." Asha reminisced fondly chasing after Nia when he was tasked with getting her home, which was more often than he liked. So lithe and quick she was—full of life—full of protest, with her muddied knees and soiled cheeks. He remembered Queen Zandile, who would join his *mbira* with her voice on those balmy afternoons in between campaigns that had seen the Piripiri dominion outspan the greatest kingdoms.

"So, tell us about your travels, Desert Sssnake. Where was your last stop in your quest of love?"

"The Eagle's Nest," Asha answered.

"How did you find it?"

Asha didn't know what to say. Sightseeing had been the last thing on his mind, so he went with, "The food is good?"

"You were there, weren't you, husband," Adina continued, "Sssculpting some statue for some obscure chief?"

"I wasss," corroborated Mariga. "The food was nice, I guess, however, I find the city's architecture rather dull. The bird statues that adorn the wall are all well and good, but they still use cow dung in some places to make their homes."

"The dung insulates against the elements and is waterproof," argued the Desert Snake.

"Pah," Mariga replied. "What good is that in this day and age, with the lackluster rains? Besidesss, we have come a long way from the days when we were no better than the animals of the wild, huddled around a fire in a cavern. Today, architecture should serve two purposes—the visual effect of construction and the practical. In my travels, prior to the Great Divide's formation, I visited a city, a conclave of poets, griots and artists that had buildings with long linear vertical linesss. When I returned home and told the builders guild about these revolutionary methods, and how I wanted to replicate them, they all laughed at me."

"Now, now, now, husband," Adina cut in. "Must we discuss architecture over supper? You are unable to discuss these things moderately."

"It's okay," insisted the sandman. "Please continue. One day I can tell my grandchildren I once discussed architecture with Mariga the Sculptor's grandchild."

So Mariga did—all night, until Adina was snoring prodigiously curled atop a cushion of luxurious animal hides. "You need to evolve, Desert Sssnake," Mariga negated. "You are ssstuck in the past and sadly so are many other craftsmen around here. Art is an evolving expression, or at least should be. Sure, I was trained in the ways of naturalism; however, I'm done with that. It's boring. These days the only thing that gets me excited isss abstraction."

"Cubism," suggested the Desert Snake. By his own admission he was a dilettante on the subject, with an amateur interest in the arts.

"Precisssely."

Mariga took the Desert Snake on a tour around his compound, showing him his private collection. The first artwork that stood near the entrance of the dinner hall was a sculpture of the Great Ophidian, and atop it, King Uturu straddled over its serpentine back. Unlike wood, fired clay did not deteriorate over time. The warrior king was dressed in military attire, equipped with a bow and quiver on his back and the legendary venom tipped spear, Snake Charmer, clasped tight in his hand.

Next was a set of terracotta heads that looked distinctly like the artist and his wife, Adina. "I used to be beautiful," Mariga opined, brushing his fingers over the male head's nose. "But time isss unforgiving and doesss not discriminate."

"Some say there is a fountain of youth."

"Tell me where this fountain isss so I can drink from it. I will drink from it until I have had my fill."

"You might have heard of the Forest of Abominations."

"Death is better than going there, I heard. I'd rather die old, wrinkly and frail."

The terracotta heads were made from grog and iron rich clay, adorned by strong formal elements and expressive qualities the Desert Snake had not seen even from some of the best sculptors at King Maghedzi's court. "So you see the necks, Desert Sssnake. Those large furrowed rings signal prosperity and power, but where is my prosperity? Where is my power?" He shook his head.

Next was Mariga's metal collection of bronze, brass and copper. Some full bodies, others heads, others masks and animals. They had an astonishing realism about them, reflecting a quiet intensity the Desert Snake saw in the carver. "Thisss one," he continued, orgulously caressing the shoulder of the standing warrior, "Isss made from copper. If you are well versed in the arts, you will know how difficult it is to work with the metal. Far, far more challenging than brass, but I think I did a good job of it."

The Desert Snake shifted himself closer and inspected the work from top to bottom, squatting so he could get a good look at the rear.

"These days I only work with metal. I am done with wood. I have seen too many masterpieces fall to the mischief of termitesss!"

The Desert Snake didn't hear Mariga as he moaned and complained, marveled and admired his own works for he was stuck in a trance, subdued by a raw expressive power that had him experience a mystical and spiritual encounter, like the ancestors themselves had touched the work with their preternatural wands. "Fantastic, Mariga," he finally opined.

"Oh, you just flatter me."

They took a walk through the purlieu across the rocky beach and sat for some moments by the pier, their fermented marula fruit induced laughter sailing into the crisp clear sky. The Desert Snake was reminded of his youth as sand tickled his toes and got stuck amongst them. They got to a monolithic statue of a man with a snake atop his shoulders. The effigy gazed into the ocean and with its left hand, pointed. "That there is King Sukukuyiri, the Tree Boa, the longest serving monarch in all the known kingdomsss." At three fists of age, a young Sukukuyiri was appointed prince regent by his father, King Anakoko. Three seasons later he succeeded him. That was more than eighty seasons ago. "I made that."

"Fine work. Must have been a handsome commission."

"It wasss, but I am now as good as broke. I have been living lavishly, way above my means. You have seen my wife. She thinks we have a pile of gold. She doesn't realize that a great drought is coming and quite frankly, I don't know how long this city will stand. The people have had enough, Desert Sssnake. There is a man called Gaya. The common folk are saying he is going to liberate them."

The Desert Snake had heard that name, chanted by the mob as guards took away the doomsday preacher, when he had first arrived at the Snake Pit. He had heard the name as he burrowed through the streets by beggars, the sick, the destitute, slumped in street corners, and huddled around fires burning whatever they could to make it through the cold nights.

"I don't know whether this Gaya is man or myth. No one has seen him, but the people talk and whisper his name like he will save them. The authorities have been looking for him, but whenever they catch wind of his location, he is always gone. Poof," Mariga exclaimed, "Like a swarm of locusts, onto the next crop field. All they find is the head of a mongoose. Some say this Gaya is descendant of the Nkala."

"I thought they were eradicated generations ago, during the Snake's Feast."

"That is the story told, but some whisper that some sons from lesser wives and concubines from the Nkala survived, and also some from the Matswi, Hovo and other mongoose clans. Whomever people think this man is, they think life will change if there is a Gaya sitting on the throne instead of the Tree Boa. From my experience, regime changes never bring anything new. Just more of the sssame." He let out a cloud of licorice-scented smoke from his elegant spiraled pipe. He offered the silver-bush to the Northman who declined. "When my wife finds out we are almost ruined, she will leave me. Here in the Snake Pit, image is everything. All these people care about is your wealth. How many cows you own, how many hectors your farm is, or how much gold you wear. That is why I have to win the Domboshawa contract and hopefully emigrate before this place implodesss."

"Where do you want to go?"

"Far away. Anywhere where I can do my work in peace and make my final masterpiece." Stars glowed from his eyes before he sighed and looked down. "I am tired Desert Sssnake."

"From what I have seen you should surely win it."

The carver nodded his head in agreement. "Few builders can rival my skill." The other carver he rated was his former friend, long dead. They had trained together as youths carving anything they could get their hands on, from raggedy pebbles to discarded wood planks builders didn't need. Both their drive to be the best had dented their relationship, but now, Mariga dedicated his work to his old friend. "It was passed down to me."

"You are not lost for confidence."

"In my profession, you cannot afford to be. I imagine it is the same as yoursss?" he finished with an eye on the Desert Snake's empty sword scabbard.

"What's the saying? When you strike, make it true?" A cold wind blew past them. "It is getting late. I should call it a night."

"Where do you stay?"

"I have to find a lodge."

"Nonsense! You shall stay the night. These lodges are filthy, with flea-ridden mats. I have several guest lodgingsss. I intend for someone to use them. My wife will insist."

"Do I have a choice?"

"I am afraid not."

Chapter 12

The Tannery

The Boroa district thoroughfare was a completely different place now that the clouds had opened up overnight. Children were playing in the newly formed puddles, and adults performed their morning duties with smiles as Tauya Mundu made his way to work, past the district center where merchants and craftsmen displayed their products. When King Maghedzi first ascended the Piripiri throne, he noted that the kingdom needed major reforms and one of them was addressing the ever-growing Pyyros population.

To solve this riddle he divided the city into several districts. He set Boroa, the southernmost part of Pyyros, to clothing and footwear manufacturing. Some of the kingdom's oldest and most famous tanneries were located in this district, where numerous stone vessels filled with different colored dyes and white liquids where a fixture, and made the district very distinct. From the wee hours of the morning, till the night lamps were lit, it was a common sight to see loincloth clad men balanced on top of the thin stone vessels, laboring to produce leather that would be exported across the kingdom and beyond.

Because soil derived from eroded volcanic rocks and ash was extraordinarily rich in nutrients, the northern most part of Pyyros, Kumputo, which was closest to Mount Pyyros' slopes, was set to producing the crops that would keep the kingdom afloat during times of famine.

The western district, Khumazulo, he set to weapons and metal works manufacturing, and the eastern district, Kum'wawa, he set to fishing, as the district was nestled by several tributaries from the river, Nhunundudu.

The river, which was the longest in the Piripiri Kingdom, cut through the middle of the vast kingdom, feeding villages and settlements with its numerous branches. It cut well into the kingdom's interior deep into the Yachonde plateau, which as a result of the inefficient rains the region had suffered in the last few rain seasons, was dry, stony and sparsely covered with hardy drought-resistant plants.

In the center, on a hill high above the districts, sat the heart of the Piripiri Kingdom's administration where the nobility, artisans and warrior class congregated.

The tannery Tauya employed was a small family establishment, and compared to the great tanneries in the district, was a dwarf. In the words of its owner, Tabonga Wachikopa, "We deal in quality, rather than quantity." The tannery was located by a tributary from the Nhunundudu, not too far from the village center, so it could be accessed by workers and traders, but just far away enough from residential areas as tanneries produced noisome smells. The complex was built many generations prior with rocks, mud and lime. The main premises consisted of two spacious compartments with wooden roofs. The first partition contained wells, presses and tubs where the hides were immerged for tanning, dyeing and washing. The second was dedicated to the finishing, and where artisans would collect the leather to create slippers, belts, bags and anything else their creative minds could conjure.

There was some new leather in that day, which Tauya wasn't expecting. He was hoping to be able to cure his hangover from the previous day's festivities. He inspected the hides thoroughly, as he reminisced about the dancers at the water plea and then soaked the hides in a concoction of cow urine, quicklime, water, and salt. This caustic mixture helped to break down the tough leather, loosen excess fat, flesh and hair that remained on them.

After three days, he began scrapping away the excess hair fibers and fat in preparation for the dyeing process. He then soaked the hides in another set of vats containing a blend of water and pigeon poop. This process allowed the hides to become malleable enough to absorb the dyes. Then with his bare-feet, he kneaded the hides for up to three hours until they were nice and soft. He was well spent when he was done, especially his legs, which were now as stiff as a corpse. He decided to call it a day and go home.

He dashed to his father's side as soon as he entered Lumambo's chambers. "Father, what's wrong? Is it your head again?" Since Lumambo was a child, he suffered from chronic head pains. Their frequency had tapered in his adult life, but not the pain. "Here, let me help you up. I'll take you to a witchdoctor."

"We can't afford it, son." He coughed. "I'll get better. I just need to rest that's all."

Tauya hated to see his father like this. He hated to think that Lumambo was going to die as well, as did his mother all those years ago. Violet images appeared before him as he went into memory lane. "Father, I'll be back, just don't die on me, okay?"

His heart swelled with nostalgia as he broke the forest's bushy threshold and followed a tight footpath, the same one he and his mother trekked when he was younger, searching for herbs and spices. Back then the path was laden with verdant and luscious vegetation and blooming flowers of various colors and kinds.

One day during one of their walks, they came upon a small violet tree with pale grey smooth bark and leaves crowded on dwarf spur spine-tipped branchlets. Its fine hairs over the leaves tickled him when he brushed his little fingers over them, and its flowers were sweetly scented, in short bunches, pink, plum and purple. Its fruits were a pale straw-color. He didn't know why his mother had collected its leaves, but he understood a moon later, when she used them to cure his throbbing head.

He stopped and looked around, trying to recall the route they had taken. He gazed up at the canopy as he probed, his head twisting and turning as he searched for the birds that sang ever so sweetly over the low buzzing sound of locusts. *That's odd.* He scratched his head. He couldn't see any birds, or any rambling amongst the leaves, just the sun's rays breaking through the cracks of the leaves exposing the outgrown roots, wildflowers and fallen leaves that crunched beneath his sandals. The singing became more distinct the further he went, until it became apparent that it wasn't the birds that sang, but a woman, who bathed in the lagoon just ahead, hidden behind the thick vegetation.

He wanted to turn back and allow the woman her privacy, but he needed to find the herbs to help relieve his father of his headache, so he hid behind a tree, hoping she would leave soon so he could be about his business. He peaked behind the tree as the woman emerged from the water, with her wet glossy hair falling over her shoulders, and her breasts glistening in the sun.

"Come out, whoever you are," the woman commanded.

Tauya wanted to run, but the voice was authoritative—enticing. He poked his head out, then his body slowly followed suit.

His whole world slowed down, the nearer he moved toward her. He couldn't even feel the thorns that dug into his skin as he made cautious way. The way she looked at him as he approached made him feel as though he was being swallowed whole. It made him forget why he was there, and the shrill screams of his father.

She was drying herself off when he arrived. "I'm done for the day, if you meant to swim." She reached out her hand and waited. Tauya was confused, but soon enough he picked up her bangles and helped slide them onto her arms. She stood there in silence for some moments and then coughed.

"Oh, sorry," Tauya apologized, before he picked up her entanglement of necklaces and helped them over her head until they were firmly over her breasts.

She picked up her basket and made way.

It's her, he fretted. He recognized her from the Water Plea. "What's your name?" Tauya shouted after her as she walked away. She didn't turn. "When can I see you again?"

"Well you know I like swimming, and with this drought on the way, there aren't so many places one can swim."

Chapter 13

Broken Chains

The next morning after a lavish breakfast of fresh milk, egg and the finest seasoned dried meat he had ever tasted, the Desert Snake was well equipped for another day of disappointment. After thanking Mariga and Adina for their hospitality, he was soon back on the Snake Pit streets, searching and probing, this time harboring a strange feeling that someone was stalking him—eyes hidden amongst the crowd, watching his every move, peering nippily from street corners like a cat hunting down its prey.

He was knocked off his feet and onto his bum as three men rushed out of an eatery, cackling like hyenas before they were one with the moving crowd. The Desert Snake stood up, dusted his cloths and crept into the inn, pulling the beads that draped the entrance to the side. On the ground was a woman tending to a boy. The Desert Snake darted to their aid and helped the boy up to his feet.

"Oh, thank you, kind man." There was broken pottery all over, calabashes, tables and stools.

"Did those men do this?"

The woman's upper lip quivered and then she finally replied, "Yesss. They are from the Kangamiti house." From the lime and gold garb they wore, Asha guessed they were from the green faction of the vine snake clan. "These houses," the woman continued, "Or should I say cartels, they control everything, from prostitution to smuggling, poaching, assassination and extortion. Sometimes I believe they control the weather. They have powerful sorcerers who protect them. Now only Gaya can save usss. I am a widow. All I have is my son and this eatery. Many moons ago, after my husband died, men would come by every afternoon and start fights, destroying property. One day a group of men came and told me they could protect me—for a small price they said. I agreed, foolishly, but now they keep coming every quarter moon asking for more and more. I have no snake-fangs to give them. What am I to do? Sssell my husband's shop?"

"I wish I could help you, but I am looking for some people. A woman of …"

"As you can see we have bigger problemsss. Leave!" She took her son and guided him to the back room. She looked up. "You are still here? Be gone with you!"

The Desert Snake did not need to be asked a second time. He was on the bustling thoroughfare soon thereafter, with eyes upon him—he could feel it. He bought himself a spit of cubed beef and casually walked around the markets. He turned into a narrow alleyway and waited. He wished he had his blade with him, but in truth he was almost as deadly without. After a few moments, he snatched a body into the dark alleyway and lifted it onto the wall and gnashed his teeth as he let his naked spit tickle the soft part of the stalker's chin. Big eyes looked down at him, petrified. "Oh, it's you." He set the former slave down. "Why are you following me, little girl?"

"I have nowhere to go. Can I come with you?"

"I am on a very important mission, girl. I have to travel light. Don't follow me." He moved along and when he turned back after a few moments, the girl was still trailing him. He sighed. "Look girl, you are making me regret freeing you." She said nothing. She just stood there with her smudged cheeks and big eyes looking up at him. "Oh, why ancestors, must you make everything so hard?" He deliberated for some moments, then finally ceded, "Fine. For now."

In the evening she made him a fire. The best fire he had ever seen from the limited tools they had. "What's your name, girl?"

There was no reply.

"You don't have a name? Then how about I give you one? How is Zara-Fe'yi?"

She repeated the name a couple of times and nodded her head and smiled. "Zara-Fe'yi."

"If you are going to be following me around, we should get to know each other, right? Tell me about yourself."

"I never knew my parents. I was raised as a slave in the Rovambira household, one of the most powerful houses in the Snake Pit. Our master was as kind as a slave master could be, and had promised to give us freedom when he died. However, he passed so unexpectedly and had many debts, so we were taken as payment. That is when you came and freed us."

"I grew up without my parents too. They were murdered."

"Do you know who murdered them?"

"Yes, his name is Farakaii."

Zara-Fe'yi dipped her head and blew at the logs, reigniting the flames. "Do you seek revenge?"

"It is all I think about—when I wake, when I sleep, when I eat. I am however growing more impatient by the day."

The girl stood up and decided. "I want to help you get your revenge, Desert Snake."

He looked at her and smiled, his luminous eyes flashing amongst the dark. "Unfortunately, revenge has to wait. My adopted father has sent me on a mission to find his wife and daughter. I assume you won't stop following me soon, so when we return to Pyyros, I will introduce him to you as my daughter. I will get us a nice little compound in the countryside and I shall instruct you in the way of the blade. You will need to learn the art if you are to help me avenge my family. I know a metalsmith here. He won't be able to match the workmanship of my shotel, but it'll work for now."

The next day, after describing Queen Zandile and Princess Nia to Zara-Fe'yi, he sent her to the northern parts of the city in search of the royal couple. His tasks consisted of further probing of the southern region, and also, to get his new progeny a blade. "We meet here just before sundown. Okay?"

The girl nodded and skipped off.

During his fruitless search, he decided to try his luck at an eatery. He sat himself down and waited to be served. Suddenly, a large figure appeared in front of him. He looked up to find the slave he had freed. He had a big smile on his face. "I have been looking for you."

"Well here I am. How is freedom treating you?"

"Wonderful."

The Desert Snake could see that, as his newly bought jewelry danced around his chest, neck and arms. "I have assembled my own fighting group."

"It seems that you have used the snake-fangs I gave you well."

"Indeed, but you never gave me the opportunity to thank you properly."

"That is not necessary."

"What is your name, kind man?"

"People call me the Desert Snake."

"And I call myself Goro. You must at least let me buy you a meal." The former slave did not give him a chance to refuse, grabbing a stool and whistling for a servant. "The day's special and two large calabashes of *umqombothi*." He turned to the Desert Snake. "You know I am always looking for new fighters and you look like you could handle a few rounds."

"No thank you. I am already on a job."

"What kind? It can't be just to save a bunch of slaves?"

"I am looking for some people. A woman with fiery eyes and rose-tinted hair. With her should be a young woman, scruffy looking and bony."

Goro began to laugh, banging hard on the wooden table sending droplets of *whawha* onto the table. "You won't believe it if I told you."

"Told me what?"

"My former master, the Prince of the Rovambira Household, was a very important man. One afternoon the Tree Boa was visiting my master as we prepared for a fighting competition. There was a woman and a girl in attendance, if I recall. After some moments, they left looking quite upset. As they passed, the girl asked the older woman what they were going to do."

"Well?"

"I heard something about them going back home."

"And you are sure that these are the people I am looking for?"

"The woman had fiery eyes alright." Goro and Zandile had caught each other's gaze momentarily, before she turned to her daughter, Nia. "Just about the most attractive woman I have ever seen. Her buttocks were so . . ."

"You better stop there if you enjoy your newfound freedom."

The former slave smiled cheekily and then continued. "Over their conversation with my master and the king, I think I heard a glimpse of her name. It was Zado? Zanozila? Za . . ."

"Zandile?"

"Yes, that is correct. If I may ask, who are these people?"

"For your sake, the less questions the better." The Desert Snake rose immediately from his stool. "Thank you, Goro."

"No, thank you. You are a good man. If you ever need anything, I am bound to you forever."

"There is one thing you can do for me. I need you to protect the widow's inn."

"The one on Bush-Viper Trail?"

"Correct."

"With my life, Desert Snake."

The Northman gave him a curt nod and exited the eatery. He waited by the meeting point, excited, as he had made progress in his search and had also bought a new sword for Zara-Fe'yi from the local swordsmith, Tuku, he had inquired. Similarly to his long departed shotel, Zara-Fe'yi's sword was semi circularly shaped, flat and double-edged with a diamond cross-section. Mastering a sword was a never-ending process, but he saw great potential in the little girl.

It was getting darker by the minute. As he placed his water skin back into his bag, a familiar voice called his name. He sighed and turned to find Sheriff Punda approaching and tucked under his arm was Zara-Fe'yi, kicking and wriggling.

"Look what I found trying to sssteal from me." In the sheriff's other hand was the Desert Snake's long-lost shotel. "A slave who for some reason thinks she was freed. I wonder who told her that?" He twisted his head left and right, looking for the culprit before he finally set his eyes on the Desert Snake and threw the girl onto the dirt.

"I did. I paid her former master his snake-fangs, bought her, and then freed her."

"Ssso, you think you can come here and free slaves?" He waved around the sword threateningly. Its edge matched the color of the Desert Snake's eyes, albeit a darker, smoky green that gleamed when the sun's rays brushed it.

"I just did, didn't I? A slave master can do whatever he likes with his slaves, is that not true?"

The sheriff looked at him. "You think you are so clever, don't you, Asha? I am going to teach you a lesson. Kwaza! Tizwa!"

The sheriff's lackeys drew their swords and before the Desert Snake had time to react, blades went into the girl.

Asha's eyes met with Zara-Fe'yi's one last time as she slowly dropped to the ground. The sheriff raised the shotel, but like his namesake, the Northman had the sheriff squirming on the ground. Without looking he ducked from an attack from behind and had the sheriff's lackeys in a twisted pile. He caught his swords glimmer on the floor and with his foot, flicked it into the air until it was firmly in his grip. He didn't have time to rejoice in the reunion as an arrow flew into his back.

He turned to discover several men headed his way. He pulled out the arrow without much fuss and surveyed the area. He pushed a man into the way of the oncoming law and leapt up onto a thatched roof. He hied across it and leapt onto another and then another until a roof opened from under him. He landed with a thud next to a woman with a babe by her breast. He apologized profusely to the flummoxed woman and child, dusted himself off and bolted out of the door.

He immediately felt hands upon him. He quickly turned startling the man, grabbed him by the arm and flipped him over his shoulder onto his back. He gave him a quick heal, surveyed his surroundings and sprang toward the eastern gate where a line of guards waited, swords in hand. He leapt well over them like a leopard, performed a double roll when he landed, and dashed through the gate as it closed.

Arrows flew past him from the battlements as he ran down the bridge until he slid into the vast swath of countryside. It felt endless and seemed to stretch on forever, but he hopped nonetheless like a springbok over newly planted mounds of millet and into a fiery tinted sorghum field, using Zara-Fe'yi's blade to slash through the stalks until he dove into a river and out the other side. He could see the sheriff and his men headed his way, on the other side of the riverbed, not far in the horizon. He turned and continued until he slid down a slope just as a hail of arrows landed in the soft damp mud and disappeared into the jungle.

The sheriff stood at the top of the slope with his fists digging his fat sides. "I think our work here is done. He won't be coming back. He will not forget this lesson sssoon."

Chapter 14

Ward Round

Prince Themba of the Akuwa drank harder than ever, the night he had his marriage proposal opprobriously spit on. He drank fruit mashes, distilled spirits and several skins of palm wine. *How dare he*, he carped. "Father sent me here to humiliate myself. This, king, Maghedzi, makes me wait all this time for an audience with this princess so I might woo her, and I haven't even had one look at her. What if she is hideous?" he complained to whomever would listen. "What if she is mad? What if she talks to stones, like her father?

"Not so loud," Munyaradzi fretted. "There might be someone spying on us." He stuck his head out of the opening and twisted it about, his eyes bulged like an owl. In the short distance were Piripiri men. Munyaradzi flashed his teeth and waved at them, before sticking his head back in, relieved no Piripiri was nearby eavesdropping. "Besides, Themba, have you forgotten our ancestor's teachings? Ugliness with good character is far superior than beauty."

The prince ignored that. "I don't care if he hears. What can he do to me? Perhaps if he heard, he would know that I mean business. These fire worshipers haven't even welcomed me with a feast! Where I will dance and show my prowess as a hunter! How can the king refuse me after that?"

"Be patient," Mutasa assured. It seemed his role as ambassador was predominantly easing the prince's anxieties. "You will have your chance. If the king had refused, I assure you we would have been on our way back to Hippo Valley with his Fireflies on our tails."

"I have been patient. Haven't I, uncle?"

Munyaradzi nodded his head as he sucked on a mobola plum, seemingly disinterested. "Yes, you've been very patient."

"You see?"

That night the prince comforted himself with a courtesan, pleasuring himself vigorously and only halting once he had spilled his seed. He rested for a few moments and then took her again, this time from behind, his hand pulling her hair like he did the reins of his equine. He gave the woman her shells and sent her on her way so he could drink some more. When he awoke it was lunchtime the next day and he still couldn't shake off the ominous feeling he had. Admittedly, he had felt like this for some time. He had been raised to be a man of action. He had to do something about it. In a fit of pique, he threw his cheetah skin cape around his shoulders, grabbed his spear and exited the room. Pikoro was waiting for him with a skin of water. Themba squinted his eyes and covered them from the sun's rays. "Take me to this Sangoma I hear so much about."

A group of owls took to the sky and the temperature dampened as Themba and Pikoro neared their destination. The gnarled trees and twisted vines that encircled the shack gave the structure an eeriness that made Themba think twice about his actions. Weeds grew from the edges and the grass besides the pathway leading up to the hut needed a good trimming. Underneath the wooden flight of stairs and around the hut was a murky pond that exuded a foul stench that had the prince covering his nose.

"Wait here," he bade Pikoro, as he put one foot on the first stair. The wood creaked as he took one step after the next, his hardened feet paying the splinters and cut wood no mind. Suddenly, he heard laughter behind him. His head turned to find the foulest hyena he had ever seen. The beast's member was so large it scraped the red earth. It snarled at Pikoro as the boy cowered.

Themba brought his spear over his shoulder and threw. Oddly enough, the spear landed flat on the ground, so he unsheathed his knife from its scabbard, but that slipped from his fingers like it had been laced with oil. He bent over and reached for the knife, but bizarrely it moved to the side. When he finally did grasp it, it slipped from his fingers again. Suddenly, his nose wrinkled, prompting him to turn around and there above him, at the entrance of the hut, the prince beheld a dreadful apparition. It whistled and soon, it had its black nails running through the hyena's thick hair as its fiery eyes flared through the cracks of its squeamish mask.

"Prince Themba," it lisped. "I was wondering when you would come to see me." The Sangoma turned and walked into the darkness of his hut.

"Master, I don't know if going in is a good idea," pled the skeptic Pikoro. Back in Shambamuto, even the name the Sangoma was only whispered by those brave enough.

"Nonsense. What can such a creature do to me?"

Pikoro could think of many things, like being turned into a frog, or worse yet, a dung beetle. "They say his magic is powerful."

"That is why I am here." With that, the prince was trailing behind the mage's array of animal skins, fastening the door behind him leaving the aspiring warrior standing guard outside.

"You should let some air in here, mystic." Themba covered his nose as he looked around the domicile with disdain. "And get some girl to come in here and clean this place up."

The Sangoma ignored that and waved away the python he hadn't yet named. "Forgive my pet snake. It is not often a prince from Hippo Valley comes to visit us." After that, he lit the dozens of lamps around the hut.

In the middle was a large cauldron. The mystic placed a large scoop in it, stirred for a few moments before he took up its contents and gave it a whiff. He sighed and then cast it back, grabbed his smoking pipe, lit it and slumped into his seat. He offered the pipe to the prince, who obliged. Soon the prince was coughing profusely and beating on his chest to the mystic's amusement. "What is this?"

"Silver-bush mixed with my own special ingredient." After the prince took another drag, he handed the pipe back to the mage. "So, young prince, why have you come to see me?"

"Aren't you supposed to know? Aren't you the great Sangoma? The witchdoctor people are calling a *muporofita*?"

"Yes, he is I, and I am him, but I want you to tell me, young hippo."

Themba looked up at the mage's display where he kept his jars and vessels, all which unsettled the prince. He gulped and began, "I don't know why I came here. Perhaps I need some questions to be answered. In truth, Sangoma, you might think I have a lot going for me, and don't get me wrong, I live a life of great privilege, but is it wrong for me to say that I am miserable?"

The Sangoma hissed.

"I have been here for ages and I have not made any progress in my mission to acquire the hand of Princess Nia. The king won't even grant me an audience. He hated me the first time he looked at me. He judged me, and he doesn't even know me."

The Sangoma lifted his chin. "Do you see those markings? That was a rope tied around my neck. When I returned from the Forest of Abominations, Maghedzi sentenced me to death. So, in my opinion, he likes you."

Themba could never get used to hearing that name, not when he was a young calf, and not today either. "YOU'VE been in the dark forest, and managed to escape?" The young prince was apprehensive. Once one entered the Forest of Abominations, there was no return, but a lot had been said about the mage around court and the various villages he and his entourage had visited on their procession towards Pyre Fortress. "What's it like?"

The Sangoma spent the next few hours recounting tales from his self-imposed banishment, from his struggles with his faith and his life as an extremophile. Early in his exile, the Sangoma had happened upon a cave filled with diamonds, rubies, topaz and other precious stones. He had danced in celebration atop the mound of his newfound riches and leisured in it like he was taking a warm bath in a hot spring. That prematurely ended when the tenant of the cavern, a grootslang, returned and chased him away. With its four tusks, elephantine body with ram-like horns and a spiked snake-like tail, the creature was so ferocious that after the species' creation, the Creator regretted making such a creature with tremendous strength, cunning and intellect, so much so, the Creator divided the leviathans into snakes and elephants. One grootslang escaped this fate and now as it seemed, lived to deny the spirit-medium enormous wealth.

Reza, who had been lying on the mat gnawing at a bone, started giggling wildly.

The Sangoma turned to the hyena, irate, and snapped, "Shut up, you lazy mutt. No, I am not going to tell him about the nyaminyami."

Themba's eyes widened, as did the mage's under his harrowing mask when he realized he had revealed too much.

"The nyaminyami," Themba inquired. "What of it? Have you also encountered the water dragon, mage?"

The Sangoma didn't want to say, but after some nagging from the prince, he finally succumbed. "I haven't . . . yet."

Themba shook his head and waved his hand dismissively. "I did not come here to be lied to, wizard!"

"True, I have not seen the water dragon with my own eyes, but I can feel it," the mystic whispered. "You see, child, I have always had one foot in the spirit realm. They speak to me. They tell me about the past, they tell me what is to come. They told me that many generations prior, when the nyaminyami roamed, magic was in abundance. I find it not a coincidence that my powers have recently grown exponentially. See for yourself." The Sangoma looked around to make sure no one was around, hidden behind a basket or in the shadows of his hut and then set his smoking pipe to the side, stood up and raised his staff. He let it twirl in his fingers for some moments before the serpent's eyes illuminated and then a draft began. He snapped his staff back and swung it over his head, sending the ball of air crashing onto the wall knocking down one of the vases that hang from it. "Prior to the nyaminyami's return I could only produce short spurts of fire from my staff, but now I can harness the power of the wind!"

Themba sat awestruck, unable to believe what he had just witnessed. He had thought the nyaminyami a fable, and heroes that had been deified like Goromonzi, Torindo the Red Arrow and Goneso the Tall, invented for children to aspire to. However, his perception was slowly shifting upon the recent revelations. After all, the mage had spoken of flying lizards, hairy imps and three headed monsters. The apocalyptic messages spewed by Akuwa oracles, the erratic weather and increased village attacks by supernatural forces began to make more sense to him. He had witnessed it himself, the night he and his half-brother, Xolani, visited General Moyo's farm—the carnage the mountain cats caused, and their paranormal ferocity. With a glint in his blood eye he now knew what he had to do—but only if he could find the courage. "Hypothetically speaking, what if one would want to find this nyaminyami. How would one go about it?"

"When I dwelled in the Forest of Abominations, the ancestors led me to a cave deep in the most treacherous part of the forest where all the creatures of your worst nightmares roam—stalking tribes of tokoloshe, feline packs of brindled furred nunda and opportunistic devouring gourds that wait in ambush—the depths of the forest with poisonous waters filled with enormous crocs and giant venomous serpents, and skies dominated by preying impdululu, kongamoto and makalala. On the walls I spied incomprehensible paintings, which after many years of observation, prayer and meditation, finally revealed themselves to me. As you know, our ancestors held the great antelope in the highest of regards, so much so they believed that in times of draught, an antelope's blood and milk helped produce rain. It is common to find artwork depicting this practice; however, in the painting I found in the dark forest, instead of the great antelope, the drawings described the capturing of a giant flying creature, serpentine and lizard like in its form. Rather than spears, the diviners wielded instruments. I identified them as a flute, mbira, marimba, harp, hosho and ngoma."

Themba's blood eye lit up. "So what does this mean, mage?"

"I was just about to get there. I entered the spirit realm, and after much pleading with the most powerful of the ancestors, they revealed to me that the diviner's music seduced the most ferocious of beasts to their will." The Sangoma shook his head and gritted his teeth. "Can you imagine such power?" He fell into a day dream, imagining what he could do with such means at his disposal. He could do whatever he wanted. Be whatever he wanted, even a king. "Unfortunately, part of the message was missing, the final piece to what would help me solve the riddle, so I set out, hoping to find similar paintings elsewhere in the detestable forest, however, one night I experienced an epiphany that led me back to Pyyros to aid the king in what is to come." He paused in contemplation. "Enough of this! I have said far too much. No thanks to my stupid mut!"

Reza cackled angrily at the mage.

"I don't even know why I keep her around. She is only but a nuisance to me. All she does is eat and leave her droppings for me to pick up. Anyway, let us get to why you are truly here. I am a very busy man. I travel in earnest. There are so many young souls that need to be purified around the kingdom and I need to prepare!"

The witchdoctor had tickled the prince's curiosity. He wanted to hear more, but he would have to do that another time. He shifted himself closer to the wizard, now unperturbed by his poignant scent. "I have been having this terrible dream, the same one, almost every night, but I can't remember it. I often wake up screaming with sweat all over my body."

"Your problem is a lot more common than you think. The question is, do you want to remember?"

The prince nodded.

After commanding Themba to rise, the Sangoma rose and shifted closer to the prince until he could see the inside of his nostrils. The mystic raised his pockmarked hand and let his fingers run down the prince's eyelashes. The Sangoma felt the crack of the prince's chest and let his hand stay there for some moments and felt his heartbeat. The mage stepped back, whipped out his staff and lifted it until it met Themba's pupils. The serpent's eyes flared a luminous red, similar to its wielder's eyes, who swayed the staff gently, left and right, round and round until the prince's gaze followed the motion. The wizard then set down it down and waved a hand in front of the prince's eyes. There was no reaction, just calm inertness on the young hippo's face. "Who are you?" the Sangoma began.

"I am Prince Themba."

"Good. Who are your parents?"

"King Farakaii and Queen Sibongile of the Akuwa."

"Excellent. Now listen to me, Themba Akuwa, I am going to go deep into your mind, deep into your soul and I am going to take it out. Let out all of your anguish, all of your burdens and give them to me. Let me carry them for you so I can cast them into a bottomless pit where they shall be devoured by a great fire! Tell me your dream."

"It begins with me toothless, treading through a dense forest until I come upon an enticing mango tree. The foliage is a wondrous green and the mangos a bright mix of coral, yellow and feint smaragdine. I walk up to it and reach out. Suddenly, I feel a crippling pain through my arm—here." He drew a line across his bicep covered with ivory colored cow-tails. "Another bolt zaps through my ankles. I turn my head as I bring out my spear, but all I see is its tail disappearing into the bush. Next, I'm trapped by a swarm of serpents, perhaps hundreds around me, swarming and flicking their tongues before they transform into waves. I'm suddenly on a canoe, you know, one of those kinds the fishermen ride. On it is my siblings, Simba, Tjingii, Nonkuleko and Xolani, my bastard brother. In the sky I see a comet, red, like those crimson red kanga cloths the Tsavo herdsmen wear. Kind of like the smudges on your mask."

The Sangoma hissed.

"Its long elegant red tail trailing behind is eerily beautiful." The prince chuckled lightly. "Like a voluptuous bride being ushered to the bed chamber by her husband with a stream of beads following closely behind. I throw in a fishing line. After a while I feel something. I pull, but it's too heavy. My brother comes to help me and when we finally pull it out, Tsitsi appears."

"Who is that?"

"Oh, some peasant girl I killed. I throw another line and this time, Yemuraii comes out. Her eagle-like nose cutting through the water. I throw in several other lines until more appear around the canoe, Sipho and Nthanda, Tariro . . . Pikoro. Then, their eyes turn violet, like a jacaranda leaf, and then they open their mouths to reveal monstrous fangs. They begin to claw at the canoe, rocking it from side to side as the sky burns blue and gold, and oceans of fire stretch as far as the owl can see. I stumble and almost fall out, into the dark violent waves, but Xolani saves me. Frantic, I pull out my trident and start stabbing. My brother and sister join me, but soon after, we are outnumbered. Simba . . ." the prince didn't want to continue, but he did nonetheless. "Simba gets pulled in. Just when he disappears under the current."

"What happens?"

"I row away." Tears began streaking down his cheeks. "I paddle away and leave my brother at the mercy of a pack of mermaids," he sniffed.

The Sangoma tossed the prince a cloth and continued sucking on his pipe. Finally, the prince awoke, hyperventilating. "What does this dream mean? Is my brother okay? I feel he is in great peril. I've felt that way for some time now. He is my twin. They say we are supposed to have a special bond."

Themba found himself in memory lane, during his rites of passage. Comrade Chengetaii had divided them into two battalions. As he jested with his comrades, something compelled him to get up from under the tree, grab his spear and run for half a day until he found Simba fending off a pack of hyenas. They fought bravely until they cut down the last of them, together as they had come into the world.

The Sangoma set his pipe down, studied the prince, and then informed, "The dream means you feel guilty for seeking your brother's throne."

Themba grabbed the Sangoma by the neck and snarled. "I seek no such thing, dark wizard! He is my brother! I love him!"

"You would strike a *moporofita*?"

The prince loosened his grip, setting the mage free. "I'm sorry. It's just, I've had this rage, this apoplectic anger inside me."

The Sangoma coughed before he regained his breath and the flames in his eyes became brighter. "What matters is what you do to make amends."

Like night to day, the prince was again the calm, unruffled figure in control of his destiny, rather than the seemingly hapless prince that had been pacing around maniacally around his lodgings. He whistled and shortly thereafter, Pikoro crept in, careful not to antagonize Reza. There was a solid thud when he laid the sack on the table.

The Sangoma relit his horn as his once blazing eyes grew cold again, took a long hard drag from his pipe, and let out a licorice scented mushroom cloud that reminded the prince of his father, King Farakaii of the Akuwa, who sat on the throne of his audience chamber as he ruled. "Forgiven."

Chapter 15

Trawling

The Kukongolas had front row seats to the stick fighting competitions. As they were husband hunting, they were dressed to impress. It took all morning but when Yananayii was finally prepped and ready, she was clad in a modest cotton garment and a matching oval flat-topped headdress. Amongst the beads that adorned her neck, arms and ankles were discreet gold and silver trinkets as well as copper and colorful stones.

Her father, Matibiri, whose moustache was silver-white, and forehead, wide with numerous lines, wore a feathered headdress over his balding, mottled scalp. This made him seem giant-like, as he was already a very tall man, and once upon a time, incredibly muscular. He was at that time considered one of the most attractive men in the district, desired by many maidens. But it was Yananayii's mother, the girl next door, that took his fancy. He never remarried after she passed. He oft said that when she was cremated, she took with her, his heart. Since then he had let himself go, piling on the pounds around his stomach, and took little if no time to groom himself. A barrage of jewelry sat over his tires of fat, as did gold, silver and copper about his ankles and wrists. His apron was a dark indigo—a color Pyyrisians associated with wealth.

"I don't understand why you men do this. It's so brutal," Yananayii cried, as the competitors lined up around the fighting ring. Brutal it was. It wasn't uncommon to hear that so and so had died or became a cripple.

"You have a soft, gentle heart. Like your mother," Matibiri replied softly. "You see, stick fighting was given to us by our ancestors. It is a way of teaching our boys social values and the worthy nature and respectability of physical endeavors. Through stick fighting our boys learn to sharpen their physical prowess and mental attitudes required in hunting and combat. It is also somewhat of a stage for our boys to assert themselves and achieve a social identity."

Yananayii nodded her head as though she understood. "Are you going to join the fighting today, *baba*?"

"I might," Matibiri jested. "Relive the good old days. You know, I was once a fearsome stick fighter. That is how I gained your mother's hand in marriage." A tear began to form around his eyes, as it did every time he mentioned his dead wife.

"Now, now, now, father," she handed him a cloth. "The first fight is about to begin."

The contestants paced around each other, wearing nothing but little loincloths that only covered their private parts, and then in a flash of a moment, leapt toward each other with their sticks raised. The spar looked pretty even until one of the fighters, frustrated at the stalemate, made a bold move that left him open to a whack across his face.

"That is a shame," Yananayii lamented. "He was once handsome," she chuckled as blood flowed from his now broken nose. After he had been dragged away by his feet, Yananayii turned to her father. "Where you really any good?"

Matibiri was incensed by his daughter's insinuation, but he was used to it. She had always been mischievous and cheeky. "Ask any of the elders, they will tell you how I whacked Wasike the king's first guard all bloody, and even . . ." He put a palm over his mouth and whispered, "The spymaster, Chiratidzo."

Yananayii's eyes widened in shock—not so much awe. "Is that so?"

Matibiri nodded his head proudly. "Indeed. That afternoon I was unconquerable."

"You must be over exaggerating, *baba*. You? An athlete? You've always been too preoccupied with your wealth for that sort of thing."

"What I tell you is true, *mudiwa*. The same dedication I have to wealth is the same I had for sport!"

The next contestants entered the ring, saluted one another, and then commenced. The reverie seemed to get Matibiri in a fond mood. "I remember my greatest afternoon. I was just three fists of age, battling men twice my size. King A'hi was in attendance that afternoon. I had never seen more people congregated in the district center. I went through the contest with relative ease, smacking my opponents in the face until they were either on their backs, or on their knees begging for my mercy. If it weren't for an injury I suffered later that night at a tavern celebrating, I may have qualified for the final and been in contention to represent the Piripiri Kingdom at the Great Flame Festival."

He pulled his daughter closer so no one could hear. "You know, people say that our king had to crown Farakaii of Akuwa champion at that festival. They say because of these events, the Eternal Flame ended up stealing Prince Farakaii's betrothal to Zandile Moto by offering her father an unprecedented number of cows." He chuckled. He put a finger to his lips. "Remember, some have lost a tongue, others their heads, for talking about that."

Yananayii nodded solemnly. She rather liked her head. She liked to look at it over the surface of a pond or a lake. "How many cows have you set for me?"

"Surely not as many, or even half," he chuckled.

"But father, you say I am far more attractive than Queen Zandile ever was."

"That is true, my sweet daughter, you are, but the queen," he paused. "How can I say this . . ." He knew his daughter well. Despite the beauty and life of privilege the ancestors had bestowed her, confidence was a resource she was short, and often left her wallowing in bouts of doubt. "The queen was a once in a lifetime gem, as you are, with hips men would run into Death Valley for, a face as if carved by Puk'yi the Sculptor himself, however, my dear sweet child, Zandile is the daughter of a high chief. The Moto were once kings and can trace their lineage all the way to the Volcan kings!"

Yananayii understood. "What do you think of him?" She used her head to point. A new group of fighters had entered the ring after a dire contest between two fighters that were neither handsome nor wealthy.

Matibiri recognized the boy. He came from a prominent family in the district. He knew his father well, having conducted business with one another for many years. "Kanji?" With his goat tails, Matibiri shooed some flies away, and then set one elbow on his knee and observed.

The boy was tall, not too slender, and not too big. The pair couldn't find a flaw on him, whether it be his face, stomach, arms or legs, but could he fight? Matibiri knew his days were numbered. His witchdoctor had told him so. He had kept that a secret from Yananayii for some moons now. He would only rest well with his ancestors knowing his only daughter had protection.

His fears were veered when with one whack of his staff, Kanji snapped his opponent's stick in half and preceded to toy with the foe, sending the crowd into a raucous frenzy. Kanji poked at the boy's feet, making him dance, and then thrashed him by the thighs until the poor challenger was on his knees. Kanji raised his stick in the air, took the adulation of the crowd and then with both hands clasped firmly around the staff, whacked the beggar across the face until teeth flew into the air and scattered.

Matibiri stood up, nodded his head in approval and clapped heartily smiling from ear to ear. "I don't want to jinx it, Yana, but I think we have found our man."

Chapter 16

A Game of Nhodo

Now that Chief Lume of Kwa'Jivu had allowed Queen Zandile and Nia to stay, the Piripiri princess was back to her old self, getting her knees dirty and making a nuisance of herself to her mother's annoyance. She didn't have Uncle Machupa's spear that she would 'borrow' whenever he got drunk and rested under the shade of one of Pyre Fortress' ubiquitous trees, so she used a stick she had sharpened at the end. It lacked the same equipoise of the obsidian tipped blades she was accustomed to, but for now it would have to do.

"Purification?" Tears were sailing down her cheeks one afternoon as bark splintered from her thunderous strokes deep in the Ngorongoro forest as she unleashed her ire against her father. "Your daughter? Dirty?" She repeated this for hours like a mantra, as she had done every day since she found her woodland sanctuary, where she would spar against imaginary images of the king. She was about to leave and return to the village when she heard a rumbling in the bush nearby. "Come out whoever you are or I'll strike!" Nia knew it was man, for the woodland critters moved in stealth. After the third command, finally someone slid out. "I know you. You are that girl from a few compounds away." She put her stick down. "It's okay. I won't hurt you. You can come closer."

So the girl did, and in no time, Nia and Amara, who also wore her hair shaggy with kernels and seeds in it, had become friends. They would play games Nia now considered childish and the princess would teach Amara the art of stick-fighting, though to her frustration, it would take a while. Nia told Amara about

Wafula, the baby-faced boy she used to play with at Pyre Fortress, and showed Amara the dagger he had given her.

"So, he is your boyfriend," concluded Amara, in a matter-of-fact tone after sliding a finger over its sharp edge.

The blade was fixed on a hilt of ebony metal covered in feint once red leather, flared at the ends like a raging fire.

"No, he is not," Nia snapped, swinging a knuckle toward Amara's shoulder.

Amara was fast. She skipped out of the way and laughed. "He is a boy, is he not?"

"Yes."

"And he is your friend, right?"

Nia and Wafula had constructed kites and flown them over the Pyre Fortress' skies together. They had climbed trees and hunted locust. They had laughed; they had cried. They had found an ancient ruin with paintings of a winged creature made of smoke and fire. He was by her side the first time she menstruated. "Yes."

"Then he is your boy . . . friend . . . right?"

"Yee . . . eess." *Wait*, Nia considered. She bridged her eyebrows and chased after Amara until they were rolling around and giggling in the grass.

Their laughter ended when a shadow loomed over them. "Good afternoon, mother," Nia greeted, as she helped Amara up and dusted herself off.

Queen Zandile was shaking her head in disbelief. "What are you doing, young women? You are no longer little girls, and here you are, rumbling in the dirt like rodents. You will never find husbands this way. No one wants a dirty wife, with grass and twigs in her hair!"

"We are sorry, Queen Zandile," pardoned Amara. "We will behave ourselves from now on."

"You better! I expect the both of you home for lunch!" Zandile turned and walked away, the tail of her sleeveless wraparound dress following behind her like a serpent.

"I like you," informed Amara. "It is a shame you are just visiting. I wish you could stay here forever."

Nia wished the same. She wished she could tell Amara the truth, about what they had been through, about all the hurdles, their trials and tribulations—the blood, *so much blood*—but she couldn't. It was too dangerous. When the princess and queen had fled Pyre Fortress, they had exchanged their royal garb for peasants' and taken aliases when needed. Nia took the name Chafu—a name that described the young princess' carefree and roguish ways. It was a nickname only shared between she and her childhood friend Wafula—her only friend, who had *abandoned* her when he moved away with his new family, leaving here in tears. Zandile took the alias Kutenda, the name of her great grandmother she was told, who had died giving birth to her mother, Tarisai. Nia had always longed for another life— not confined by the limitations of Pyre Fortress, but not like this. "It is a little different from home, and I do miss my brothers, but I am really happy here."

Amara took out a couple of marula fruits and offered one of them. "You and I will be friends forever." They sunk their teeth into them and smiled as the juice trickled down their chins. "I have an idea. Let's play *nhodo*."

"What's that?"

"It is really easy. I will show you." The girls searched for pebbles and dug a large hole, about half a foot in diameter. They sat down on the red earth and Amara elucidated, "Usually we play with ten pebbles." She handed one to Nia, slightly larger than the others with a darker tint. "This is yours. It is called a *mbuga*."

Nia looked rather bored. "Are you sure this is fun?"

"I promise. You will love it. The objective of the game is to eliminate all of the pebbles over ten stages. You understand?"

Nia nodded her head, but in truth, she was still rather confused.

"I'll walk you through it. In the first stage, you toss your *mbuga* into the air and drag more than one pebble out and catch the *mbuga* like this before it falls." Amara tossed her *mbuga* in the air and as quick as a mamba, grabbed a couple of pebbles from the pit just in time to catch the *mbuga* before it fell.

Nia's face animated, impressed by her new friend's lightning reflexes. She stuck out her tongue in concentration, threw her *mbuga* into the air, reached into the pit, but failed to catch her *mbuga*. She frowned. Amara had made it look easy.

"Usually you miss your turn if you drop your *mbuga*, but since it's your first time, I'll forget it," Amara smiled. "I should also mention that if you fail to drag out the minimum number of pebbles, you also lose your turn. When you drag and miss the pit, you also lose your turn and conversely, if you fail to leave the minimum number of pebbles outside . . ."

"You lose your turn," Nia finished.

"Good. Let's continue. Then you toss the *mbuga* in the air again and drag back all the pebbles except one. You keep that pebble and repeat what I just showed you until all ten pebbles have been eliminated from the circle. Got it?"

They played all morning, even forgetting to go home for lunch. When they remembered they were supposed to be home for their afternoon meal, Queen Zandile was standing behind them sporting a smile and in her hands, two bowls. They ate heartily until they were full and snoring under a coral tree.

When the girls awoke from their afternoon slumber, with little bright red leaves covering their bodies, they returned home to help prepare the evening meal. "Weh," Zandile exclaimed. "I am glad you have made friends like Amara. Usually you never want to help with the hut work."

"That's not true. I help sometimes," Nia protested.

"Barely." Zandile reached for her ear playfully, but Nia evaded her fingers.

"What's it like being a queen?" Amara inquired.

Zandile wanted to reply trapped, bound to another's will, *to play second fiddle to a mountain—and a stone,* but she smiled and replied, "It is a great honor being a queen. It is a great responsibility. You are not just a mother to your own children, but to every person in the kingdom."

Amara looked at Zandile with starry eyes. The queen had regained her weight, a far cry from the gaunt physique she and Nia had arrived with. She was every bit the great queen Amara had heard about in stories and songs that hailed her unparalleled beauty. "I'd like to be a queen one day."

Zandile reached into the vase that was hanging from the ceiling like a vine and plucked a leaf from the fire lily. "Take this, kindle it at night when you are alone, and make a wish."

Amara thanked her. "I have to go home. Thank you for the food." She knelt, clapped her hands and left.

"That new friend of yours," Zandile praised. "Such a well-mannered girl. You could learn a few things from her!"

Moons later, laughter filled the hut as the chief, who after a few calabashes of *doro,* occasionally considered himself a jester. "What about this one?" The crowed waited with bated breath for another of the chief's rib-tickling zingers. Zandile and her mother sat quietly, laughing moderately compared to others, as they had heard them countless times before and in truth, Zandile didn't find them funny at all. "A husband was troubled, so went to a spiritual healer. When he returned home, he lifted his wives on each shoulder and carried them around the compound. The wives had never seen their husband so energetic. Bewildered, they asked, 'Husband, what advice did the clairvoyant give you? To be more romantic?'"

Princess Nia on the edge of her stool hollered, "I know this one, I know this one."

"No," continued the chief, snorting like a pig first. "We must carry our burdens!" The king waited for the raucous to subside and then went for another joke, but as he began, a man appeared at the entrance.

The room was dimly lit, with only the fire that blazed in the middle, lighting the spacious room, but the eyes of the visitor seemed to illuminate the chamber, as did the pale white kanzu that hang loosely over his frame. Zandile turned and looked at her father, unable to conceal her disappointment—her heartbreak. "Zandile," cried the chief. "I am sorry. I had no choice!"

"Grandfather," exclaimed Nia. The chief did not raise his head. "Grandmother?" There was no response there either. Tarisai's eyes swelled and tears broke down her cheeks.

Zandile shot a last resentful gaze at her parents and surrendered herself to the Desert Snake.

Chapter 17

The Thief of Time

Lumambo Mundu's final rite of passage was performed atop a wood fueled pyre by a stream from the Nhunundudu River. *This is the same place mother died*, Tauya reflected, as he gazed down at his father for the last time. He didn't want to see him like this. It was the third day since Lumambo had passed, and nature had not spared him. *At least you are with mother now, in her warm embrace*, he comforted himself.

He had slept in the same room with his father as he lay in state, bathed him and clothed him. He would even bring his father food, to appease him, so Lumambo had no reason to cause chaos upon him in the afterlife as a malicious spirit. *I tried to be a good son*, he sobbed. If he wasn't in life, he meant to be a good son in his father's death, so he took great pains to ensure the cremation ritual was done correctly, as the process signified the transition between life and death.

Lumambo's funeral procession was a humble affair, with perhaps only a handful of drummers, friends, neighbors, and relatives, so Tauya had to hire professional mourners, who wailed loudly, ripped their hair out of their heads and scratched their faces bloody. A strong throng of mourners signified that the deceased was once a wealthy and powerful individual. *You once were, father!* Tauya lamented, but that was a thing of the past. A man who lived by the land depended on it to be fruitful, but the sporadic rains and poor judgments made had seen an end to his status as a respected man in the district. *Where are the Uyaba and Mamharwe? They all abandoned him!* Tauya carped. *After all he did for them! I shall call upon them to get back those shells they loaned!*

As the only son, when he lit Lumambo's body aflame, he began to wail, even louder than the professional mourners. "Goodbye father, now I am truly alone," he wept, as the peculiar smell of burnt flesh engulfed his nostrils. "And you are with your beloved ancestors." He wanted to follow his father into the flames, and almost did if not for Rafiki's last moment intervention.

"You need to calm yourself. You are the man of the house now," Rafiki whispered. "Everybody is watching!"

"It's my fault," Tauya sobbed inexorably.

"What did you say?" Rafiki's eyebrow was raised in suspicion. One had to be cautious at funerals, for few deaths were ever seen as natural.

"Nothing, I just miss him so much." In truth, Tauya oft missed his father when he was alive. Lumambo was a man who favored the company of the ancestors rather than people, including his only son.

When Tauya had returned from the forest looking for medicine, he had found Lumambo unconscious. "Wake up, *baba*," he had begged, but Lumambo was gone, now one with the ancestors he had dedicated his latter years.

After the body burned, Lumambo's ashes and remaining fragments of bones and teeth were interned in a funerary urn. No funeral was complete unless there was a ritual feast at the end of it. It ensured the deceased's passage to the ancestors and allowed the bereaved to move forward; however, much like in life, Lumambo was also unlucky in death, as it began to rain, ending the feast prematurely.

"What did your prayers accomplish, father," Tauya asked as he scurried to the safety of a tree's shade with the urn tucked tightly in his arms like an infant.

That question was answered later that evening at the inheritance ceremony, where Tauya took the mantle of the man of the compound. He would inherit a dozen or so cows, several goats, chickens and a donkey, some barren lands, a compound of four huts and a kitchen, a rusty old spear his father was not famous for wielding, several headdresses, some cheap jewelry and his father's widows who were now his burden to bear.

"I wish I could have given you a daughter in law as you wanted," Tauya grieved to Lumambo's urn cradled in his arms as he sat in the chamber his father once enjoyed meditating upon. "I bet you will be smiling when you see what I have in line. Maybe finally you will be proud of me." In retrospect, his father had been proud of him once . . . *wait, no.* His father had always treated him with criticism and disrespect. 'Mother's boy', was what Lumambo liked to call him the most, and often accused him of hiding behind her skirts when he wanted to give the boy a good hiding.

Tauya turned to Rafiki, who had his fingers deep into his calabash of sorghum pap and meat from the goat he had slaughtered in his father's memory. "Come, let's go for a walk."

They walked in silence. Rafiki found himself losing breath as Tauya walked with a blistering pace. "Where are you taking me? It better not be to find another fire lily. What was that nonsense by the way? Looked like witchcraft to me!"

"Just be quiet, and follow me."

They passed the district square, which was illuminated by the eternal holy fire that burnt hot ribbons of light. The smell of wood smoke drifted through their noses as shimmering embers leapt from the mound of pyre and snaked in a blazing dance, flickering like stars and crackling like dry leaves in the forest. After entering the northern residential areas, where the finest and largest homes were located, they arrived outside a compound and hid behind a large tree posted just outside of the perimeter.

"What are we doing now?" Rafiki whispered.

"We wait."

"For what?"

Tauya didn't reply. After some moments, a figure appeared through the window. Tauya's eyes livened, and his cheek bones rose unlike anything Rafiki had seen before. When the window shut, Tauya, with his back on the tree trunk, and hands by his breast, slid down the tree overwhelmed with happiness.

Rafiki was very annoyed. "You took me out here to linger outside some girl's compound?"

"Quiet, Rafiki, or we'll get caught. That isn't just some girl. That is my future wife. Just one look, that's all I needed, one look to cure my heart of all my unhappiness."

Rafiki shook his head and began to walk back. "You are insane. Get up, let's go to the tavern."

Tauya arrived at work late, to his overseer's dismay. "Why are you late again?" Sibile Wachikopa's arms were crossed, as were her eyebrows. She did that in the same way her father, the owner of the tannery did when he was unsatisfied with the season's yield.

"My father died, remember?" In truth, Tauya had been by the lagoon where he had first met the girl of his dreams. He had been there every day since he had met her, but she hadn't appeared.

"My condolences," offered Sibile. "Do you need some more time away?"

"That won't be necessary. I think work will be good for me, to help me forget."

"Very well. Anyway, we have some new hides." She threw one Tauya's way, landing over his headdress, now with elaborate ostrich plumes, symbolizing he was the head of a household.

He inspected the hide and then looked around. His colleague was nowhere in sight. Like him, because of the barren soils his family tilled, Tumelo also had taken up tanning to help add food to his family's table. "You can't expect me to do all this by myself?"

"If this is too much for you, just say so and we can find someone who is willing to put in the work," Sibile replied.

Tauya's newly inherited lands weren't producing any crops, so he got to it, beginning the rigorous and odious process by separating the hides into several mounds. It took most of the day, and when he was done, he ran to the lagoon to find, as he had found every day for the last half moon, no one in the waters. To make matters worse, no one appeared at the window despite him lingering there until the wee hours of the morning.

The next day he put one mound of hides into a dying pit containing natural vegetable dyes. This pit had sumac, which would turn the hides into the color red, a shade that had made somewhat of a resurgence in the district. They could add a few more shells to the price of their hides. He also added some marula oil into the pit, to give the hides a shiny quality, but because of the lackluster rains, the tannery couldn't afford to be munificent with the oil, leaving the hides somewhat inferior.

When the rains were plenty and agriculture was bountiful, they would use darkwood from Domboshawa for their brown dyes, but in these times they had to rely on common acacia wood. For the verdant dyes, he added mint, and for the yellow dyes, he added pomegranate. He worked the whole day and through the night, even sleeping at the tannery. He awoke early and continued his duties until midday. Tumelo was back now, so he left him preparing the hides for drying. That was the easiest part, for unlike other products like vegetables, fruit and meat, the sun was in abundance.

He went to the lagoon and sat on the bank with his feet in. He sat there for hours on end, despondent, apparently impervious to the sun's hard-hitting rays and ruminated on the girl he had met. He was about to call it a day and return home when a voice giggled behind him, "Aren't you going to jump in?" A cool wind billowed around her skirt, exposing soft, pale thighs.

He looked to his side, and there sat beside him was the girl looking out into the distance, perhaps at the pair of ground hornbills that glided toward Mount Pyyros' clouds, with their wings stretched out, ivory tipped and flared. She was as beautiful as ever. As beautiful as the first time he saw her strut her stuff during the Water Plea. "I can't swim," he finally replied. "But I like dipping my toes and peering into the water. It is strange, isn't it? Considering my mother drowned? My father, he is also dead now. He passed half a moon ago, that same day I first met you."

The girl put a hand over her mouth and gritted her teeth. "I am so sorry."

"Thank you for the kind words. My mother and father are now together, resting, with their ancestors."

"My mother, she died also, but I was too young to remember her."

"I'm sorry," Tauya replied, putting a hand on her thigh and rubbing it softly.

"It's okay, I guess you can't miss something you've never had."

"It's still sad though."

She nodded her head in agreement. "What's it like, having an *amai*?"

Tauya looked into the sky and pondered for some moments. He remembered his mother applying some herbs on his throbbing knee after he had scraped it climbing trees, and concocting a brew whenever he had fallen to the elements. All the time she had a smile on her face, and whenever he would look up at her, he knew he was safe. "I cannot explain it. There is nothing like it."

A soft wind blew between them and a salubrious beam of light shone through the cracks of the canopy above like the ancestors had showered their ethereal glory upon them relieving their keen grief.

"You asked for my name. Yananayii," she revealed as walnut and pecan eyes blent silently for some moments.

Most men could not stand Yananayii's gaze, nor could Tauya in most respects, but something, perhaps his father's spirit, gave him a courage he didn't know existed and spurred his fingers to cautiously, tenderly stroke the back of her neck. Her lips were as soft as the sensation of her hair on his fingertips when they parted, and the smell of her sweet vanilla scent helped him guide her wraparound beside her. Her eyes blinked, allowing her eyelashes, longer than any he'd ever seen, to flutter like a firefly. *Ancestors*, he gasped. He was spellbound, trapped, and he knew there was no escape, not even with the aid of all the kingdom's greatest enchanters.

"This is my first time," she revealed.

Tauya dipped his head low, brushed her earlobe with his lips and whispered to her. "Me too."

Chapter 18

The Grand Tour

Prince Themba of the Akuwa spent the following days gawking at the Sangoma as the mage performed the ancestors' work around the palace grounds. It seemed that his consultation with the witchdoctor had left an indelible mark on the young hippo prince who looked on like a love-struck pubescent as the mystic conducted ceremony after next. He could barely contain himself when the mage thrust his gnarly staff high into the sky, and professed him to be an unequaled man of the ancestors when he saw how skillfully the mage slashed sacrifices from ear to ear, thus, when it was the day of the Lamentation, a ceremony the flame peoples had observed since the first Piripiri descended bearing fire, Themba made sure to be present with all his Akuwa entourage. They arrived just as the Sangoma's staff spat a flame from its fangs lighting the pyre until the holy smoke glided toward the mountainscape, overrunning malevolent spirits that oft visited wielding spears of chaos and mischief. Amongst the tribes that had descended from the Volcan Kings, an eternal holy fire was kept in the middle of every village and city. The throng that had congregated, warriors, artisans and farmers alike, performed the Piripiri fire-dance, hissing as a snake cries upon a mongoose's birth. Only by invite were outsiders allowed to feed the fire, so Themba was startled when he was called up and handed a log of wood. He accepted it circumspectly and then cautioned up to the ten-man high pyre. Smoke soared skyward from it with a southern wind toward Hippo Valley—toward home—toward his family and friends—toward everything he had ever known. He performed a silent prayer, hoping the Akuwa ancestors could hear him, so far away from home, and cast the log into the raging flames.

A loud cheer erupted as the crowd chanted, "Gyiku'o! Gyiku'o!"

Things had turned for the better for the Akuwa prince. He felt as though an albatross had been unburdened from his shoulders. Cathartic sleep came easily at night now that the Sangoma had prescribed him some herbs. The nightmares that had plagued his journey and stay in Pyyros had seized and had now been replaced by mauve-tinged wet dreams.

In it, he was lying on a large luxurious mat covered by purple and lilac jacaranda leaves. One by one women appeared around his mat. He lifted himself and balanced his body on his elbows, as all the girls from his past appeared: The innkeeper's and metalsmith's daughters, General Moyo and General Shato's daughters, the Chitemo chief's daughters all the way from Mazowe, as well as other numerous, faceless women who had shared his mat. They all smiled at him, their breasts all looking at him in their various forms and sizes, bouncing up and down as their excitement to see him overcame them. Then lastly, a figure appeared in front of him with her face draped behind a beaded mask. She was a lodestone figure with a magnetic force the prince could not deny. She walked up toward him seductively, stopping by the edge of his mat and took off her mask.

"Nia," Themba asked before he woke up. "Holy ancestors," he cursed. It seemed the dream always ended before he got a glimpse of the face under the beads, but whoever it was, his spirits had turned for the better and it was all thanks to the wizard.

He was even finally granted an audience with the king, this time at the palace thoroughfare. Beside Maghedzi snapped his new pet ngiri'mamba he had named Kuluma, now about four meters in length. The juvenile had grown into a fine specimen, well armored with thick, olive-green leathery skin with bony plate-shaped scales. Kuluma lifted himself and snapped at the air when the king dangled a large fish above him. After the pleasantries, Maghedzi gave Themba a tour around his palace grounds as the boar-croc wobbled behind them, the king seemingly oblivious he was walking a vicious reptile.

The palace boasted numerous courtyards, each surrounded with alcoves and verandahs. Fine artwork and stone monoliths were a staple around the fortress with lush verdant gardens and perfectly trimmed hedges. Themba noted the security, which he calculated could withstand a season under siege; however, more than anything, he was mostly impressed by the Fire Shrine.

By the entrance, statues of the Ifirit, the winged King of the Kongamoto stared at them as they walked down the tunnel with walls and statues covered with gold leaf. According to Maghedzi, his ancient ancestor, Puk'yi the Sculptor, who had resistance to fire, molded the statues of the fearsome creature that blazed in smokeless fire. Puk'yi's uncanny ability allowed him to fashion the molten rock to his will before it solidified. Hanging from chandeliers, kongamoto statues created shadows that complemented the eeriness of the room. The offshoots led to smaller chambers with multiple rooms of several levels that contained a series of traps and obstacles to be overcome as part of a trial, for only the wisest and truest deserved to be in the presence of the ancient ancestors.

The foyer was a large cylindrical room with offshoots connected by tunnels. A large flame raged in the center that was kept alive by a lava flow that channeled through the temple. "The lava runs from Mount Pyyros," informed the king as he knelt and slowly pushed his fingers toward the stream, as if bewitched. He grimaced from the pain after an unusually long abhorrence to the scalding, then snapped his fingers back and rose. "They say the lava comes from the center of the mountain. Every day I have gone up there and peered into its streams of fire. Is it strange to you that I find peace there? Amongst the burning rocks and steaming lava?"

Themba could relate. He was Akuwa, with the blood of the river lords rushing through his veins. He oft found himself seduced by gushing currents that took fishermen and careless rovers to their deaths. He would linger riverside, sometimes for hours on end until the day had passed, peering down into the effervescent waters—deep and murky like an otherworldly abyss. "Not strange at all," the young prince finally answered.

"Up on the mountain I have men digging every day. The gold, silver, and iron ores they pluck is well and good, but I seek something greater. Something that will bring peace amongst all the tribes, and even amongst the beasts of the wild."

"That is why I am here, Raging Inferno. Your daughter . . ."

"Enough with that." Maghedzi turned and moved toward the exit. Themba had to spring to catch up with his brisk strides. "One of these days, I shall take you up to the volcano, so you can see for yourself. It is also the best place to view my kingdom."

They took a walk through the various Pyyros district markets, passing stalls selling local pottery, imported glass beads, crucibles, spindle whorls and among others, grinding stones. At other stalls hung various textiles on display—imported natural yarn, domestic fabrics of cotton, wool, zitenge, mudcloth, barkcloth and kanga to name a few—red and black the main colors in vogue. The stall keepers bowed and saluted the king as they passed, some falling on their faces in reverence of their king. One man was so overcome by his love for his liege he began to cry, joyous tears flowing down his cheeks.

They halted their tour by a footsmith's stall in Boroa. The cobbler stopped his threadwork, rummaged in his chest, and presented his latest creation to the prince. Themba looked at Maghedzi for confirmation, and after that, the prince was brought a stool. He sat and let the smith slip on the sandal and buckle the straps. They were similar to the king's very own pair, but where the king's had red-beaded flame toe bars that connected the parallel straps across his feet, and little red leather threads flaring sideways, this pair was less grand but none the less studied with colorful gemstones. After Comrade Chengetaii's training, he wasn't used to sandals, but it did feel good. "How much," he asked, twisting and turning his foot as he inspected the footwear. He thought he would return to Hippo Valley with a pair each for his siblings.

"For you, nothing."

Themba didn't know what to say. "Thank you?"

"No need, Prince Themba. It is my honor having my sandal worn by royalty!" The cobbler bowed as the king and prince continued their walk amongst the plebs, like two immortals descended from the firmament to bless the harvest.

The next morning, Prince Themba and his entourage were summoned to the palace gates. A regiment of Fireflies waited with the king, black shiny spears and oblong shields tucked close to their bodies. "I hope you are ready for a short trip," notified the king.

"Where to?"

"Death Valley"

Chapter 19

Trials of Love

Tauya Mundu and Yananayii Kukongola frolicked over the canvas of dried leaves, rolling around laughing. Tauya gazed upon her flawless, naked chassis, like he had seen a rainbow for the first time. Her skin glistened with a sensual sweat, skin so smooth and silky, almost as if it was tailored from gold fabric. She sat on top of him and gazed down at him. Her eyes were a rapturous paint of hazel-auburn. In them inhabited a coruscate twinkle that augmented their splendor, a tenderness that cut through the very fiber of Tauya's soul. Usually Yananayii wore simple studs in her ears when she met him, but today she had copper hoops that sat perfectly on her bare shoulders. "You are so beautiful," he confessed, a little ashamed, for those words couldn't justify what he saw. He couldn't believe it. Here she was, the girl of his dreams, and she was his, all his, in every way possible except one.

She got up and fastened her wraparound.

"Same place, same time tomorrow?" he asked her.

"I have some plans with my father. We will have to meet another day."

"Can't you cancel them?"

"If you'd meet my father, you'd know that that is impossible."

"Well, why don't I?"

"What?"

"Meet your father?"

She laughed, but soon stopped when she saw that he meant what he said. "Things are complicated right now. You will meet him one day. I promise."

Tumelo was outside the tannery when Tauya arrived at work. "Where have you been?" he whispered. "Sibile has been looking around everywhere for you."

"I thought you said you'd cover me."

"Yes, I did, but I can only cover you for so long. You've been away for three days! What in Gyiku'o's name have you been doing?"

Tauya smiled and looked into the heavens as though a wondrous bird with flowing golden feathers was gliding through the sky. "Tumelo, I am in love."

Tumelo was bewildered. "That's why you haven't been coming to work?" He shook his head and laughed, for that was the only thing he could do. "Make sure you have a better excuse when Sibile asks you about your absence!"

Luckily enough for him, Sibile had been preoccupied with the selling of the finished hides. She could procure an exorbitant sum for them, as these luxury goods were becoming rare. That day Tauya was a model employee, and a better colleague, allowing Tumelo to take as many breaks as he wanted, and insisted on carrying the greater loads, but the next few days he was a nightmare to be around as Yananayii hadn't showed up for days on end.

"Go and get yourself some sleep," Tumelo told him. Now dark shadows surrounded Tauya's eyes. His clothes weren't up to their usual standard and he looked like he had lost quite a bit of weight. "You look like you need some!"

Instead, Tauya went to the store to buy Yananayii a gift on his way to their secret conclave.

He couldn't believe his eyes when he arrived at his sanctuary of love. In the distance he spied a man sat next to Yananayii, exactly where they would sit by the lagoon—where they had first made love. He dropped the copper earrings he had bought and thundered toward the couple with haste, trying his best to exude calm, even ignoring the thorny bushes that brushed over his skin.

Yananayii was the first to spot him approaching. She smiled and waved. When he arrived, he couldn't believe it. It was his best friend, Rafiki, smiling from ear to ear. "Tauya," Yananayii greeted, "Why didn't you tell me you had such hilarious friends?"

Rafiki was still smiling. "The best company," he winked at Tauya. "Isn't that right, Yananayii?"

She giggled, "Indeed."

"How did you find this place?" Tauya asked, barely masking his irritation.

"Everyone has been wondering where you've been lately," replied Rafiki, "So I decided to follow you, and this lady here, is what I found." He turned around and looked into the waters with his arms spread out. "I can see why you like coming here so often. The view is so beautiful, isn't it?" Mount Pyre loomed in the distance, below the low-lying clouds and heavy mists that lay in the mountain's hollows.

Rafiki didn't hear the reply, just a cracking sound over his head. Tauya picked up the bloody stone and struck his friend again, this time sending Rafiki to his knees. Tauya leapt onto him and struck, over and over again until Rafiki's face was unrecognizable, just mush and splintered bone.

When Tauya was done, gasping for air, he sat atop his old friend and that's when he heard her screams.

"Calm down!"

Yananayii was about to run, but Tauya grabbed her and held her tight by his breast. "Look at me," he pled, "Look at me," this time less a plea, but more of a command. After some moments she did. His face had bone marrow and blood splashed over his tanned complexion. "He was trying to get between us, okay?"

It took some convincing but soon enough they began to kiss, wild, like two worms tangled in the mud, and all the while, Rafiki's lifeless eyes stared at them as he was spread out over the leaves with his arms and legs spread out. Against their religious customs, they buried the body in a ditch like a pauper and fled for their homes, promising to lay low for a while, for there was sure to be a search for Rafiki's body.

After an agonizing couple of full moons, Tauya and Yananayii resumed their courtship, however, something had changed. Tauya could feel it. There wasn't the same laughter in her eyes, nor the sharp-tongued wit he had grown so fond of. Hers was a face that didn't hide emotions easily. "You are not yourself, *wangu*. What's wrong?" Tauya finally asked after she had turned down his advances several times.

She didn't want to say, but finally she explained, "My father, he has found me a husband." She told him the story, of how she was so beautiful that no man was ever brave enough to approach her, so she asked her father to find her a husband. "That was before I met you," she pled. "Please don't be angry."

Tauya gritted his teeth and contemplated. "What are you going to do?"

"I don't know." She looked down and began to sob. "Father says he is the perfect husband for me, and has offered many cows."

"How many?"

Tauya gritted his teeth when he heard the number. His whole world was beginning to crash, slowly, like an injured cub stuck in the pathway of a wildebeest stampede.

Yananayii's eyes lit up. "My father, above all, loves wealth and me. He cannot bare to disappoint me, so if I beg him to consider another betrothal, he might accept it, if . . ."

"One offers more cows," Tauya finished.

She nodded her head as she stroked his chest, flat, but with sparse hairs. "And then we can be together, forever."

<h1 style="text-align:center">Chapter 20</h1>

<h2 style="text-align:center">Death Valley</h2>

Prince Themba of the Akuwa and his entourage followed the Fireflies as they marched toward Death Valley. After passing through the majesty and wonder of the Piripiri capital, they were in the countryside where barley, nightshade, amaranth, okra, spider plant and black-eyed peas were cultivated. They marched past children playing, women carrying water back to their villages, and young men guiding livestock back to their cages.

They passed travelers who would duck out of the way upon noticing the large feathers and tall spears that glimmered in the sun. They passed by the source of Piripiri wealth—several quarries and iron ore deposits where men struck at the rock in search of copper, silver, or gold. After the mines, farms and villages were no more, they were in the extension of the Piripiri Kingdom. They continued deeper into the interior for half a fortnight before they arrived at the foot of a chasm infamously labeled Death Valley.

Themba could smell the deceased and see their dry bones scattered around the valley from battles long past. He felt like the ancestors were swirling around his very presence, battering their shields in an eternal battle, and high above, glided a winged puff of smoke, casting a shadow over the battlefield. On the other side of the valley, Themba could see a diversity of elaborate coiffures, feathers, spears, and hear the bawdy singing of men. Their leader, Chief Umlilo, stood in the front, garbed in an ensemble fit or a king having proclaimed himself one, according to Piripiri spies. His headdress clung close to his head and down to his shoulders decked with cowrie shells, glass beads, little copper plates and other fine accoutrements. Gold, silver, and copper rings adorned his neck as well as various amulets and precious stones. An ivory and gold ornament fell down his chest and over his swollen belly where it hung by his buffalo skin apron.

"Who are they?" inquired Themba.

"Infidels," spat Maghedzi.

"Or the Ashu, if you like," added Prince Machupa, the king's more diplomatic brother. "The Raging Inferno made a decree that all of their unmarried women should submit themselves for purification. Chief Umlilo, or should I say, king, refused the request, so here we are." He took a long drag of his *whawha* and produced a bored sleepy-eyed burp.

"Isn't there some way this can be solved? More…amicably?"

"Obviously you do not know my brother well, young Akuwa."

As a child, Maghedzi saw in his flames that the survival of the Piripiri depended on the expansion of his father's kingdom, thus when he became king, he submitted the region to blood, and mostly, fire, reducing opposing tribes to ash. This period was followed by the Great Dry, which resulted in the exodus of many groups to neighboring kingdoms. It seemed that lesson he had taught all those years ago had been forgotten. He was in the mood to remind the Ashu why his subjects dubbed him the Raging Inferno and the Bush Fire. "You'd think they'd be grateful for my ancestors' benevolence," he spat.

In the age of old, an impoverished people known as the Ashu dwelt. They ate food raw because their chief had lost the fire that his daughters kept in a sealed horn. Hunters from the north, led by Chief Mberevere, a Piripiri ancestor, came into the land bearing fire, ritually smoking a pipe to sustain their magical force. Mberevere gave fire to the Ashu in exchange for the hand of the chief's beautiful daughter, uniting the tribes by marriage.

The king took a few paces and thrust his spear into the earth causing a small cloud of dust. "Tonight, we camp here. At sunrise, we live, or we die."

Dinner was made from the wildebeest Themba had felled on their way. It was a clean strike from a nearly impossible distance. If the king was impressed, Themba couldn't have known. The king skinned it himself as he unleashed wisdom. "It is like fire," he claimed. "People take it from others. My father, for all his faults, bestowed some wisdom upon me, as did my tutor and other wise men in Pyyros." In Maghedzi's eyes, his father, King A'hi, had almost seen the tribe fall into obscurity. He spent his whole life correcting that, reforming the mining sector and eradicating the kleptocracy that his predecessors had allowed to prosper in his dominion. "Where do you get your wisdom from, young prince? What have the wise men of Hippo Valley taught you?"

"Erm… lots of things, like…" Themba had to scratch his head as if to dig up the wise teachings he had buried deep in his brain. Truth be told, all the prince had ever cared about was spear, and who would lie on his mat. "When a king has good counselors, his reign is peaceful?"

The king lifted an eyebrow, now with his hands deep in the wildebeest's cavity. "A good king only listens to the ancestors. There is no one wiser." There was silence for a while as the king pulled out the wildebeest's intestines and now with its heart gripped in his hand, he inquired, "I suspect you shall lead your own regiment one day."

Themba nodded his head proudly.

"And what is your strategy for leadership?"

"My father taught me," he explained confidently, "If I treat my men like equals, they will run into the dark forest for me."

The king looked amused, like it was a strange concept to him. "What else has your father taught you?"

"He said our family has ruled the Akuwa Kingdom for countless generations because the people consider us legitimate. If our family is to thrive we must have legitimacy, and this can only be achieved through justice."

The king chuckled. "Your father, he likes to prance around festivals like he is such a righteous man. Shaking his hips and singing to the girls. Let me tell you something, boy, the Akuwa have ruled for eons because of fear. Your father is no different from me, nor the rulers at the Snake Pit, the Lion's Den, or any other realm. You hear me, boy?"

The next morning, the Piripiri forces took their place at the foot of Death Valley. Adjacent were the Ashu, standing in a tight formation, with large shields that did well to fend off any arrows and javelins the Fireflies might unleash. Maghedzi walked a few paces ahead to the edge of the chasm, a hollow barren decrepit wasteland, and surveyed the battlefield with Kuluma by his side, snapping at the air, enthralled by the smell of old blood and rot. "Prince Themba, ready your forces," commanded the king.

Themba looked around. *What forces?* It was just he, his uncle, a few bodyguards, Pikoro, a few foot runners and the chief-treasurer—if you could count him. "This is not my war."

"You see it is, Themba. Your father wants a friendship does he not? Is this not what friends do for one another? Help each other?"

"I am sure there is another way the prince can exhibit his worthiness, your majesty," rationalized Chief-Treasurer Mutasa.

"No, this is the only way. Princess Nia is a fiery one, like that mountain our ancestors gave us." He pointed his shiny black blade in the distance where Mount Pyyros sat, proud amongst the lesser mountains and volcanoes that sat under it, its peak hidden behind dark shadows. "If I am to give her away, especially to an Akuwa, I need to know that that man is truly her match."

Such was his life, Themba perpended. He felt he had to prove himself all the time, to his father, to his brother, to his clan and now to the man he meant to call father-in-law.

He whistled for his shield, magnificently lined with large nearly symmetrical crescents in red, white and black, fastened his ivory scabbard around his waist and brushed his finger over his knife's edge before re-sheathing it. Pikoro came with his leopard skin cape and fastened it around his shoulders till it hung to his calves. He snatched a batch of the Sangoma's herbs from his cloths then sniffed it thoroughly. After he washed it down, with a long drag of his *whawha,* he exhaled, then pulled out his spear from the earth, and to the bewilderment of those who stood watch, marched down the valley by his lonesome.

What will the griots say of this battle that awaits me? Themba wondered as he strode down the valley. He could see the chief-griot, Sekuru Katswiri, from the corner of his eye, with his sharp inquisitive eyes observing from a safe distance away. *What will the future storytellers sing about Prince Themba?*

When he got to the middle of the chasm he yelled, "There is no reason for all of you to die. We have more men, more steel, and, we are better trained. When all of you are dead or enslaved, we will take all your livestock, rather than the virgins your king requires. Your boys will be sent to work on the slopes of Mount Pyyros, your huts will become ash and rubble, and your possessions will become our possessions." The prince paused. "However, there is no need for this. I know a better way, one where there will be only one casualty."

At the top of the hill the rest stood watching, waiting in formation. Prince Munyaradzi tried to make a run down the hill and stop his nephew's foolishness, but the king put a stiff hand on his chest, so Munyaradzi shouted instead.

Themba did not hear the words. He was stuck in his own world and could feel ice water flowing through his veins. He had decided he wasn't returning to Hippo Valley alive without accomplishing his mission. "Send down your best warrior so we can settle it, man to man."

There was silence for a while and the singing and battering of the Ashu shields had seized. The wind brushed his face and his cow-tails followed the motion of the wind as one by one, he could see Ashu after Ashu look to the ground and at each other.

The prince almost produced a smirk but the mob suddenly parted, revealing a man nearly as big as Tulu the Water Dancer, but more muscular—more fiendish.

He had an entanglement of ivory-colored hair that grew from his face like a lion mane. His eyes gleamed red, matching the paintings that covered his body from his zebra-like jaw to his heel. His spiked knuckle busters gleamed in the sun and under them tightly in his palms, the largest spear Themba had ever seen. With its metal frame, from top to bottom, only a man of consummate strength could wield such an instrument.

With his eyes close-set and thick eyebrows bridged, the Ashu giant charged toward the prince as his shiny white teeth gleamed in the early morning sun. Themba casually pulled out his club and with one fluid motion flung it toward the galloping Ashu champion, knocking him off his feet. The giant tried to get up but Themba sent a whole quiver of arrows toward him, pinning him down. Themba strolled to the subdued warrior, pulled him by his mane and gauged out his eyes with his fingers. The giant's screams echoed into the empyreal tapestry of the sky. Themba looked up toward the circling vultures. "I know you were expecting a feast, but for now these eyes will suffice." He threw them on to the dirt and hauled the Ashu back toward the waiting Fireflies, in front of the king. He pulled out his spear and waited behind the kneeling warrior. When Maghedzi nodded, the Ashu's head landed with a thud and rolled till it came to rest by the king's heavy soled sandals. The warrior king did not smile. He never did, but Themba could see in his eyes that he was satisfied when the Ashu tossed their weapons and ran for the hills.

Chapter 21

Millet and Barley

Yananayii Kukongola led the singing as she and her friends weaved cloths they would wear in the winter. They made them nice and thick, for the oracles had predicted a harsh winter, colder than any in the last generation, with frosted grass in the mornings and nights. Batsirai, whose father's compound courtyard they had made their place of leisure, was her usual garrulous self, talking about anything and everyone. It sometimes amazed her friends, how she acquired the latest scoops, like she was a mystical sleuth, who lorded over a crystal all seeing ball. Yananayii thought she had escaped the prier, but soon enough it was her turn in the ring of fire. "How are things going for you, sister?" Batsirai inquired.

Though it was a question, by the look on her face, Yananayii knew Batsirai knew more than she was letting on. She took her time to answer, first piercing the cloth on her lap with a needle and then forming a nice clean knot. "I am guessing you have heard."

"You know how things are in Boroa, news travels faster than a dog with a big juicy bone."

"Clearly. It doesn't help that my father is telling everyone he knows about it."

"As all proud fathers do. Are you not pleased with the betrothal? I thought this is what you always wanted?"

Yananayii finally put her tools down and sighed. "It was—is. Father has done well by me. Kanji is very suitable indeed."

"You are so lucky, Yana," Mukai confessed. "You have no idea. I can only dream to find such a match. Kanji is sure to give you plenty of sons, strong and masculine ones, like their father. Did you see him at the stick fighting competition?"

"I was there, in the front row seats."

"That must have been the moment he won your heart, wasn't it? He was so merciless and oh so handsome."

"And wealthy too."

"Very wealthy," Mukai corrected.

"Those were the terms father set for me," Yananayii expounded. "Wealthy and handsome. You should have seen some of the men who approached poor Matibiri with a proposal. A pathetic bunch! What would they do with a wife like me? Have me grind my own millet and live in a two-hut compound?"

"I wish I had a father like yours," sulked Mukai. "The other day, some tanner came to the compound. He revealed that he had been watching me from afar and as a result had fallen enchanted by my natural grace and beauty. I thanked him for the compliment but when I arrived home, my father informed me that he had been visited by a tanner armed with a proposal!"

"Well?" Yananayii was on the edge of her seat, as was Batsirai, who lived for such things.

"My father accepted." She shook her head incredulously. "However, I declined the offer stiffly. My father does not love me. If he did, he would never suffer such a proposal. All he wants is for me to be married off and locked somewhere far away, even if it means selling me to a man of such mean birth. I wish I had a father like yours, Yana."

Yananayii pitied her friend. "I will tell you like this, it may look like Matibiri Kukongola is the perfect father, and only the ancestors know how much he has tried to compensate for me not having a mother, but he does have his flaws." She picked up her needle once more and continued with her threadwork.

Khamukelo, who was newly married, was also in attendance though circumspect. It had been a while since she had seen the girls, such a while Khamukelo now sported an ample round belly.

She had been silent throughout, steadily working on a zitenge baby shawl she would have to use in the coming moons. Most soon to be mothers usually performed this task with glee, but Khamukelo went about her threadwork with melancholy. She wasn't going to voluntarily join the conversations so Yananayii tapped her on the knee and inquired, "How is marriage treating you, Kelo?" Yananayii had stars in her eyes, as it was a dream she was yet to realize. "It must be amazing," she conjectured. "No wonder you never have time for us anymore."

Khamukelo took her time to answer, never looking up, her eyes obsessively fixated at the shawl she sewed. The way her needle weaved in and out of the cloth was maniacal, like a malicious spirit had afflicted her. When she did raise her head, her eyes lacked the luster they once had, like her soul had been ripped from her now copious breasts. "It's wonderful," she lied, woefully, for everyone knew something was amiss.

Yananayii placed a gentle hand on her shoulder and rubbed it gently. "Kelo, my *mudiwa*, what is the matter, dearest?"

She took a deep breath, hesitated and then began, leaning her head against her hands in a disconsolate manner, "Marriage . . . It's not what I expected!"

That took Yananayii by surprise. From what she had seen and heard, there was no greater union than that of a husband and his wife.

"Everything was wonderful in the beginning," Khamukelo continued. "Kambarange was so sweet. We would spend so much time together, joking and laughing and always in each other's embrace, however, once I became pregnant, everything changed, so much so he doesn't even touch me anymore."

"Oh, don't worry about that. He is just afraid for the baby." Mukai reassured. "You have nothing to be worried about."

"It's not only that. Now, he hardly ever speaks to me. His mother is so cruel to me and expects me to do everything around the compound whilst she sits all day with her friends gossiping about me. Kambarange has also started talking to me roughly. He is often drunk and from what I hear, he is already looking for a second wife. I am truly wretched!"

Khamukelo continued revealing her woes detail after the next, as Yananayii pitied her despondent and mortified expressions. She tried to listen, but as Khamukelo went on and on, now with tears flowing down her cheeks, perspiration began to crack by the side of her temples. She rose from her stool, ready to pardon herself and return home, but finally unable to support her frame, her knees buckled sending her backward onto the red earth.

When she finally gained consciousness, Khamukelo was by her side, as was Mukai and Batsirai. They had tears in their eyes, and their voices were sore from the zealous praying they had performed. "Praise the ancestors," Khamukelo exclaimed.

"Gyiku'o is so so good," Batsirai added. "We thought they had taken you."

Yananayii helped herself up onto her feet and inquired how long she had been unconscious.

"Not long at all," Batsirai revealed. "The ancestors must have been nearby when they heard our pleas."

"I thank you, my sisters, for your intervention."

"We must take you to a healer," Mukai decided. "Let us not test fate. Your health is of the utmost importance to us, dear *mudiwa*!"

Yananayii looked at the sun. It was beginning to set. "Oh no," she fretted. "I have to go . . . Father . . . must be wondering where I am." Despite her friends' protests, she gathered her things and charged off.

She stopped in her tracks when she broke through the thick vegetation that secluded the lagoon she and Tauya Mundu had made their secret haven. It had been a colorful amalgamation of the dyes of the wild, rich greens, violets and luminous pastels during their brief courtship, as the Sangoma's intervention at her purification during the Water Plea had resulted in rains. That was however short-lived. The clouds had now ceased to weep, so the once luscious and vibrant enclave was slowly fading back to the taint of the dry, and once proud and healthy leaves and wild flowers were now wilting from the sun's unrelenting jolt.

In the short distance, Tauya's ostrich plumes shook wildly as he threw his arms about, pointing at someone, something, as though he had been severely offended. Yananayii moved cautiously toward him and then tapped him on the shoulder. When Tauya turned around and saw her, he looked surprised and his eyes became two gigantic balls of joy. If he had seemed troubled, by the way he was gesticulating at nothing, like a dog barking at clouds, now he couldn't have been happier. Their trysts had become less frequent. It had seemed like an eternity, the time they had spent apart, so it felt like the first time, when her breasts pressed on his chest. When he held her, she felt like everything was okay. All her anxieties, insecurities and the recurring pains from her purification seemed to vanish—just for a moment. Tauya sunk his head for a kiss, but she moved her face sideways, so he had to be satisfied with her cheek. Excited by her presence, Tauya reached for the knot that held her wraparound, but she pushed his fingers away. "Not now, *wangu*. I have something important to say." She looked up at him for a strangely long time and then with a torrent of tears forming down her cheeks she announced, "I am pregnant."

Tauya took some moments to digest what he had just heard, and his eyes seemed overwhelmed by a mixture of emotions. It wasn't quite happiness, Yananayii saw, nor was it quite fear. It was something betwixt. "Are you sure?"

Yananayii was certain. "I have performed several tests and they have all ended the same way."

When she first suspected she might be with child, she obtained some millet and barley and urinated on them. After a few days, the millet sprouted, indicating she was pregnant with a girl. To be sure, she performed the test three times more before she visited a witchdoctor for confirmation. After observing the color and characteristics of her urine mixed with palm wine, the seer confirmed what she had already known.

"Tauya, are you listening?"

He wasn't. His head was already in the clouds, fantasizing about the child he was going to have with the woman of his dreams. It all seemed unreal to him, like the ancestors were playing a big joke on him that they would ultimately reveal. *Alala*, Tauya decided. He would give the child his mother's name. The prettiest name he could think of. He thought of his father, Lumambo, who had questioned his attraction to women. *That smirk of yours must be firmly wiped off that face of yours*, he smiled.

"I need shells to visit a healer," Yananayii pled.

"What do you need to do that for?" Tauya finally replied after coming out of his reverie. "I love you, Yana. It is what I have always wanted. What you have always wanted."

"Yes, but not like this. If Kanji were to find out he would kill us all to protect his honor. Not to mention the shame it would bring on my father's name."

In a sudden movement, Tauya grabbed Yananayii by the back of her head and leaned closer so his nose ran along her neck. "Listen," he snarled as he jerked her head backward, "And listen very carefully. You will not harm my baby. Are we understood?" When she agreed Tauya let her go and then held her by the side of her shoulders, this time tenderly. "I will get those cows I promised, and I will approach your father with an offer he cannot refuse. You just have to be patient and trust me. Just keep the baby a secret, for just a little longer. Okay?"

Chapter 22

The Champion of Pyyros

When the Pyre Fortress gates opened, a garish roar erupted. King Maghedzi and the vaunting Themba were the first through, the Akuwa prince with his prize in hand, the head of the Ashu champion. He raised it into the air as he threw his leg over his equine's back and marched past the whistling, tambourines and *hoshos*. Themba could get used to this, and to a small extent, already had. It seemed he was making heroism a habit, first in Shambamuto and now in Pyyros. He just wished his father had been there to witness it, as well as his mother, Sibongile, Simba and his other siblings. In his eventual return to the Stone Houses, with his bride by his side, he would tell them all about it. He would tell the whole clan so that Sekuru Rwizi, the Chief-Griot of Hippo Valley, could compose songs of how Prince Themba the Brave had defeated the Ashu singlehandedly and won the hand of the most beautiful maiden in all the kingdoms.

But in reality, he was torporific. All he yearned for was a calabash filled to the brim and quiet relaxation in his chambers. However, paws were upon him—strangers' hands, all trying to get a piece of him, like touching him would give them good fortune and health. He looked around as his arms stretched out in a hero pose, as fire lily leaves laved over him. Below him, wrist bound Ashu girls shuffled through the gates toward their purification in a slow-moving chain. He could see in the distance a Piripiri soldier set his *sjambok* on a girl who wouldn't walk, over and over, across her legs and torso as the Firefly cursed and spat.

Themba was suddenly gripped by melancholy. Everything seemed to go in slow motion, from the fist one man thrust into the air, to the mother who lifted her child toward him, hoping he would rub it on its cheek. He thrust the Ashu champion's head into the air one more time and then tossed it down to Pikoro waiting on standby and hopped down from the high pulpit.

There was a fete later that evening, which oddly enough to Themba, was not performed by the Sangoma, but a new clairvoyant. The priestess began by sacrificing a bull in Themba's name, praising his prowess as a warrior, and bestowed a Volcan name upon him—Umuzi. Themba found the name fitting, for the ancient Piripiri ancestor he now shared a name with, through his intellect and grit, had saved a small primitive people by rechanneling a stream of lava into the path of marauding reavers that had emerged from the mountains, killing many of them and halting their incursion.

After cutting the bull open, the priestess reached into its cavity, grabbed its heart and with her clawed fingers, squeezed until the carcass was filled with blood. She lifted the organ over her entanglement of silver hair and let the sound of the people wash over her, as did the blood over her head till she looked more beast than man in the young Akuwa prince's eyes.

Despite the fanfare, Themba couldn't work up an appetite. On most occasions, he was the first in the dance circle, waving his cow-tails carelessly, lifting his feet well over his head, but today, he sat quietly, with his barely molested calabash of brew on his lap. He looked on, rather than participating in the bull-leaping competition, clapping his hands lightly at the end of every turn. Illicit eyes from Pyyros' finest maidens flew his way, the daughters of chiefs, generals and men of great wealth and title. Several had asked the prince to dance, but the answer was always the same, "No thank you. Another time."

He looked around for King Maghedzi. He had been at the banquet during the purification of the Ashu girls, but now the king was nowhere in sight, nor his queen or the princess. Themba put a hand into his cloths and took out a batch of the herbs the Sangoma had prescribed. He sniffed it first and then tossed it into his mouth and chewed. After a few moments, he stood up in the midst of the jamboree and stormed toward the king's chambers with the same ice-cold determination he had exhibited when he marched down Death Valley to face the Ashu champion. Wasike, who was standing guard, tried to stop him, but the young prince was resolved, leaving Wasike writhing in pain, regretful he dared lay his hand on a prince.

The king was brooding over a fire as he scrutinized the veiny entrails of his Heart Stone that reminded him of the many tributaries and streams that flowed from the Nhunundudu. Kuluma rested in the shallow pool of freshwater the king had built in his chambers, enthusiastically chewing on a massive hippo leg, but Themba was unfazed by the creature, shackled or not. "I know she is not here, Princess Nia," barked the Akuwa prince. "I know your wife has left you."

Maghedzi turned his head and raised himself slowly, the look on his face, the apotheosis of bewilderment. He fastened the stone back over his chest and stammered as he struggled to find some words, some explanation for the prince, but Themba didn't need one.

"I have spent all my life in my brother's shadow. I've spent countless nights devising ways to impress my father. I've come here trying to impress you. I have realized that I have never done anything selfless."

"Speak plainly," gruffed the king.

"It means from now on I shall do what is best for me."

"And how do you intend to achieve this?"

"Not marrying your daughter for one."

The king's jaw rippled and a look that once would have subdued the young prince did nothing but reinforce his resolve.

"I leave in earnest."

"Where are you going?"

"On a pilgrimage, where I shall find myself. Where that is I do not know. It may be the Lion's Den, Wolf's Lair or even the Forest of Abominations."

"You will die there and your spirit will never rest."

"Maybe so, but that is all my soul has ever known."

"If you mean to throw away your life, that does not matter to me."

"Good."

"So be it!" Maghedzi strolled to the back of the chamber and rummaged through a large chest. The room was dimly lit, but it illumed when the he opened the package revealing a spear. The blade was in the shape of a flame, the emblem of the Piripiri. "Take this." He handed it to Themba. "This is one of the three blades forged by the mystic, Zoromango, in the age of the Volcan kings, up, above the clouds on Mount Pyyros. It is called Torch. When surrounded by darkness, say these ancient words, *moto unopisa*, and the fireflies inside will awake and omit light."

Themba reflected on his reflection as he peered down at the shiny surface. His blood eye was still gleaming, but not as much as before. Simba had been awarded Hippo's Nail-claw by his father, whilst he had to make do with plain steel. *But he is the heir*, Themba had rationalized. The king's bastard Xolani was not, but despite that, he had been awarded Night Slayer, forged with *masimbi* steel atop the Sacred Hills by the all-seeing Sisters. Themba repeated the Piripiri words, his dialect better than ever, and immediately, the blade illumed.

"I cannot take this," decided the prince finally. "This spear has been in your family for generations!"

"You defeated the Ashu champion, ending their rebellion. You saved hundreds, if not thousands of Piripiri lives. You have earned a place in our family."

Themba was taken aback, humbled by the gesture, that the only words he could muster was, "Thank you."

Maghedzi put a hesitant but fatherly hand on the prince's shoulder and nodded. "Be careful though. Some spears receive the qualities of their forger. Since Zoromango was an insane and violent man, this spear is imbued with unrestrained qualities, especially the ability to possess its wielder. That is why I do not wield it myself."

Its first owner, Kinjan, in a fit of rage, slew his best friend with it and then turned the blade on his mother. He would have killed his only child if it weren't for his wife's last-minute intervention. Bereaved, he locked up the blade in a chest until his great-great-grandson rediscovered it. The other two spears went to Kinjan's brothers Kijani and Kimani. Kijani used his to slay the Ifirit in an epic battle of bravery and cunning, casting it into an unknown river after he saw the full strength of its malicious intent, concluding no man could wield such power. Kimani committed suicide, as was custom, after dropping his spear during battle. The spear was never seen again, only spoken of in nighttime tales over a fire. "May the flame guide your blade, Umuzi."

Themba bowed, clapped his hands and crept out of the hut. Chief-Treasurer Mutasa was waiting for him outside. "So, did you do it? Have you secured the hand of the princess, Nia?" he inquired, as he pulled up his sarong, struggling to keep up with the prince's purposeful pace down the King's Way toward their guest lodgings.

Themba laughed. "How? She isn't even here. She and her mother ran away."

The treasurer looked perplexed. "How do you know?"

"Ask Pikoro. It seems someone here has made himself useful." The boy's orgulous and crooked whites were in full display.

"But what about your mission? Your father's will?"

"If my father wants a wedding, he can have another one himself."

Chapter 23

Collection Day

Tauya Mundu was on the verge of tears after counting his compound's inventory as the scarcity of tangible wealth to barter had deflated all of his hopes of raising enough cattle to poach Yananayii's betrothal to Kanji. Not to mention, the bride price had risen because now, as Yananayii was pregnant, he was liable to pay damages. He lit up the pipe he had inserted some dhob he had acquired from a street peddler and inhaled. It was the only thing that helped cure his anxiety. "There is no way I can raise enough cattle to even start talking to Yananayii's father," he complained at Tan, a mirror image but with buffalo horns about his temples and locusts spewing from his mouth. He had asked his new friend where he had come from.

Tan had replied from a faraway land, in the past, in the present, in the future. "Perhaps in your head, perhaps not."

Tauya had no time for riddles, so he continued his rant. "The number of cows I have won't even get her father to look at me, even if I sell the entire compound and all of its contents." A wicked thought crossed his mind as he looked at his father's widows who had their pot lids out that expressed discontent. *They're not even my wives, yet they complain to me like I paid their* lobola!

Tan had spoken about a group of slavers he had met on his travels. It was still prevalent in places like the Boaboa Kingdom. Tauya shook his head and extinguished the thought. His father's widows were old and frail. They were likely worth a handful of shells. It wasn't worth the hassle.

He set his dhob pipe down and set his ostrich plume headdress over his head and brought out his father's spear. It hadn't done anything noteworthy, nor did it gleam or glisten, like he saw others do. Somehow Lumambo had always found a way to avoid conscription, but Tauya meant to change that. *From now on this spear shall be something my future children with Yananayii will be proud to wield*, he vowed.

He beckoned Tan who had pledged to make him a warrior with no peer once Yananayii's lobola and damages had been settled to follow behind him. "I'll be back," he barked at his father's widows with a new sense of destiny, his eyes now bloodshot red and head quite light, but it didn't seem like anyone was paying him any mind. He cursed at his wretched crew and stumbled out of the hut toward Kum'wana, Pyyros' eastern district, to settle his father's unfinished business.

After acquiring the shells owed to his father from the Uyaba at spear-point, word travelled fast around the district that he was a serious man, so when he inquired upon the Mamharwe, they returned what they owed with haste, and even added an extra bag of shells.

He went to the markets immediately after and managed to acquire ten more cows with the recovered shells.

The next day his efforts took him through Khumazulo, Pyyros' western district until he was in Kumputo, which was closest to Mount Pyyros' slopes. It was a long walk, a picturesque one, where the sun's light streaked through the violet and crimson boughs that lined the walkway laden with pedestrians going to and fro between the districts.

Tan kept Tauya entertained throughout with his wicked sense of humor that had the tanner laughing throughout the journey. "Men," Tan whispered, in that lispy yet raspy voice of his. "They are more eager to copulate than a pygmy chimpanzee. It is the shells that restrains them."

Indeed, Tauya smiled wryly. If he had a bigger kraal, he and Yananayii would be laying on his mat right now as man and wife.

He arrived outside a compound. "I think this is the place," he told Tan, before using his spear to knock on the gate.

A little boy, about two fists of age clad in a loincloth and wielding a miniature spear came up inquisitively.

"Chiyembekezo," Tauya greeted. The boy looked at him confused. "It's me, Tauya," he smiled. "I am your cousin. Will you open the gate for me?"

A young man walked out of one of the numerous huts that laced the large compound of tiled walkways and little ponds scattered around. He marched up to the gate menacingly, splendidly dressed in a cream loincloth embroidered with beads and copper trinkets of various kinds that rattled when he walked and ordered the boy to return to its mother. "Who are you?" he barked.

"It's me, your cousin, Tauya. Don't you remember me, Rondo?"

Rondo scratched his little goatee for some moments, and then his face softened revealing a handsome face, as handsome as any on any thoroughfare. "Yes, you are Lumambo's."

"That's right, cousin," Tauya smiled, full of teeth.

"Please do come in." He used his massive arms to push the sliding gate open and ushered in the guest. "Can I offer you anything? Some beer? Water? Cow blood?"

"Oh, that won't be necessary, but if you could alert your father to my presence I would be grateful."

"Of course, cousin. I'll take you to him right away. He has just returned from overseeing his livestock."

Rashidi Mchoyo was sitting under a shed as he dispensed wisdom upon his numerous wives and their young when Tauya and Rondo arrived. Rashidi looked tall when he sat, but it became apparent that he was a short man when he stood to greet them. Tauya found that funny. He had always remembered his uncle as a towering man.

Rondo clapped his hands and then announced, "*Baba*, look who has come to visit."

Rashidi squinted his eyes, unable to place the Boroa boy, but soon his eyes lit up. "Tauya! You're so grown now! When was the last time we met . . ?" he put his hands to his chin and counted the years. ". . . Not since your mother passed." He looked down and put a hand on his heart. He and Tauya's mother, Alala, had been close. They were born a season apart and Tauya could see a lot of similarities between them, like the nose and the skin tone, which he had also inherited. "I heard about your father. We pass our condolences."

"Thank you, uncle. He is with his ancestors now."

"We did not hear of his passing until well after his funeral. Otherwise we might have attended."

"No apologies needed. Father always wanted a small ceremony."

"So, young man. What brings you to visit your uncle after all these years?"

"Do you think perhaps we could talk somewhere more private?"

"Why? I do not hide anything from my family members, and them, from me."

Tauya looked around. Sweat began to break from his temple when he began. "Uncle, I would like to marry."

"I'd hope so young man."

"I have found a girl."

"That's great, however, I sense there is a problem?"

"You could call it that." Tauya fidgeted as everyone looked at him. He felt a rush of embarrassment that almost crippled his tongue, but he thought of Yananayii, his unborn child, and his vexatious situation. Now was not the time for vanity. "The girl I intend to marry requires a large amount of cows for her father to sanction the marriage."

"How many?"

He shuffled forward and whispered in Rashidi's ear.

If Rashidi was shocked, one couldn't have seen that by his reaction. "That's quite a lot. Not even my first wife, whose father was a district chief, was worth that much. Who is this girl?"

"Yananayii Kukongola."

Rashidi raised an eyebrow. "Matibiri's daughter?" He and Yananayii's father had been business associates for many years, and were well acquainted as part of the district's elite.

Tauya nodded his head.

There was silence for a while until Rashidi broke into laughter.

Tauya wondered if there was something on his face.

"Are you sure you mean Yananayii Kukongola?"

"Yes."

"I know losing one's father is a huge disappointment. Sometimes one can...imagine things." Rashidi was no fool, and was once young himself. There was no mistaking the smell of dhob that wreathed from Tauya.

"I am not imagining things, uncle. I love her, and she loves me."

Rashidi stopped laughing, drank a cup of water and then calmed himself. "It's just that, Yananayii's beauty is a rare kind. Do you know how many chiefs' sons would jump at the chance of marrying her?" He looked at Tauya and saw the conviction in his eyes, plus the boy was beginning to unsettle him, like a cold mist had descended. "Very well, young man. I shall loan you some cows."

Tauya's eyes livened and his teeth gleamed. He couldn't wait to run to Yananayii and tell her that he had managed to raise the lobola until Rashidi revealed the number of cows. "Half a dozen cows?" Tauya spat. "How will that help me? Even with the number of cows I have, I am well short. I am running out of time!"

"That's all I can give you. In case you haven't noticed, things are rough right now."

"Won't you give me more, for my mother's sake? Your sister!"

Rashidi looked down, as his eyes reddened. One could see the sorrow the name Alala caused him. "I'm sorry if you wanted more, but that is all I have to give."

Tauya was about to unleash a furious rebuke, but Tan's silky hands caressed his side, and from behind, whispered, "We will find another way to get those cows."

Tauya nodded his head, dropped to his knees and clapped his hands. "Thank you uncle for your generosity. I will repay you in kind when my lands become profitable once again!"

After Rashidi performed a prayer, Tauya was led by Rondo to one of Rashidi's numerous cattle enclosures to select his cows.

"Six measly cows," he muttered as he made his way home. "Six measly cows! Father said he was a stingy and selfish man, but I would have never thought this tightfisted. The man owns hundreds and he gives me six measly cows?"

"The ancestors frown upon selfishness," Tan whispered to him. "Your uncle will finally get his payback."

"What do you mean, finally?"

"That's for another time."

Now that Tauya's uncle, Rashidi, had loaned him half a dozen cows, when Tauya arrived back at his compound in Boroa, he whistled and commanded his father's widows to take them to the livestock enclosure. After also claiming what was owed to his father from the Uyaba and Mamharwe, he had a dozen and a half cows, which was still not nearly enough to prize Yananayii away from her betrothal, especially now that he had to pay extra for getting her with child, but at least he was making some progress. He had to get creative.

He ordered some food and sat himself in his chambers. He fiddled with his father's urn and waited as he sent dhob smoke into the thatched roof. He set the pipe down and went into his father's chest where he kept his precious belongings and emptied the contents into a sack. He went around the huts and snatched the ornaments from the walls and then went to the shed. There were several pickaxes, sickles, scythes, pitchforks, spades, shovels, trowels, hoes, forks, and rakes for farming. His lands weren't producing anything soon, so he gathered them and with the help of his only donkey, took them to a pawnshop. After the trade was complete he was now shy of three dozen cows.

The next morning, he pushed one of his father's widows off a stool and snatched it. He was going to sell that too, plus other furniture, cooking utensils and clothes. She landed on the stone floor with a thud causing several pairs of eyes looks of dismay. "Why don't you old wenches do something for a change, instead of sitting in here and gossiping," he barked. Tan advised that their jewelry would help raise the funds he needed, so he gleefully relieved the widows of their jewels, nothing fancy, just beaded, copper, wooden and leather bracelets, anklets, bangles and necklaces. Some he had to take by force as they were loath to part with them. His father's widows were old, frail things, no match for a man his age with a righteous cause—love. He stripped himself of his own jewelry too. Now all he had was the clothes on his back plus his spear.

After pawning the items, Tan appeared in front of him again and shook his head in pity. "You should see yourself. You look a mess. You need a drink." Tauya thought he needed sleep, which he hadn't achieved for days, but nonetheless, he gripped his spear tightly and made way to the local tavern, where he and Rafiki had shared a few over the seasons.

He was well into his third calabash of *umqombothi* when he noticed a man standing at the foot of his table. "You're Alala's boy aren't you?"

Tauya's eyes widened. "How do you know? My mother drowned many years ago."

"Your mother and I were once friends. You look like her, and you probably don't remember me, but I used to play with you when you were a little boy."

Tauya bridged his eyebrows trying to place the familiarity about the man. "Yes, I remember you. You are Tiyamike. What brings you back to Boroa? Last I heard you had moved to Kwa'Jivu."

"I am here to settle a family dispute."

Tauya sighed and welcomed him to sit at his table.

"I have been watching you since you came," revealed Tiyamike. "I do not think I have seen a sadder man. Your mother too, had a melancholic heart. What has been troubling you, young man? It is matters of love, isn't it? Only that can distress a man as much as you are troubled."

"Is it that obvious?" Tauya replied.

"As clear as the blue sky."

"You have it correct. I am in love with a girl, and she is in love with me, but . . . I cannot afford to marry her."

"That is unfortunate."

"Indeed. I have loaned some cows, sold most of my possessions and I still don't have enough. I might even have to sell my compound."

"I see." Tiyamike scratched his head, not sure what to make of the revelations. "You know, some things are not meant to be. You would sell your home for this girl? Where will you stay?"

Tauya hadn't thought about that. "Love is all that matters. Isn't that what the ancestors say?"

"I think you misinterpret the meaning. You need to live in the real world, or you might suffer the same fate as your mother."

"Drown?"

Tiyamike looked at him until he realized that the boy was clueless.

"Do you know something that I don't? Tell me, if my mother didn't drown, then how did she die?"

Tiyamike took some long sips of his calabash, sighed and then revealed, "Your mother did drown, but she drowned a witch."

Tauya's eyes enlarged in bewilderment. "A witch? Never! My mother was a good woman—a woman of the ancestors. She prayed all the time."

"And spun spells too, young man. Since she was a young girl, she had always been fascinated with the occult. As she got older she became more introverted and spent her time concocting things in her cauldron."

Tauya went into memory lane. Those excavations and the herbs and spices they would collect on their long treks, and sometimes he would find his mother speaking in odd languages he couldn't understand.

"When her father got ill, it drove her to madness. She started seeking answers in the dark arts."

"That's not true."

"Ask anyone. I thought your father would have told you."

Lumambo had been tightlipped about the circumstances of her death. All he had told Tauya was that she drowned whilst collecting water from the Nhunundudu.

"A plague had taken over the district," continued Tiyamike. "Many people began dying and there was nothing our healers could do about it. Your mother had quite a following. One day as they tended to the sick at their secret lair, they were ambushed by the sheriff and chief witchdoctor and charged with causing the plague. From what I heard, her own brother, Rashidi, perplexed by what he had discovered one day, repeated what he saw to the wrong people." Tiyamike shook his head. Even though these events had played out a long time ago, one could tell it still pained him greatly. "He didn't understand the implications."

Tauya's eyes darkened. "That snake!" he snapped, overcome with dander.

"She and her members were taken to the Nhunundudu. Their hands and legs were bound and led into it. If the water rose enough overnight to drown them, they were witches, and as it turned out the following morning, they were."

Tauya's whole world was turning around. His mother was kind and sweet, not a wily old witch.

Tiyamike looked at him with gritted teeth. "Sorry, young man, but now you are old enough to know." He got up wobbly from the brew and threw some shells onto the table for the next round. "For your troubles," he apologized before shuffling off.

Tauya was now several calabashes in, drinking with a rage as the feeling of betrayal poured through his volcanic veins. "How could father keep this from me?" he carped as *whawha* splashed over his lips. "How could Uncle Rashidi do that to his own sister?"

"I told you to trust no one didn't I? Not even me," whispered Tan.

It now all made sense to Tauya why Rashidi and his family had been estranged when they were once so close. "All my life I have believed a lie. My mother was a witch!" He began to weep.

As he did, an old man approached him at his table. He greeted Tauya warmly and announced his name as Tsolofelo. "I couldn't help but overhear your conversation with that man. For that I apologize, but what if I told you there are ways a man can solve the problem you are having?"

Tauya wiped away his tears. "There is no way to solve this. I am doomed. My mother was a witch, and the woman I love shall be married off to another man."

"There is nothing we can do for your mother. She is with the ancestors, if they have accepted her," Tsolofelo gulped. "What matters now are the cows you are looking for. I can help you with that."

Tauya looked up, skeptical. He was about to leave until Tan whispered to him. Tauya nodded his head, turned to the stranger and asked, "How?"

"There is an order. They are called Matsotsi. They specialize in… how can I say this…acquiring things…Free of charge," he coughed. "I can arrange a meeting with them if you like?"

Tauya had heard about this order. Depending on whom you spoke to, they were either loved or despised. Some believed them to be nothing but petty thieves . . . scavengers if you will, that made a living off the backs of other people's efforts. To others they were philanthropists, who returned to the masses what was owed to them from the corrupt thieves that dwelled at the king's court.

Tauya studied Tsolofelo's face. It was lined with wrinkles by the forehead, and had deep creases along his mouth. It had that friendly, grandfatherly look about it. Tauya couldn't say the same about the rope burn around his neck that suggested the old man had been once hanged and lived to tell the tale.

"What are you hesitating for?" whispered Tan. "Isn't this what you've been looking for? The salvation of all your troubles?"

Tauya studied Tsolofelo a while longer, even taking a couple of sips of his drink in between. He thought of Yananayii, at her wedding bedding, and inside waiting for her in the tent, was Rafiki, as happy as that day when he struck him across the head by the pond. "Take me to them."

Chapter 24

Ukweba's Hall

Tauya Mundu knew they had arrived at their destination when Tsolofelo, the old man he had met at the tavern, removed the blindfold he had placed over his eyes. He had no idea where they were. It couldn't have been far off from Pyyros as they had left Boroa in the early morning and it was now just before midday. All he knew was they were perhaps near the chain of rocky hills west of Pyyros toward Phulusa, where the Utsi reigned, or toward Kilumu, where the Kilumulimu chieftaincy governed, a family that had tight links with the Piripiri since the days of the Volcan Kings.

The Kilumulimu's first chief, Masizi, the bastard brother of King Nokuduma of the Piripiri, was awarded the rocky lands after helping his half-brother in his conquest of lands northwest of Pyyros. The Kilumulimu, with Volcan blood running through their veins, often intermarried with the Piripiri, to ensure that the fire bloodlines remained pure. King Maghedzi had taken two wives from the Kilumulimu, and one from the Utsi. Princess Vusi of the Utsi was infamous as she was the girl that the Raging Inferno took at the feast many seasons prior, celebrating the birth of Prince Alinafe, third in line to the Piripiri throne. Those that witnessed the scene testified that despite not being much of a drinker, the king that night became so drunk he mistakenly entered the Usti girl's hut, rather than his own wife's, Queen Zandile.

Tauya and Tsolofelo stood surrounded by scattered leaves amongst the heavy loam that housed unhinged bushes, some that grew taller than an average man, and thick trees older than time itself with blade-like leaves of crimsons, indigos and blues.

The enclave had a voice of its own, the hooting of an owl and the flicker of a creature swinging through the branches behind them. Tsolofelo looked around and over his shoulder to make sure no one was lurking hidden amongst the vegetation. When he was satisfied, he reached into his bag and brought out a bamboo flute. He put it to his mouth and began playing a tune.

As he played, the disconcerting sound of gibber and chatter suddenly accompanied the wafting and ethereal melody, and up above them appeared a monkey on the monolithic one-eyed hyena shaped into the mass of vined rock. "Xixi," hollered Tsolofelo coercively, as one does to a stubborn donkey. "Open the mouth, will you."

The monkey replied with an aggressive barrage of chatter so Tsolofelo threw a marula fruit its way. The primate sniffed at it and then threw it back at the old thief's head causing him to rub his forehead.

"I have nothing to give you," he shouted at the monkey irately. After Xixi gibbered angrily for some moments, Tsolofelo reached into his cloths again and brought out a shiny nugget.

The monkey began to chatter frantically causing Tsolofelo to throw the nugget toward it. Xixi savored it for some moments and then nippily placed it into its little sack strapped across its chest. It then climbed down onto the hyena's snout, stuck its hand into the eye and after a short rumble, the hyena's jaws opened.

"This monkey," Tsolofelo ceded, "Has more riches than all the Matsotsi combined."

Tauya found that amusing, but soon fear and regret engulfed him as they made way down the hyena's jaw and into a paved tunnel with gorgeously engraved walls and roof. *I should have never agreed to this. I should turn back,* he decided.

"Turn back if you want to lose that girl of yours . . . and your unborn child," Tan whispered by his ear, so Tauya carried on with hope in his heart that soon he would be able to amass enough cattle to persuade Matibiri Kukongola.

It was a short walk before they could hear voices arguing in the short distance like wild dogs amidst pack politics. The calmer voice belonged to Mnyakuzi, the leader of the Matsotsi of Pyyros, and the louder belonged to Wanugu, the largest, bald of head and barrel chested.

It was a spacious chamber of walls made of rock engraved with carvings of vultures, jackals, hyenas and other opportunistic creatures of the wild. It was called Ukweba's Hall, in honor of the third leader of the Matsotsi. As a former mason, Ukweba the Builder was credited with overseeing the initial construction of the hideout, as well as other Matsotsi hideouts across the kingdoms. The lamps ornamented on the walls shimmered, creating a discomforting and sinister atmosphere. There were several offshoots that connected from the main chamber, and in the middle was a stone throne formed from the floor with two great stone vultures perched on each armrest. There was a somber mood, as the gang of thieves had just returned from a botched heist. Everyone was painted black from head to toe, with matching loincloths, aprons, vests and cow-tails.

"We could have had all the jewelry, but instead, all we have is this," Wanugu complained as he slammed an empty sack onto the floor. He was visibly angry, and he showed this by laying his fist into a wooden table in front of him, causing it to crack in the middle. "I have a family to feed!"

"We all have families to feed," retorted Mnyakuzi, almost half Wanugu's size. To mark his position as leader of the Piripiri Kingdom's faction of Matsotsi, on his right arm he wore a gauntlet with a shiny black stone.

Mnyakuzi's was one of several mystical gauntlets passed on from one leader to the next. It was constructed by an oracle whose name has been lost to history under the command of the order's forefather, A'khungu. Labeled the Lost Chief, A'khungu distributed the gauntlets amongst his lieutenants on the Mystical Aja Hill, and there proclaimed them princes under a sprawling jacaranda tree. Each amulet sourced different powers, specific to the characters his lieutenants possessed. As the king of thieves, A'khungu bade the mystic construct a special gauntlet for himself encrusted with replicas of all the amulets.

Wanugu spat on the floor and thundered toward Mnyakuzi menacingly. "You're getting soft, prince! Your time is over! We need new leadership! We haven't made a score in ages!"

Whilst Mnyakuzi had been with the outfit since the start of King Maghedzi's reign, Wanugu was a relative newcomer, but had quickly risen amongst the Matsotsi ranks and gained influence over a good portion of the members.

The first prince of the Pyyros Matsotsi, Uvunjaji, was a very paranoid and cautious man, so his amulet was imbued with the power to pulsate and thrum when it discerned danger, so now Mnyakuzi's amulet was thrumming violently. "If you're asking me to step down as the leader of this faction then you are gravely mistaken."

"I'm not asking, I'm telling you to," spat Wanugu as he raised his club ready to strike.

"Then you know what you have to do," replied Mnyakuzi as he calmly unsheathed his twin daggers and assumed a fighting stance. It seemed to be a variant of the nshiko stance that mimicked the freshwater crabs of the seas. Tauya could tell by the way Mnyakuzi had his arms arched with his daggers pointed forward. He had seen his love rival, Kanji, use the same technique out on the Boroa sparing circuits, and had witnessed him cripple and maim many a man with it. Xixi, the monkey, who was an ever-present fixture on the current and former thief-prince's shoulders, began to chatter and hop angrily.

"Enough," commanded Tsolofelo, whose booming voice echoed through the room. The feuding pair did so, but not as a result of Tsolofelo's might, but respect. He was the oldest member of Matsotsi, having served the order since the days of King Nuru. A thief's life was oft short, but Tsolofelo's was long despite participating in some of the order's most daring capers. His favorite activity was recounting his various escapes and scraps with the law to the newer recruits.

Due to his old age, he did not participate in the banditry, but acted as a recruiter, spy and advisor to the prince. He was often tasked to deliver messages and conduct the prince's business, which he had just returned from. Whilst Mnyakuzi was referred to as the head of the gang of thieves, and Wanugu the arms for his strength, Tsolofelo was regarded as the nose, because of his unrivalled aptitude at smelling a potential score. "The prince is right in this. In the age of old, our numbers dwindled down to just five of us after King Nuru waged a war against Matsotsi when our thefts began ignoring our order's second and very sacred rule."

"No blood of the innocent!" echoed the crowd as they watched the drama unfold.

"Our ancestors had forsaken us," Tsolofelo continued, with a stern index finger pointing skywards. During that era, under the leadership of Nyoretsoeng, killings were a common occurrence. Such was the lack of respect for life that it wasn't uncommon to hear a man or woman had been stabbed at a local market, or a family had been slain during a burglary. "Returning to our old ways will only alarm the fury of the Raging Inferno who would march here himself and give us to the flames."

Wanugu's shoulders dropped as he brooded toward the comfort of his closest allies, Wacucu, Lesholu and Nkosazana, who was referred to as the princess of thieves by her peers, not for anything noteworthy, or because of any relation to the prince other than as a subordinate, but because she was the only woman in the order.

When Wanugu was gone, finally Mnyakuzi and Tsolofelo embraced. "Good to see you again old friend. You look well." Tsolofelo was incredibly fit for a man his age, and still boasted a headful of hair that raced into the sky like a white flame. "How fares the king of thieves? I trust he was pleased with the tribute?"

"He was, however, there is another matter he means to speak to you about, in person. A job he says, of utmost importance."

"I see." Mnyakuzi fondled his chin hairs in contemplation. "We shall discuss this more after you have supped and rested. It is a long journey from the Canine Free States, especially for an old thief like yourself." He noticed Tauya lurking in the corner. "What do you have there?"

"A young man. He wants to join our order."

"Does he now? Bring him forth." The prince of thieves looked Tauya up and down and laughed.

Tauya was getting tired of this. All his life he had been underestimated, by his father, his friends and family members, but he meant to make them pay for that.

"A bit soft this one, don't you think?" Mnyakuzi poked Tauya around his sides.

"The boy is fine."

"I'm not so sure about that. I've seen a lot of thieves and this man is not one of them."

"All he asks for is a chance. We took a chance on you to lead us didn't we? And everything turned out fine."

When the order's former leader was killed during a heist, three members were considered to succeed Mareka and don the black gauntlet of thieves. One was Kubarashe, who died shortly after under strange circumstances. Some say it was poison. Others say the ancestors struck him down after leading a heist in a sacred temple. Muzinga was the favorite to become the new prince of thieves, as he was popular amongst the various factions, however, the elders of the order deemed him too greedy. There was no heist too daring for Muzinga. After the purge of the Matsotsi led by King Nuru, the order needed a calm head to lead them forward and regain the order's former glory. That man was Mnyakuzi, though it had proved difficult. He had inherited a roguish crew whose motives for joining the Matsotsi were far off from what the founders intended.

"That depends on who you ask, as we have just seen." Mnyakuzi put a hand to his chin. He had a smile on his face, somewhat amused by Tauya's stupefied demeanor. "What can you bring to the table?" he barked at Tauya.

Tsolofelo replied for him. "He says he's a talented tanner and can also help us make new scores. He says he has access to many potential heists."

"Like what?"

Tauya was about to explain when Tan put a hand over his mouth and whispered, "Not until you've been accepted into the order."

Tauya relayed the message to Tsolofelo who in turn relayed the message to the prince of thieves.

Mnyakuzi studied Tauya some more for what seemed like an eternity until he nodded his head. "Very well. In order for him to join Matsotsi, he must perform the challenge, as was decreed by the founders of this ancient order many generations ago atop the Mystical Aja Hill. One in and one out."

That took Tsolofelo by surprise. During one of the order's heists, a rhinoceros had killed one of their members. The vacant position had been filled whilst Tsolofelo was away on the prince's business. "I see. Then a challenge it is isn't that right, Tauya?"

"Why, yes, of course," he replied, after a slight elbow on his ribs, even though he had no idea what this challenge entailed.

Many made way to the center circle, but Wanugu with his massive arms pushed them out of the way and took his place in the middle and announced, "I shall be the one to test him."

Tauya finally pulled Tsolofelo to the side and inquired on what the challenge involved.

"Oh, when our roster is full, and a person wants to join our order, they must challenge a member to a duel . . . where there is only one survivor."

Tauya's heart froze. He turned around and tried to run to the exit but there was an armed man standing guard. He had no chance—he was in the company of seasoned criminals, some with military backgrounds. He had never been formally trained in the arts of combat.

"This is a secret order. We cannot allow you to leave. You might tell someone about what you have seen. Today one man shall die, and another, shall live. Make sure that is you, Tauya Mundu, if you want to see your beloved Yananayii again." Tsolofelo pointed to a chamber. "You may go in there and pray to your ancestors and prepare yourself for what is to come."

Tauya gulped and then slowly stepped into the room. Above him was a statue of A'khungu the Lost Chief, tall, lean and cleft jawed with a monkey perched on his shoulder. Sat beside him on the right was the first Queen of Thieves, on his left, Uvunjaji with his suspicious eyes, and scattered around the room stood smaller statues of A'khungu's other lieutenants. Tauya set his ostrich plume headdress on the small podium in front of him and let the light that shone through the circular gap up high beam onto his face as he raised his head toward the ancestors. He asked for forgiveness for killing his friend, Rafiki, he begged the ancestors for Yananayii and his unborn child's protection in the event of his death, and asked them to reunite him with his mother, that he lost all those years ago. *It must have been a mistake.* There was no way his mother was a witch. He meant to ask her himself and learn the truth. When he was done, he returned into the main chamber where the order waited for him.

Wanugu who stood in the center circle grinned and raised his weapon. As soon as Tauya entered the ring, Wanugu attacked, swinging his large club toward the tanner's face. He ducked backwards, falling into arms behind him before he was heaved back toward Wanugu's onslaught. To Tauya's own surprise, he was nimble of foot. He skipped out of the way and dodged several strikes, even running away from his pursuer before he was pushed back into the center.

"Coward," barked Wanugu. "Fight me, woman," he bellowed as his strokes became slower and his breath, heavier. He finally almost managed to catch the tanner but Tauya managed to dip low and kick out at Wanugu's legs, causing him to fall.

Tauya was amazed by the sheer strength of his kick. *It must be all those hours kneading hides*, he decided, taking a short moment to celebrate his minor achievement.

Appalled, mouth ajar stupefied, Wanugu leapt to his feet and made another move for Tauya, but the Boroa boy dashed backward, and with his spear, sliced him on the thigh. Wanugu snarled and swung his club blindly, this time catching the tanner hard around his chest.

The crowd cheered as Wanugu menaced toward Tauya who was writhing in pain as he lay on his back, struggling to breathe. Wanugu took the applause of his supporters and knelt over the Boroa boy. "Kill him," yelled Wacucu, as did Lesholu and Nkosazana, as they threw their fists into the air over and over again, whistled and clapped.

Wanugu grabbed Tauya by the collar of his apron and began raining a barrage of blows to his face with his hammer like fists. Whilst Wanugu took a pause from the assault to regain his breath and raise a fist into the air for the onlookers, Tauya saw a glimmer of hope by the side of Wanugu's hip. He stretched out his arm, willing his fingers to grow longer, and just before Wanugu continued the onslaught, with a speed he could have only summoned by his desire to see Yananayii's sweet face again, he latched onto the dagger and planted it into the side of the barrel-chested thief's neck. Frantic, Wanugu rose and desperately tried to stop the blood from oozing out, but soon it was seeping through his fingers and down his chest and torso before he staggered for some moments and then fell onto the tanner beneath him.

With the little strength Tauya had left, he managed to squeeze himself from under the large man and rose to his feet. He could see the look of disbelief on Wacucu and Lesholu's faces. Tears were already flowing down Nkosazana's. There was silence for a while that seemed like an eternity, until a raucous applaud erupted from the thieves, hailing their newest member.

Chapter 25

Judgement Day

King Maghedzi of the Piripiri Kingdom leisured over a canvas of lilac and violet leaves, and above him, a large jacaranda's branches relieved him from the treachery of the sun. His nose was well in a fresh wildebeest's cavity—his snout and paws blood red. When he was full, he tossed the carcass to the side for his pride to finish, Atakachi, Alinafe, Mukina, and all the several dozen lesser children he had sired, but there was no Nia, nor his queen, Zandile.

As he licked his paws, sharp and glistening, in the distance approached a young male, fully grown with a spikey pale mane that trickled down its back, lighter than the tawny grey that flowed over his head and back. Behind it, Pyre Mountain spewed molten rock into the air, and red clouds rained down black rock. The ground splintered as the nunda dodged balls of fire, and hopped over the fissures formed. The air followed its strides with ash, smoke and fire so ravenous even the wide winged kongamoto in the sky were consumed. The king felt dread as the nunda's claws thrashed at the earth, thundering toward him, his pride behind him looking on and the mokele-mbembe and chipique filled waters nearby boiling acid.

"Zandile," Maghedzi cried as he woke, but to his annoyance, his queen was still at large. So was his daughter, Nia. He wiped the sweat from his forehead and cursed the Desert Snake's name as he wondered why his mission to retrieve his wife and daughter was taking so long. His adopted son had never failed him in any task he had bade. *Maybe they are dead*, he pondered. Perhaps Asha was chasing ghosts. The wild was a treacherous place, especially for a woman and girl as softly bread as the princess and queen. He then leaned on his elbows and turned his attention to his recurring dream and the conversation he had had with the Sangoma in what seemed like a generation ago. "You are the architect of peace," the mage had told him. "The ancestors have chosen you, to save mankind from annihilation. You shall unite the tribes under the flame and save us from the real threat."

He had had his reservations. What the Sangoma had placed on his shoulders was a ginormous burden to bear, but he had come around to the idea. His kingdom was vast, but mostly included barren hill and mountain chains. He needed the other kingdoms' recourses to orchestrate man's salvation, but the will of the ancestors, he had learnt, was not always an easy path. He poked his finger into the light he kept aflame bedside. He let his finger stay there exceptionally long until he latched back and grimaced from the pain. He got up and moved from his bed chamber to his living quarters linked by a short tunnel, chucked down a calabash of water and then set himself on a stool by the great fire that roared and got to business.

"What do you see," asked a soothing voice lurking in the shadows next to the king's collection of skulls. It belonged to Nabii, a Priestess of the Temple of the Flame Bearers. She had long silver hair that almost touched the ground. Her eyes were an unnerving shade of yellow, and on her side she carried a long gnarly cane, as black as the night.

"Nothing," the king lied. In the flame he saw the strapping young nunda that had been plaguing his dreams, thundering through jungle and flat plains towards him, its roar reverberating through the clouds and canopies. Furthermore, his excavations deep into Mount Pyyros were proving fruitless. He had thousands digging for long hours that stretched from dusk to dawn. He was beginning to think he was looking in the wrong place, but by the ancestors, he would tear down the volcano before he gave up. He would stop at nothing to reveal the mountain's cloaked parts.

Nabii rose from her stool and strolled around the fire, disappearing momentarily behind the flame and then reappeared, a necklace made of miniature human skulls rattling as she strolled behind the king. She ran her fingers over his flagellated back and then massaged his shoulders, digging her nails well into his flesh. She kissed the open wounds and then set her bloodstained lips by his ear. "Relax, Maghedzi. You can't force the ancestors to speak to you."

The king took a deep breath and tried again but the result was the same. It was against his nature. Everything he had gained had been achieved through force.

"You need to stay calm. That is the only way."

With the help of Prince Themba, the Piripiri had triumphed over the renegade Ashu. Its maidens had been captured, purified and sent back to their villages clean. Peace and calm had been returned to the vast Piripiri kingdom. Despite that, the water reserves were low, and no rainy clouds were in sight. *Do I need to purify more?* He contemplated. "There IS one way you could help me calm down."

"Is there now?" The priestess had to pat away the thick fingers that probed her way, but the Raging Inferno's wide-eyed glare remained. "Is this a command, my king?"

Maghedzi nodded solemnly. Nabii smiled as she looked down at him, her sharply filed teeth gleaming. She offered a hand, which the king took, and followed her back to his bed-mat.

The priestess was gone by the time his servants were rubbing shea butter over his body. His personal guards were waiting for him outside his private chambers, a line of oblong shields and obsidian spears that beamed in the sun. The king nodded his head in approval as he marched down the tunnel of his personal guard, his crocodile skin cape so heavy and long that a servant scurried behind carrying the tail at great pains.

After being greeted by Wasike, they were on their way toward the audience chamber, down the King's Way.

The Sangoma, who had been waiting in one of the trees, hopped down and slithered toward the king, his wicked staff thrashing at the earth as he hurried. "Eternal Flame," he hollered, unable to get past the guards. "Good morning. I trust the ancestors kept you well in your sleep?"

Maghedzi squinted at the sound of the mage's lisp. His sleep was almost nonexistent, and when he finally did find some, the same dream came to him, and followed into his consciousness. He could hear the sound of nunda paws thundering his way but only he could hear it. "Do you hear that, Sangoma?"

"I hear many things. The ancestors, they speak to—"

"Enough!"

The Sangoma's back curved and his head bowed as he fell into the fetal position, his arms raised to protect his head.

"What do you want, wizard?"

"Nothing much. I just haven't heard from you, that's all."

"Have you found the location of my wife and daughter in those flames of yours? And what about the rains you promised once we performed the purifications?"

The mage had nothing to answer.

"I'll call for you when I need you."

A host of people were waiting as Maghedzi and Kuluma entered the audience chamber—a congregation dressed in fine cloths and luxurious jewelry. The overindulgences disgusted him. Some days he wished to flog the greatest perpetrators at his court, make them an example, a lesson on modesty, but there were more important things he had to deal with.

In the front row sat some of Pyre Fortress' most powerful characters. The chief-griot, Sekuru Katswiri, occupied a seat near the king. He wore a long wraparound with gold lace in between, trimmed on two sides like a carpet, with a gold fringe sewn in place with a two fingers wide ribbon woven with gold roses. By his waist was a bag where he kept his drum and *mbira* in case he had to narrate a tale, or sing a song praising the king's sensibilities. Maghedzi enjoyed those the most. He meant to give the griots the greatest tale of them all—the tale of the malevolent leader, who had saved humanity from total annihilation.

Next to the griot sat General Kamau, a lean and balding man with a short, bristly grey beard. He made up for his small countenance with the same cloths and gold Sekuru Katswiri sported. Maghedzi had grown to rely on him with his shrewd and capable advice in times of war.

The Spymaster, Chiratidzo, was also amongst the front sitters, the cautious, pensive, and subtle man, hugging onto his staff he needed to walk. Despite that, he was well feared at court due to his spy network that extended to the outskirts of the kingdom and beyond.

Nabii stood behind the king, with her hands placed over his wide caped shoulders. Since the priestess had arrived at Pyre Fortress, in the taverns, people were saying her powers were greater than the Sangoma's—that the little mage's magic was obsolete. Tavern talk had it that the priestess had killed a nunda, taken its semen from its scrotum and had slipped it into the king's cow blood unawares, binding him to her will.

After Sekuru Katswiri's drum had thundered, the procession began, petitions and complaints from officials, soldiers, merchants, artisans and farmers. The former king had been a quiet man of gentle disposition. He was so anxious to prevent bloodshed to such a degree that executions at his court were almost unknown. However, in his desire to spare or to conciliate people in his judgments, he often attempted to show that neither disputant was solely in the right, or that both were in the wrong. During Maghedzi's reign, this was not the case. Trials were swift and judgments severe. After a series of tiresome processions, which the Bush Fire adjudicated only after the mysterious priestess had whispered in his ear, lastly, a group of prisoners were tossed in front of him.

Sekuru Katswiri, who was an expert on Piripiri law and custom rose and announced, "Eternal Flame, these prisoners have been accused of attempting to steal cattle. The accuser is one Rashidi Mchoyo from the northern district, Kumputo."

Rashidi rose from the crowd of observers. He was clad like your average successful man in Pyyros, a combination of gold and crimson cloths, indigo dyed skins, feathers about the head, silvers around the neck, as well as coppers and golds. His eldest son Rondo sat next to him, as did other members of his household.

"The Mchoyo are a very well-respected family in Kumputo," Katswiri confirmed to the king. "The aggrieved man, Rashidi, the head of the family has served his kingdom well, as did his father, giving his spear to King A'hi's cause during the false king's rebellion, as well as several other minor campaigns. His son and heir, who is with him today, Rondo, has already served in your regiments despite his youthful age, most recently in your victory against the Ashu at Death Valley." Now that he had concluded the introduction of the accuser, the griot turned to the crowd. "Is there anyone who questions this man's honesty?"

When no one raised their hand in the crowd, Rashidi genuflected, clapped his hands, and then began his appeal. "In the middle of the night, I was awoken to hear that there was commotion at one of my numerous cattle enclosures. When we arrived, we found thieves attempting to steal my livestock. Some of them managed to escape, but my sons managed to capture a few. Two of them committed suicide using poison as we waited for the sheriff to arrive." He looked down and sighed. "It turned out that my very own nephew, Tauya Mundu, was involved." He shook his head in disbelief. "The boy came to me not a fortnight ago asking to borrow some cows. He said he wanted to marry but didn't have enough cattle to pay the lobola. I gave him half a dozen, but I guess it was not enough."

Maghedzi fidgeted in his throne as his nose rolled into a tight knot and then flared as the revelations unfolded. In his eyes, stealing one's cattle was akin to seducing another man's wife. It was an unsavory act of turpitude that demanded the harshest of judgments. Katswiri, who looked similarly repulsed, turned to the accused.

Before the boy from Boroa could explain himself, Nkosazana, the sole female member of Matsotsi testified, "It was all his idea," she began with a weep, pointing a finger at the tanner. "Tauya Mundu forced me to join him. He said he would kill me if I didn't help him. He told me about his uncle's vast wealth and told me that he had been around the cattle, so they recognized him. He assured me that the cows wouldn't make a commotion."

Tauya knelt mouth agape as Nkosazana went on and on and placed all the guilt on his shoulders. He really wished Tan was there to counsel him, to whisper something that would get him out of his bind, but Tan had fled like a snake in the grass with the others once Rashidi and his men and dogs were upon them, gone miraculously, in a cloud of soft, muzzled buzzing locusts. He looked into the crowd. His father's widows were in attendance, as was Yananayii Kukongola. Even in her sorrow, she was still as beautiful as ever, sitting there with her arms curled softly over her belly.

Sekuru Katswiri shook his head in pity when Nkosazana had finished her theatrical teary-eyed testimony. It was clear to everybody congregated that the bubbly eyed girl had been misled by bad men. After the other defendants had said their piece, the chief-griot rose and asked the crowd if there was anyone who would vouch for the accused.

After a long silence, one of Tauya's father's widows struggled to her feet, set her walking stick to the side and expounded that since her husband's death, the boy had been feeling unwell and insinuated that his father's spirit was responsible. "Lumambo was not a happy man in his final days," she explained. She believed it was no coincidence that right after his passing, Tauya had begun talking to himself. "At times he would demand that we cook him and his friend supper. When we would ask, which friend? he would get angry. One day we found that he had burnt the roof of one of his huts, saying there were shells he was looking for up there. Another time I found him with a broom shooing away what he said was a little fairy Abatwa hiding behind some furniture." She waited for the hearty laughter to subside and then continued, "Tauya was a very sweet young boy, but after Lumambo's passing, he transformed into someone we did not know. He would harass us and took all of our jewelry away from us. He even took our bed mats away, so we are sleeping on the floor! The Tauya I watched grow up would have never done something like this. I appeal to you *mambo*, Raging Inferno, Bush Fire, my king, my Eternal Flame, to show this boy mercy for this is not a crime of the mind but of a possessed spirit." She clapped her hands and sat down.

Katswiri let the crowd absorb everything they had heard that day and then rose. "Do you have anything to say Tauya, Mundu?"

The tanner could have mentioned Matsotsi and exposed the order in the hope of saving himself, but once he had defeated Wanugu and claimed membership, he was a brother of the band of thieves, and had made a solemn oath of silence in front of the statue of A'khungu and his followers, at pains of forfeiting his afterlife—his chance of feeling his mother's soft embrace again. He even saw his like-form rise from the smoke, after Tsolofelo had sprinkled his blood into the flames that roared, and captured it in a vase that remained sealed in Ukweba's Hall. Resigned to his impending fate, the tanner raised his head and said, "Yananayii Kukongola, I love you. I shall be waiting for you and our child in paradise."

After the priestess had whispered something into the king's ear, without word Maghedzi fastened Kuluma's chain around his throne and menaced toward the kneeling Matsotsi. His crocodile skin loincloth bopped over his front and side, and his jaw, rippled. With his hands on his hips, he turned an eye at each of the accused and then with sudden speed, grabbed a *tsotsi* by the neck and let his nails dig through the flesh. The thief tried to break free but the king's grip was resolute, tight, like a boa constrictor. There was silence in the room, the only sound coming from the thrashing of the *tsotsi*'s feet, and the desperate croak for air. The king's raging Heart Stone was the last thing Tauya Mundu saw, and the last thing he heard, was Yananayii's cries.

Chapter 26

The Guardian

King Maghedzi was returning from his daily trek up Mount Pyyros when the Sangoma spotted him and his convoy marching down the Pyre Fortress gates. The mage, who had been muttering to himself under a large sprawling tree of various shades of red, took from the rock he sat upon and rushed toward the king. *Too late*, he sighed. Again, as he had become accustomed to, the king's private chamber door slammed hard in his face. He raised a fist to knock, but instead he hunched his shoulders and sulked back to his hut. "The Temple of the Flame Bearers is but a corrupt band of thieves. Their leaders are fat and are only interested in gold and cattle. They live in their luxurious compounds with abundant servants whilst we, true messengers, perform the ancestor's work. What does this false prophetess have that I do not?" he asked as he walked down the King's Way and onto the offshoot toward his little abode near the Fire Shrine.

Reza skipped beside him and giggled, seemingly bewildered that the mage hadn't figured it out himself.

"My magic is far superior than that treacherous witch. Isn't it, Reza? I've come back from the Forest of Abominations! What has she done?"

The hyena cackled again, this time, more sinister than before.

"That's not true, Reza. I haven't lost my hunger. I'm more dedicated to the ancestors today than I have ever been."

Reza gawked at the mage with her customary blank expression that never failed in its task of upsetting its master.

"Perhaps you are right." The wizard sighed. "I should have stayed in the Forest of Abominations and found the final piece to the riddle." He rolled a tight fist and gritted his teeth. "Just you wait. I will show them. I'll show her. I'll show you! I have this new concoction I am working on, far greater than yours—better than any dream-root in all the land. Once I gain the final ingredient, I will be back in Maghedzi's good graces!"

Moons came and went without the Sangoma seeing the king, nor creating the new, revolutionary elixir he had promised. He reached for the vase containing Reza's elixir, opened the lid and sniffed it before reaching in and pulling out its contents. There wasn't much left, just enough for one spirit walk—maybe two. He cursed his luck and went about his business.

He went to the Eternal Flame's compound every day, only to be denied by the armed guards that manned the compound entrance. "The Raging Inferno is expecting me," he would lie, but when that failed, he turned to flattery, but the guards' hearts remained abhorrent. "Please?" he would try before he was picking himself and his mask from the dust. *How the mighty have fallen*, he sighed. *Chief-Witchdoctor*, he spat. *Pah! Is this how they treat a man of the ancestors?* He waved his fist and slithered back to his ramshackle hut.

"Where is that mutt?" he muttered as he entered his domicile. "Oh, there you are." He patted the beast on the head and produced a juicy bone. "Do it again. Make more of that elixir!"

Reza just stood there, looked up at her master and giggled.

The Sangoma sighed. "The ancestors have forsaken me, Reza." He reached up to the shelf and took down the vase containing the hyena's elixir. "This might be my only salvation now." He grabbed his horn and inserted a batch of the mixture, using a small twig to pump it in and lit it aflame. The hyena cackled. "Don't be afraid Reza. Yes, yes I know what happened last time. As long as you stay out of my visions, everything will be just fine, okay?" The hyena got up on all fours and began giggling angrily. "Sit!" the mage commanded, flashing his twig like index finger. "Sit!" Reza just looked at him as drool slowly dangled from her glistening fangs. "Fine, stay as you are!" He sat down and took a sip from the horn. He coughed a little and then lit it again. He took another drag as he held the horn with both hands, exhaled, and then slumped into his pile of rugs. He tried to relax but he couldn't. "After all I did for the king. He works me like a slave, you know? He makes me perform all those purifications. Day and night I'm purifying, travelling from village to village, and for what? To be called Chief-Witchdoctor of the Piripiri Kingdom? I do not feel like a chief. You know what I feel like Reza?"

The hyena giggled.

"I am not a loser you poor excuse of a dog! Take it back!"

Reza cackled mockingly so the Sangoma jumped to his feet and with arms extended, leapt for his pet. He landed with a thud, rubbed his side, and then sprang for the hyena around the hut spewing obscenities. Just when Reza was at the tips of his fingers, the mage froze, erect like a Firefly on salute, and then headfirst, collapsed onto his dusty floor.

He woke up to a knock on the door. He sniffed around. Several days must have gone as flies had gathered around a rotting calabash of food. In his white path, he had returned to the same giant mountain, reddish copper, and followed the same labyrinthine footpaths he had marched during his previous trance, till he came to the same thin perilous barrier-free pathway. The fires that burned violently below, an entanglement of scarlet, blues, gold and ambers was as ravenous as ever, as was the hopelessness that emanated from it. He had hurried along but instead of a host languidly frolicking in a murky pit, this time the chamber of dust was bleak and wild, and buzzing locusts in a solid humanoid form sat sunken in a colossus throne atop a barp of bones.

Undead ground hornbills with burning eyes covered the top rail and manchette of the seat that spewed evil so unrestrained it was visible. It whirled around the entity as it solidified into flesh and bone, round its neck, arms and through its long slender fingers that wielded a spear so wicked it was but a shadow. The Sangoma cautioned toward the throne so that he might kneel and declare his service, wading through the tormented bones, minding as animated skulls snapped at his feet, but before he could reach his goal, suddenly, the entity burst into an uncountable swarm of pests. The ground moved producing deafening noise from below, many magnitudes louder than thunder, a roar so terrifying, paralyzing, that his white path would end, and had replayed over and over again.

"Something is interfering with my vision," he decided. "It's that witch, Nagii" he spat.

Reza giggled.

"Nagii, Nabii, what's the difference!"

There was another knock on the door. The Sangoma picked up his mask that had escaped his face during his white path, tried his best to make the hut somewhat decent, and then opened the door.

A royal messenger was waiting by the porch steps. He kept a good distance away. Such was the trepidation the name and vision of the Sangoma caused. "The Eternal Flame demands your presence at once," he said with his eyes turned downward lest he be transformed into an ant.

The Sangoma licked his lips. This is what he had been waiting for, a summoning by the king, yearning even, but something, perhaps a disturbance in his spirit, made him anxious. "For what purpose?"

The boy did not say. "He is waiting for you up on Mount Pyyros."

The mage nodded his head and entered his chambers, returning shortly after in his full ceremonial witchdoctor attire, the finest animal hides he had in his possession, his miniature skulls, necklaces and ground hornbill feathers that announced his title as supreme mage of the Piripiri Kingdom.

Reza rushed out, whining as his master followed the messenger down the pathway. The Sangoma turned, knelt and caressed the hyena by the head and chest as it giggled alarmingly. "It is okay, Reza. I will be fine. Go gnaw on that juicy bone I gave you. Understood?" He stood up, patted the hyena on its snout and continued down the pathway as a parliament of owls took to the sky, a mixture of brown-greys, blacks and whitish cream feathers. After a few steps, he looked back to find Reza still trailing behind. His finger flashed. "Sit, dog," he commanded. "Don't follow me!"

The hyena did as it was told, whining and giggling as its master disappeared around the bend.

Led by a trail of royal guards, the Sangoma trudged up the mountain trail towards his waiting liege. They had braved the mountain pass for half a day, yet still, its crater was still an eternity away, hidden above the violet and luminous clouds. They passed burnt and blackened corpses as the living mined, obsidian, gold, silver, hematite, and iron ores—some picking in shafts so low, they had to crawl or bend, the stench of death their only distraction as overseers paced about and brandished weapons where needed. The higher they went, the hotter it became, the scree burning so hot they penetrated the mage's thick foot calluses, the only solace, the sporadic thorny boughs arched over the pass and the view below the mage savored behind his harrowing mask, a view that took him back to the good times—to the festivals, the miracles, the healing and the purification ceremonies he had presided.

The music played in his head, the hard-beating drums, and the marimba's velvety, wooden and earthy tones. He could hear the sonorous sounds of the mbira as though he was playing it in his own hands, and the sharp rattling hoshos that accompanied them. His smile became broader as he saw himself in his prime, darting left and right and executing effortless back flips and cartwheels and thrust his stomach forward and back, falling to the ground as he shook violently as the ancestors engulfed him, and always, Reza the hyena by his side.

The Sangoma's halcyon was interrupted when a horde of pickaxe and shovel-wielding workers appeared before him, all flesh and bone, dark shadows under their eyes, sores and sun-beaten backs. He strode through the tunnel they had formed until he came to an opening. He hesitated and defied like a stubborn beast of burden, but with the butt of his spear, a guard nudged the mystic into the ravenous gap and left him alone to continue down the speleothems that formed a mouth of razor-fanged teeth daring him to proceed.

He should have been excited. This is what he had prayed for, to be in his sire's presence, a luxury he was malnourished since the advent of the priestess, Nabii, but as he broke from the void, his armpits grew moist despite his charges with beads of sweat sailing down his torso like the Nhunundudu. Such was the effect of the Raging Inferno, whose back was turned when he arrived, more creature than man, as the cape wrapped resembled a ground hornbill anticipating death. Under his cape, rather than his customary loincloth studied with precious gemstones, he wore plain leather and had discarded the crocodile skull that hung over his crotch and shoulders. He did not address, nor acknowledge the little wizard when the mage took his familiar place by the Eternal Flame's side. The king was fixated on the massive statue in front of them carved out from the mountain side.

"Do you know what his is?" the king gruffed. He was strumming his Heart Stone, which gleamed brighter than the mage had seen yet.

The Sangoma wanted to skip and dance. He had longed to be once more of use, whispering in his liege's ear, advising him, the king and the mighty witchdoctor, working in tandem to fulfil the ancestors' will. He scrutinized the sculpture. Its face was wide, and its chin, narrow, with a long nose with flaring nostrils. Its eyebrows were furrowed and blazed outwards like a flame, as did its hair that spiraled upwards in intricately cut curls until they were one with the mountain side. The mage took his time to answer. He couldn't drop the ball. Not when his future was at a knife's edge. "I believe this to be the Guardian."

"Believe?"

The Sangoma moved closer to it. He could feel a celestial presence emanating, like it was imbued with the soul of an ancestor. He cautioned his fingers towards it and retreated with a howl when he touched it. "Yes, Eternal Flame," he confirmed as he tended to his charred finger. "It is as I suspected. This is a gateway. You will find similar structures around the kingdoms."

Maghedzi lifted an eyebrow. "A gateway to where?"

"Your guess is as good as mine. But in my estimation, into the Lost City of the Volcans."

Maghedzi stroked his chin and nodded his head in apprehension. "How do we get it to open?"

"We must awaken him."

"Who?"

"The Guardian!" The Sangoma shook his head, disbelieving the king's aloofness. He backed off a few paces, spread his feet and with both hands lifted his long-crooked staff over his head. He twirled it around in a circular motion as he spoke at the statue.

"Are you spinning a spell, mage?" The Raging Inferno was a paranoid man. He never ate without a food taster and surrounded his self with the best and most loyal of his guard— warriors that had been bred from birth to protect his person.

As the Sangoma hissed and clicked, almost as if he were in a quarrel, the scree amongst them began to jitter and then slowly, Mount Pyyros began to rumble until the statue's face moved, left and right, sluggishly, like a crone, then downwards, towards them. "Who seeks entrance into the land of the Volcans?" it bellowed, its voice deliberate and as horse as the ash and pumice stone it was formed. "Only the worthy may enter." Its eyes, two pits of molten rock, were unnerving, cross-eyed with one looking right at them and the other like a sentry, surveying the vicinity.

The king nudged the wizard to the side and bowed for the first time in a generation, as reverently as he did all those years ago when his father, King A'hi sat the Piripiri throne. "I," he pronounced proudly. "King Maghedzi of the Piripiri and all its dominions, and my witchdoctor, the Sangoma, wish to enter these holy lands."

"So be it." The ground shook once more revealing two short podiums decorated with flame sigils.

The king and the mage spread out and stood atop the platforms antithetical to each other. The mystic shook his staff around like it were a calabash of beer, causing its eyes to light, and then shot a pair of little spurts of fire into the Guardian's eye sockets until they were lit aflame.

"I don't think anything is happening," said Maghedzi after some moments.

"Patience, mambo." The mage was about to unleash a proverb on the virtue but suddenly a blinding light beamed over them from the clouds, and Mount Pyyros began to quake more aggressively than before.

When the tremors calmed, and their eyesight was once more restored, the Guardian's mouth began to quiver and then slowly opened. "You may enter, descendants of the Volcans. But harken, some protect their earthly possessions, even in the spirit realm. Be warned!"

The Eternal Flame's face dropped at the day's unfathomable revelations. "YOU have Volcan blood?"

The Sangoma shrugged his shoulders. "I always had a hunch." He inhaled and exhaled the hot air and then fixed his headdress. He wanted to look his best in the hallowed confines of the sacred mountain. He patted his cloths and animal skins down and wiped the smudges off his staff's serpentine head and stepped forward past the Guardian of the Lost City's gaped teeth. "Shall we proceed, mambo?"

The king took some moments to recollect himself, ensured he had all of his weapons and equipment for the journey, and then at last, after all his efforts that had taken a near lifetime, kissed his Heart Stone and then followed the Sangoma into Mount Pyyros' interior.

Chapter 27

The Migas

"We need to pee," demanded the renegade queen, Zandile, of the Piripiri. "Set our hands free so we can relieve ourselves." Her tone was similar to the one she used fostering a young Asha when he had first arrived at Pyre Fortress and thrust into her care. The child had been full of defiance and fits of rage, but as the seasons went by, his angst was somewhat honed, refocused, and their relationship blossomed to such an extent that Zandile and Asha had become friends, rather than mother and son.

As the journey back to Pyyros wore on, the Desert Snake had grown weary of Zandile. He wasn't sure if this was another one of her ruses. Since he had found the princess and queen in Kwa'Jivu, as he guided them back home, throughout their journey, Zandile's neck twisted and turned, as did her eyes, searching for an escape route. "You can urinate with your wrists bound," he declared.

So Zandile put her thumbs by her waistband. "Well aren't you going to turn away?"

"Not a chance, mother." The last time he let the queen urinate unattended, he found her trying to set herself free with a sharp rock she had found somewhere along their journey, so he had to be more vigilant, even if it meant forsaking sleep.

So Zandile squatted. "If I may," she asked as her water flowed and seeped into the dry soil. "How did you find us?"

"When I was at the Snake Pit, I freed some slaves." Zandile could see that recanting this chapter in his journey steered a melancholy inside the Northman. "One of them was a fighter in the Rovambira household. He said he saw a pair as I had described and said he overheard you saying you were returning home."

"Then why did you come to Kwa'Jivu?"

"I know you well, Zandile. You have never really accepted Pyre Fortress as your home. Not truly."

"Neither have you."

It was vague, but Asha still remembered the square palace, whose halls he would skip up and down, investigating the numerous figurative frescos and reliefs that depicted people and animals. He remembered the bathhouse where he and his siblings would play, the water reservoir, and the agricultural enclosure his uncle was in charge of. His favorite was a man-made oasis his grandfather had built, where he would dip his toes and leisure under a date palm as his sisters' voices complimented his harp strings. Soon this beautiful image changed to carnage, when Zandile informed him that Maghedzi had burnt down Ido looking for them. He could see the charred frames and blazing roofs of his home as purple-eyed hordes descended upon them.

"He has begun purifying girls from neighboring villages and is expanding into the far reaches of the kingdom," Zandile continued. "His blood lust is unquenchable. Tell me Asha, is this the man you serve so faithfully?"

The Desert Snake set his eyes upon Zandile momentarily, before jerking the ropes tied around his prisoners' wrists.

Their journey from Kwa'Jivu led them southwest from the Moto lands to avoid bandits and prying eyes, through flat flavescent common-finger-grass valleys with isolated clumps of trees and clusters of granite-rock hills, some scenes Nia and Zandile recognized from their flight from the Piripiri Kingdom toward the Snake Pit which lied east of the fire tribes' dominion. They travelled well into the night and continued the morning after until they were at the threshold of a cave opening.

They crept in one by one, doing well to dodge the spider webs that manned the threshold. From the cave entrance you could smell the mold, and goose bumps lined their arms from the cold that swept through the dank hollow. It was a cave mouth of impenetrable blackness, and the only sound was the monotonous sound of dripping water. Thus, the Desert Snake reached into his bag, brought out a jar and opened it, brightening the passageway as fireflies flew out omitting a powerful amalgamation of bright yellow, green and amber. It exposed walls that arched several dozen feet up toward gargantuan stalactites and bat roosts. "This way," he beckoned as his voice echoed on forever, waving his hand in the air and directing the lightening bugs down deeper into the cavern as they flashed synchronized, giving the way an air of gloom, bright then dark, over and over again.

When they were out of the cave, a long wooden bridge was before them. According to the position of the sun, it led them east again. On the other side across the Yerera River congregated a flamboyance of flamingos, a mixture of bright pink and reddish feathers, stilt-like legs and serpentine necks. Nia wrinkled her nose as a foul stench permeated her nostrils. The water was still and on it, she could see the reflection of the sun, though peculiarly, thick lenticular clouds dominated the skies.

"It's not me, if that's what you're thinking," denied the Desert Snake.

"What do we do now," asked Nia.

"We cross, that's what we will do."

"On that thing?"

It looked like the bridge hadn't been used for eons. Its wooden planks were splintered, and it swayed uncertainly. Ginger seemed to think the same thing, growling and kyoodling.

"I'm afraid so," replied the Northman. "I'm sure it'll hold up. We just have to be careful." He latched onto the upper rails and stuck a foot out to make sure the bridge was sturdy. When he was satisfied, he moved along, turning back to make sure his prisoners were following behind. When he got to the middle of the bridge, the rope securing Zandile snapped, and then, something latched around her foot and dragged her into the waters beneath.

The Desert Snake moved his head about, instinctively surveying the environment. "Untie me, please," pleaded Nia. He contemplated for a short moment, and then sent his blade through the rope, with one clean stroke, freeing the princess. He reached into his bag, took out another rope, and tied it around the bridge-rail. With that he followed the queen, rope in hand.

"Mother," Nia whimpered as she stood there, atop the bridge searching the waters like a fish eagle in flight. "Asha?" There was no response, just the still waters and Ginger's whimpering. Suddenly, she saw the rope jerk, then out from the water burst the Desert Snake and under him a hideous migas.

The cephalopod had thick tentacles as big as an elephant's leg. It fixed Nia with a gaze before it let out a loud screech from its parrot-like beak that had Nia clutching onto the bridge rail as one of its tentacles landed with a thud in front of her. She kicked it back into the waters beneath and searched for her mother. Zandile finally emerged from deep and made to swim to shore, but a tentacle took her from below and carried her into the air.

Amidst Zandile's wails, the Desert Snake slashed again and again, his other hand tightly gripped around the rope, cutting off one tentacle after the next. Pieces of meat flew through the air, but miraculously each time the Northman cut, another tentacle grew back.

"Stab it in the eye," Nia yelled. She hoped the Desert Snake could hear her amongst the monster's shrieks, the splashing of water, and her mother's screams. She ransacked Asha's bag and brought out a bow and arrow. She pulled the string back but instead ran across the bridge to the riverbank, Ginger by her side, her tail flapping wildly from side to side. Maybe she would have a better shot from there.

The Desert Snake gnashed his teeth as a tentacle embraced him. He could feel his life force departing as the migas heaved. It let out a deafening screech as an arrow flew into the tentacle, and then another, allowing the Desert Snake to wriggle himself free and slash, chopping the tentacle into two. Now free, he gripped the rope tightly and swung toward Zandile as she kicked and screamed, wrapped in a tentacle. He brought his sword out as he approached and hacked. As he swung back he scooped out a limp Zandile thrashing under the current and left her on a rock protruding from the waters. He pulled out another long rope and tied it around her wrist and cast it toward Nia. "Pull," he cried.

She did. She pulled with all her strength. "I am too weak!" Her palms were shredded bloody from the hauling, but she clenched her teeth, closed her eyes and heaved until finally Zandile was out of harm's way. Nia dove into the shallow waters and dragged the queen onto dry land with her bloodied hands.

Meanwhile, the Desert Snake was powering through the waters, black ink obstructing his vision under water. He latched on to the migas and pulled himself toward its giant eye. When he was above it, he raised Zara-Fe'yi's sword, and with it, stabbed the cephalopod multiple times, again and again, its razor's tip cracking the monster's hard crust over and over, as black ink splashed all around until his kanzu matched the color of his hair. As he gored, a bright light appeared, and the creature shook as violently as Mount Pyyros' tremors, and not long after that, the monster exploded, sending the Desert Snake through the air, landing with a splash just off the riverbank.

He groaned as he lifted his head but immediately awoke when he remembered Zandile. She was as pale as a cadaver when he arrived by her side, wet as a fish, as Ginger laid her warm tongue about her face. Asha went onto his knees and gave the queen the kiss of life, leaving black ink over her perky lips.

Nia watched, stiff as a log. The Desert Snake pumped at her chest and then kissed her again. He did this a few more times until water erupted from her mouth.

When Zandile's coughing had subsided and her breath returned, suddenly, the Desert Snake looked at Nia and squinted his eyes. "It's strange. I can see three of you." Then, his smile turned and knees buckled.

Chapter 28

The Lost City

The Sangoma could feel his age as he galumphed behind King Maghedzi as the odd pair descended down the Guardian's staired throat into Mount Pyyros' network of volcanic caverns. The Raging Inferno however, with calves the size of pumpkins, and a stomach that put adolescents to shame, moved in his customary brisk, with heels that hardly touched the ground, manic, like he was living on borrowed time, sometimes seizing the mage by the arm and guiding him on onwards, towards the hidden secrets he had devoted his life.

When they were at the bottom of the stairway, a lava filled chasm sprawled, bridged by a labyrinth of rock footpaths that led towards several portals in the distance. The fire ahead roared in tempest, blazing, filling the cavern with a tangerine sheen. They cautioned over the trail as heat blew upwards like a furnace blast till they reached a fork prompting the Sangoma to kneel in deep meditation as he summoned the ancestors' guidance. He stared intently at the several mouths, pointing at each before deciding, "This way," springing up childlike, with a new sense of courage, but the king was suspicious.

"How in the name of our ancient lords would you know what path we must take?" His nose wrinkled, like he was ready to thrum his spear butt across the mage's face.

Since they entered the volcano's interior, the Sangoma had been plagued with a sense of familiarity, like he had been here prior amongst the perilous pathways and lakes of fire. "The ancestors, they showed it to me, in my white path."

The king was not convinced. A false prophet is what he had branded the Sangoma. The mystic had failed to locate his wife and daughter's location despite his claims, and the purification campaign they had waged across the kingdom had not brought back the rains. Still, the diminutive creature had resurrected his son, Alinafe, and despite his shortcomings, the king had met few, if any, with the wizard's zeal and attachment to the spirits. "So be it, but know thy penalty for failure." He ceded navigation and followed behind with his arms spread-out and eyes firmly set on their goal as violent and acidic fumes mushroomed into miniature clouds.

After a series of twists and turns through arched passageways, they were peculiarly back in the same cavern albeit on another side. "I should have known better than to put my faith in you," said the king as he grinded his teeth. " . . . With your history."

The Sangoma scratched his head and pondered. "Patience, Bush Fire. Do the ancestors not say that one acquires a chicken from hatching an egg, not by smashing it?" The mage put a finger over the king's lips, jerked his head back and forth and listened to the air as he cupped his ear. "I think that's the way," he pointed, over the lava pool and towards a portal sandwiched by two others, all identical.

"Think?" The king was growing more fractious the longer their journey wove along.

"As you know, mambo . . ."

"Yes, yes, the ancestor's way is not always clear." The Priestess Nabii had uttered the same thing.

Maghedzi followed the mage back where they came from, to the fork in the middle of the cavern and onto the winding tributary until they reached the portal and down its dark passageway until they were stopped by a circular stone door. The king brushed the dust off the panel revealing the Volcan symbol, a torch flaring upwards like a trident. He moved his hands over it, shifted to the side and then with his shoulder, applied gnashed-teethed-effort that broke the sweat from his temples, but the door would not budge. "You've led us to another dead end, vile creature!"

"What force cannot accomplish, the spirits may." The Sangoma took a few steps back and raised his staff. When its eyes lit, he slammed it down, and with all his might willed the stone door till it rolled enough to squeeze past. Weak and exhausted from the exertion, the mage collapsed, and when his eyes finally opened, Maghedzi was standing over him.

"Get up," the king barked. "And put this on." He threw the mask over the witchdoctor's belly and hauled him up. "You look hideous. Let's get moving. We have much work to do."

When they cautioned over the doorstone the odd pair's eyes burgeoned. "Behold!" the Sangoma beamed, with his arms stretched and staff raised high in triumph. "The Lost City of the Volcans!"

Two winged statues, shiny obsidian black stared down at them as they crossed the city threshold. They couldn't help but be awestruck by the vast roof and stone hewn pillars that stretched upwards like baobab trees. The Sangoma had heard tales of this city, its song recited to him by his mentor, the spirit medium that had taught him everything he knew, about its sprawling halls, lava falls, shiny walls, glistening with obsidian, polished, smooth as the wind-swept hills overlooking the Yachonde plateau.

In its glory the advanced civilization consisted of several levels all linked by glistening obsidian carved steps. It was paradisal, with natural archways complimented by tiled walkways, little ponds of lava scattered symmetrically, and statues shaped from the volcano's interior. The higher they went, the more outstanding it became with the remnants of a city that boasted shiny black colonnades, terraces, courtyards, alcoves and verandahs decorated with imposing monoliths, but now, the city was but a carcass, a remnant, overrun by time's dust.

The Sangoma closed his eyes. He could hear the sound of beating drums, whistling and tambourines, singing and dancing and the sound of commerce, blissful families and a compassionate community working in tandem, a society that had no knowledge of dishonesty, nor violence, and devoid of hatred, arrogance and avarice.

A nudge from Maghedzi ended his reverie. He followed behind the king as they moved down the gold paved thoroughfare, cautious, yet marveling and absorbing the unfathomable, falling with melancholy as they peered into the abandoned homes and markets that had been replaced with emptiness. They proceeded up the flight of stairs towards the upper level, all the while, the Sangoma's ear twitching. "Did you hear that?" He had asked the king several times.

When they reached the final level, the Sangoma couldn't help but notice something in the shadows, gliding through the row of buildings and statues that lined the corridor. He was thirsty and only his strong connection to the spirits prevented him from succumbing to the heat. He decided he was growing delirious. They moved down the long pathway until they were stopped by a large door, more than twice the king's height, heavy, made from darkwood and reinforced by gold beams. They lifted the gold shaft that barred the door, and together, heaved until it creaked open revealing a stone vault with a beam of light that shone from above and over the middle of the oval pool of bubbling lava.

Their necks twisted as they surveyed the chamber. Amongst the artifacts scattered around was mountain piles of treasure, riches beyond the king and mage's wildest and most fantastical dreams. In the midst of the gold statues and mounds of diamonds, sapphire and assortment of precious gems was the jewel of them all—a statue of Gyiku'o.

They looked up and marveled. It was indeed a fine piece of work. Naked as one's born day, the glass statue was unlike anything they had seen. Its muscles were pronounced, with every cut carved with prodigious detail. Its waist was slender and hands and head remarkably large. Another man might have gasped at the size of its genitals or the vastness of its calves, but Maghedzi was certain this was no exaggeration. The ancient ancestor looked like a lion poised for action, watchful and concentrated, spear in hand and pointing onwards with the other. The king tickled his cleft in deep contemplation. He followed the finger's projection towards the beam of light that shone in the center of the vault. He looked back at the statue and noticed a cordiform aperture in the center of its chest. Without much thought, like he was being guided by a celestial force, he snatched the Heart Stone from its link chain, and in his palm it glinted, shimmering exuberantly with pulses of light that shone over his face, giving him an appearance more sinister than his usual self. He looked up and began speaking to the statue.

"When I was in the northern desert lands before the Great Divide formed, I met some merchants," he told the Piripiri's most revered ancestor, like they were enjoying a pleasant conversation under a jacaranda tree. "They presented me with goods they were selling. When I told them they had nothing I needed, when they turned to leave, something fell from one of their many bags. Somehow, despite myself, I was immediately drawn to it. Now I know why." He lifted the Heart Stone and inserted it into Gyiku'o's chest and stepped back. "When I asked how much they were willing to sell it to me, I knew it was worth way more than any gold or cattle could buy by the way they defended it. Despite their admirable efforts, I took it for myself, and since that day, I have been looking for its home."

After ordering the Sangoma to set it aflame, he stepped back and watched arm folded as amber streaks began flowing through the statue as it illumed. Soon thereafter to the king's barely disguised delight, the ground began to rumble and then up from the lava pool slid out a tall looming pillar, and atop it, a rectangular stone sarcophagus. The king and mage looked at each other in disbelief. Not much for words, the Bush Fire hasted headlong towards the flight of stairs that had formed and crept up towards the light.

Maghedzi was caressing the surface of the coffin when the Sangoma joined him at the top of the pillar. "After all these years," the king pronounced, licking his lips and wriggling his fingers like a child upon a pot of honey, "Finally, I…"

"We…" the Sangoma corrected.

"…Have found it! The hidden secrets of Mount Pyros!" He moved his fingers to open the lid, but something compelled him to stop. He took a step back, twisted his neck towards the Sangoma and calmly ordered, "Open it."

The mystic froze as his past flashed before his eyes, to a time he had buried in a deep pit of sand. He began to stutter. "The Guardian . . . he warned us." He looked at the sarcophagus' surface and then at the king's face. It was stern—resolute, like a galloping bush fire. It made the mage picture the barp of skulls the king kept in his throne room, and crowned at the top, his very own mutilated ugly mug. He moved closer to the pall and saw the painted eyes which the occupant could spy. They were oppressive and tore a trail through his heart making him look away. "The ancestors forbid it!" he decided, hoping invoking the yester men would sway the pious king. Disturbing the dead had been the cause of all his problems and had ushered a lifetime of misery, but the king was determined. The mage dropped his shoulders defeated and stepped forward, gulping, all the while thinking of the punishment he would face this time around. He had suffered the ultimate price for his past crimes, but at this point in his life, he felt that there was no curse he could not endure. Misfortune was a condition he could live with, even in the afterlife. He did as he was bade, running his claws along the sarcophagus' side and searched for some groves, slowly, in a way to buy time. He took a deep breath and with some effort, slid the crown a nudge open, and to his surprise, nothing happened.

Encouraged, relieved he had not been struck down by lightning, or suddenly turned into a pillar of ash, he calmed himself and then applied more effort until the sarcophagus revealed a body, as old as time, somewhat preserved, dried and withered.

Resting on its chest was a long flute cradled in the corse's fingers. When the king saw what it was, his face changed, like a man looking lustily at a beautiful woman. Despite himself, in the plain view of the ancestors swirling around them, he snatched at the flute, brought it aloft and marvelled until he began to cackle, more sinister than an orchestra of hyenas. "Soon, everything in the world shall belong to me." He looked down and gave the mage a supercilious smirk. "My spies thought it was useless tracking you, despite my urges. They thought you too cowardly to betray me. All you did was empty your soul to that nasty beast of yours, but I insisted and soon enough, the depths of your betrayal was revealed."

That Reza, the Sangoma cursed. It was not the first time he had got him into trouble, but it looked like it was the last.

"In your discussions with the hyena, you mentioned a final piece to a riddle, and now, it is finally in my hands."

The Sangoma raised one of his eyebrows behind his harrowing mask and even more so when he felt the pillar begin to shake unsteadily. "My lord, that is not the final key to solving the riddle!"

But Maghedzi was deaf to his cries, cackling and too enthralled by the flute to hear him, nor care for the dust particles that began drizzling from the ceiling. He could feel the ancient instrument radiating on the tip of his fingers. It was heavy, way more than it looked. He licked his lips as he grew in confidence and moved it up, closer to his eyes for a more thorough inspection and then motioned to throw his large lips over the mouthpiece, all the while, the tremors in the chamber more ferocious, and the lava pool bubbling more violently. He took a deep breath, but before he could blow, the Sangoma snatched it out of his grasp. The king looked at him, like it was the first time he had set his gaze upon him. "Mambo!" the Sangoma heeded. "We need to leave, immediately! Can't you see? The ancestors are very very angry! This place is about to implode! We must flee!"

The Sangoma fastened the flute on his back and raced down the stairs as the king followed after him. As they fled the chamber, despite himself, the mage scooped a handful of precious stones from a mound nearby as Maghedzi retrieved the Heart Stone from Gyiku'o's chest. After he slipped the gem into his satchel, the king followed the mage back through the Lost City, leaping over the fissures that had formed, fallen debris and now rampaging streams of churning lava.

All the while the Sangoma's ear was twitching. He could feel something in the hot air, like something was following them, hidden in the shadows like a phantom. They made their way down the stairs that connected the Lost City levels, but just when they were about to reach the next they turned their head to a deafening roar.

Screeching towards them was a winged behemoth, blazing in smokeless fire. Its flickering eyes glared at them with burning rage. "THIEFS!" it roared as it towered well over and brandished a flaming spear. It raised the weapon over its head and brought it down forcing the pair to hop out of the way and scurry towards the level below. The creature stabbed and then swung again as they rushed down the stairs, demolishing the stair case causing the king and mage to tumble to the ground. They picked themselves up as the monstrosity wheeled around them before hurtling their way, smashing through pillars and buildings until it was above the fleeing pair. It raised its spear and swung, but the king and mage hopped out of the way and took refuge behind a giant obsidian statue. It came again, this time with its fist, a ball of blazing fire, heavy, until their refuge was no more, a mound of rubble and stone. With no obstacle to hide under, the creature's next strike was blocked by Maghedzi's sword, shattering it into molten fragments. It swung again, this time catching the king's cape that disintegrated exposing his bare back, broad with the numerous scars of flagellation. The king and mage ran as fast as their lungs could take them, down the steps until they reached the first level of the ancient city. With their hearts beating, they surveyed the area. "That way!" the Sangoma screamed.

They took sanctuary in one of the abandoned homes and enjoyed some momentary respite. "What in the ancestors' name is that?"

"It's alive," the Sangoma fretted. "It lives, it lives, it lives!"

The king gave the mage a swift feel of the back of his palm and then grabbed him by the shoulders and shook violently. "Who lives?"

"The king of the kongamoto! The Ifirit! Mambo, what should we do!?!" The Sangoma's teeth were rattling and his heart pounded harder than the numerous times he had to flee vicious packs of nunda in the Forest of Abominations. He could feel death approaching. "Mambo, why didn't you tell me that the Heart Stone once belonged to Asha's family?"

"Where I found it matters not," Maghedzi snapped. "What matters is that we escape this city, body and soul. As powerful as the Ifirit is, it is still a beast. Do as I say, and we might have a chance of seeing tomorrow." The king searched the area. Sandwiching the main pathway were rows of buildings and behind them were backstreets that also led to their salvation. "If you take the left route, I'll take the other through the main corridor. Its confusion will give us a head start and give us just enough time to make the exit which is too narrow for the behemoth to follow."

The Sangoma wanted to protest, but the winged creature's poised spear prompted him into action. It took to the air and followed after as the mage scurried down the backstreet like a rodent over a shiny kitchen floor. When the Sangoma was finally cornered, it raised its spear. "*Tsotsi,*" it vociferated, "Thief!" Just before it made its killing blow, Maghedzi's obsidian tipped spear pierced through the creature's wing. It howled as it searched for its assailant, who was whistling and waving his hands hoping to attract the beast's attention his way. When the Ifirit found him, it took flight and charged after him allowing the mystic to race past the exit. The king followed suit. The spear lodged in the creature's wing had severely slowed it, giving the king just enough time to roll past the exit and into safety behind the stone door.

They fell to the ground, exhausted. Their lips were parched and the Sangoma was sobbing. A trail of mucus was falling from his nose as the wall behind them juddered as the Ifirit's fists banged hard in solid blows over and over again. They summoned the last ounce of strength they had and braved the thin labyrinth of footpaths over the chasm of now leaping lava until the Guardian's throat was in sight. They scurried towards it as unbridled heat hissed and smacked from below.

They began their ascent up the final tunnel as the steps began to crack and devastation followed behind them, rocks and boulders raining down as the ground shook under them causing the Sangoma's mystical staff to tumble back down the stair case. "Noooooooo," he screeched as his source of power rolled down the stairs towards the lava that was rising behind them. He wailed like a widow and stomped his feet in agony, his feathers raving wildly as the staff sat momentarily over the lava then foundered with an explosive hiss. The mage turned and scuttled back up the stairs after the king, but right at the penultimate moment, the Guardian's throat gave way and crumbled into its stomach below.

Chapter 29

The Orphan

I have always had an affinity towards the woods. Perhaps because that's where my mother died as she brought me into this world of woe, amongst the critters, eerie darkness and vines that bowed from the untouched trees. As for my father, I can't be certain, but I heard rumors that he perished in one of King Nuru's failed incursions. Soon thereafter I was raised in Molora, a village near where I slayed my mother. I grew into an inquisitive and earnest boy, always helpful around the community, lending my services where needed, whether it was herding cattle, repairing leaking huts or giving joy through storytelling, song and dance at festivals.

At the Fire Festival that coincided with the birth of Prince A'hi, the Coming Flame, who would one day ascend the Piripiri throne, is where I first fell in love with Tawara. Even after all these years, through the various kings' reigns and the Great Dry that brought the kingdoms to their knees, her face is as vivid as the last time I saw her. She was an orphan just as I was, born a few winters prior. Perhaps it was pity, but she took it upon herself to be my protector, my own benevolent ancestor in the flesh. Molora was no place for the motherless, not with the group of local boys that prowled, who would spit on us, call us names and gave me a good beating whenever they could. Through Tawara's protection, that was not often. When she was not around to curse them away with her fiery temper I'd run to the nearest tree, climb up like a monkey and throw fruits at them and any stones I kept in a small pouch on my side. So, as you can imagine, it wasn't always pleasant being in Molora, so whatever time I had for myself I would dedicate it to excursions.

Since I can remember, we were told to stay away from the Mukuvisi Woodlands that lied north of the village walls. They said it was enchanted with evil spirits, ghosts and goblins. However, I was inquisitive by nature, and always questioned things to my peers and elders' annoyance. Unlike other children my age, I often pondered how and why things worked, so when I crossed the wood threshold, rather than be petrified, I was awestruck by the light that faded as soon as I entered and embraced the darkness I was born, the shadows that darted and the perpetual feeling that something was watching me. Exploring these woods that stretched far and wide became a daily habit despite the peril I was warned.

On one occasion that would change my life forever, up ahead in the distance, I spied a peculiar looking woman talking to no one. I came to learn that she was a spirit-medium named Yazuru, whose powers some villagers used in times of crisis. Diverted from the birds and insects and mystery of the varying trees, stalking the mystic became my everyday activity. Always with her was a raggedy satchel tucked under her armpit, and on her side, a large, dark and shiny horn, slick with graceful curves. She was such an enigma to me. I came every day and spied on her and took to imitating the way she moved, the way she jerked her head and the way her tongue flickered around and tasted the air like a lizard slipping through the bush when she spoke to the wind. The first time I saw her cup her fingers and then produce a ball of fire in the palm of her hands left me awestruck. It was a moment I would never forget. I went home trying to replicate what she did, willing my hands to do the same but nothing happened.

The following day I found Yazuru in the company of several diviners exchanging a calabash of umqombothi as they listened to a woman speak. She seemed the most senior of the congregants, with a head covered in a lengthy woolen wig of serpentine vines festooned with wild feathers and flowers. From a raggedy satchel she unveiled a coiling snake, and with a sturdy hand tight around its neck, pumped its venom into a small bowl. She let the viper slither away into the dense forestry and let the venom drip over a batch of herbs she had prepared. She then cast the meld into a stone block mortar and then accepted a chicken from one of the diviners. After slitting its neck, she let its blood cascade into the meld and then one by one, each mystic brought forth a root and cast it into the blend. She then raised her hands and led the diviners in a prayer. She asked the ancestors for infinite wisdom, vision and the welfare of their kind. After she concluded, Yazuru rose from her stool, produced a wisp of fire from her finger and cast it into the mortar lighting it aflame. In unison the mystics clamored over the rising smoke and disappeared under its mushrooming cloud.

When the smoke settled, the festivities began, an orchestra of frantic drums that produced a visual of energetic leaps and head banging I had then yet seen, not even at the Flame Festival in Pyyros I was fortunate to have attended, where the most skillful dancers from the kingdom descended like a mass bird migration, hoping to earn a place at the king's court.

Perchance it was twisted fate, but as I watched the action unfold, I felt something brush my ankle. I looked down frantic and saw a snake, poised and ready to strike. I scrambled for a stick nearby and lifted it over my head, but thankfully, the serpent turned and slid seamlessly into the verdure. As I wiped my forehead and settled my nerves, having forgotten the proceedings I had been spying, my heart froze when I heard someone call my name. "Yatima," it cried, velvety and lizardry. "Show yourself, child!"

The first thing I wondered was how they knew my name and who to call for as I was well hidden amongst the vegetation. My first instinct was to run away but refusing a sorcerer's request was a gamble. I had heard stories that they could turn people into a tokoloshe, so I slipped out and cautioned towards the conclave.

Yazuru was the first to speak. "What are you doing," she hissed at me.

She didn't look anything like I had imagined from afar. I didn't know what to answer, but after my time hidden, observing the spirit-medium hidden amongst the bushes, I knew that I wanted to be like her. "I want to be able to produce fire from my hands, just as you did," I told her.

Yazuru chuckled as she looked down at me. She turned to her peers. "What do you think about that? The boy wants to learn our ways."

One of the mystics, the stoutest of them circled and sniffed at me like I was prey. Another took me by my head and leaned over me as he glared into my eyes. When he finally set me free, the most senior of them stepped forward and hissed as she snaked around me, slowly, stalking on tipped toes. "Aren't you afraid, Yatima?"

Everybody was, from the humble tanner, butcher, cattle herder and even the village chief. I shook my head truthfully and told her no.

"Well you should be."

I told her that I couldn't fear something that I admired.

She hissed and then looked at the others. "Do you know that to be like us you must forsake your life? You must die and be reborn again. Are you not afraid of that?"

I thought about it for some moments and then shook my head once more.

"Lies!" she spat. "You are as clear as a fountain. You are afraid. You have always been afraid, since you were born. You are afraid of loss. I can sniff it on you."

"How can I be afraid of loss?" I told her. "I am an orphan. I have no family, no station, no wealth. I have very little to lose."

"That is a lie. I am sorry, boy, but you cannot join us."

I was crushed, I could feel tears begin to swell about my tear ducts. "Then what is to happen to me?" I gulped.

"Well, we can't just let you leave, after you've been spying us. Our order is one of secrecy."

I knew what she meant. In the future I would learn why she did what she did, but Yazuru, who had been silent throughout stepped forward, grabbed me by my jaw and inspected my face. "He reminds me of Ruwa," she said. There was an uneasy murmuring after she said the name. She released me and then tickled her chin as she looked down at me. "He certainly has her strong connection to the spirits. More than anything I have ever felt."

"Even more a reason for us to do what now needs to be done," the senior witchdoctor said.

"That is not necessary. He is too handsome to be turned into a warthog. I shall train him," Yazuru declared. "I think it is about time I took an apprentice."

I couldn't believe it. I thought my fate had been sealed.

"He is too old," one of the mystics decried. "And too attached to the world. This boy's mind is clouded by his personal attachments and the loss of his parents."

"Indeed," said another. "He is angry. The life of a motherless child is an unfortunate one."

Tempers flared and raged as the diviners argued into the night as I sat there and prayed for my salvation. Yazuru remained defiant throughout and through his rhetoric, managed to gain sympathy from some of her peers forcing the senior witchdoctor to cede and reluctantly allow me to become Yazuru's apprentice. "So be it," she declared. "But be warned, this boy will bring you nothing but trouble." She cast a batch of powder onto the floor causing a cloud, and when it had subsided, all that was left was Yazuru and I.

Chapter 30

Ngorongoro

"Help us," Princess Nia screamed as she and Queen Zandile hauled the limp Desert Snake past the Ngorongoro village barbican.

"Nia?" stuttered a young man stopped dead in his tracks.

He looked like someone she knew, albeit much taller, less boyish, with spares hairs about his chin. "Chafu," Nia corrected. "Don't just stand there, Wafula, help us!"

"Of course . . . Chafu," Wafula redressed perplexed. Whenever he used to call her that back at Pyre Fortress, she would strike him with whatever she had in her hands. He peered down at the Desert Snake. Even as the Northman lay there unconscious, innocuous as a babe, Wafula was still afraid, petrified from the tales he had heard growing up over open fires—tales of the soulless fiend from across the divide who drank children's blood from his collection of skulls. He had heard it all, stories of how the Desert Snake was actually King Maghedzi's bastard, the fruition of the king's tryst with a mermaid.

Wafula remembered playing as a babe watching mouth agape, hidden behind rocks and trees, as blade in hand the Northman on his blood eyed zebra thundered past. He had never been this close to the enigma, for his mother had warned him to stay well clear, so he summoned all the courage he could, set his hands upon the Northman warily like his kanzu was made of poisonous substances and surveyed his wounds, wrinkling his face immediately with worry. "He is lucky to still be alive," he declared as he grabbed Asha by the armpits and with help dragged him into a hut. "What happened to him?" he commanded as he set Asha onto a mat and felt his ink smudged forehead.

"We were crossing the bridge over the Yerera River when a migas dragged my mother into the waters. He went in after her and saved her life."

Soon the village healer was on the scene, a short man with a big belly and feathers all about. He felt the Desert Snake's slick forehead and announced, "Only the ancestors can save him now."

"Then get to it," barked Wafula, his hands waving as he gave instruction.

The whole village stopped what they were doing that day, as they anticipated what many thought inevitable, but later in the evening the healer finally emerged from the hut and informed the waiting crowd on the Desert Snake's condition. "He is a strong one. Touched by the ancestors."

"Can I go and see him?" asked Nia.

"You may not," the healer lisped. "He is still in great danger." He looked up into the sky like he was watching something. "Life and death are in a great struggle for this man's fate," he declared. "I have dressed his wounds and given him an anodyne. Hopefully that should ease his pain. Now rest, and most importantly, pray."

Later that evening, Chief Ilahle, the young potentate of the village, summoned Zandile and Nia to his audience chamber. Wafula was stood next to him when they arrived, as he had been taken as an attendant to the young chief.

"Wafula tells me that you are his relatives," Ilahle began, after Zandile and Nia had performed their pleasantries.

"That is correct, most ferocious chief," Zandile replied. She was well versed in the arts of flattery, especially that of royalty, being one herself. "My name is Kutenda, and this is my daughter, Chafu."

"What relation are you to Wafula?"

Zandile had to think quickly. "Wafula's deceased father's sister is my aunt."

The young chief pinched his face and stroked his invisible beard, trying to decipher the relation. "How long do you intend to stay?"

"Until our travel companion is well enough to continue our journey."

"Very well. You are welcome here for as long as you like. Do not hesitate to ask me for anything."

Zandile and Nia clapped their hands and exited the room.

Wafula caught up with them as they made way to their new lodgings. "Nia," he whispered. "Why are you calling yourself Chafu? You used to hate that. You even gave me a black eye once that I had to lie about to my mother. And you . . ." he stooped his head in reverence of her title, the Queen of the Piripiri Kingdom . . . "Kutenda?"

Nia quickly put a finger on her lips. "Not so loud, Wafula!" She waited for a group of passersby to stroll past before she finally revealed in a hushed tone, "Mother and I ran away from home."

"You what?" Wafula was now visibly flummoxed.

"Calm down." She grabbed him by the arm until he stopped fidgeting. "We've been wondering around the kingdom since then looking for refuge. We even went as far as the Snake Pit in the Boaboa Kingdom, but they denied us asylum there. We finally found refuge at my grandfather's *kraal* in Kwa'Jivu, but he betrayed us. That is where Asha finally caught up with us. We were on our way back to Pyre Fortress when we were attacked by the migas."

Wafula stroked his chin as though a voluptuously flowing beard resided on it and contemplated. "You must have gone through a lot."

Zandile was now visibly older than when they set off and Nia was no longer the bony legged girl, but a woman, with a hardened exterior.

"What shall you do now?"

"We pray that Asha heals from his wounds," Zandile answered skeptically, and it was apparent all over her ink-smudged face. "Then after that..." She looked into the distance. She was still resolved to save Nia from the Sangoma's blade, even at her life's cost... *even at a whole village's cost* ...and the penalty for murder in the Piripiri Kingdom was death. "...We will see."

"Will you keep our identities a secret?" implored Nia.

Wafula contemplated for some moments. Lying to one's chief was an offence many had lost a head for, and the young chief had placed a great deal of trust in him. "With my afterlife."

It was now half a moon since Princess Nia and Queen Zandile had been in Ngorongoro, and the Desert Snake's life was still in peril. To pass time, Nia took company with a group of local girls. She was often silent as they took part in storytelling and bawdy gossip. Eniola, a wide hipped young woman was the loudest, only halting her chatter to let the other girls' chortles wash over her.

A group of boys howled and whistled in the near distance, thrusting their herding sticks into the air in dramatic fashions.

"Who are they?" inquired Nia.

"The one on the left is Bushiri," answered Eniola. "He is the son of a very important man in the village, the chairman of the village council. The really tall one is Bomani. Their family runs the village's shea butter production. The other is Idi, an apprentice to his father's metalsmith shop, and the shortest one is Boitumelo."

"He is so handsome," purred Toni, another one of the local girls whom Nia had grown most fond of.

"This one," laughed Eniola. "I personally don't see what she sees in him." She put a hand over her mouth and whispered, "And his family still prays to the Great Ophidian!" She smiled.

"But, who am I to judge? The heart wants what it wants." She batted her eyes.

In truth, the villagers practiced many similar customs as the snake people of the Boaboa Kingdom. Nia also noted that some of the people bore some of the snakelike features she had seen at the Snake Pit—elliptical pupils and stretched limbs. Thus it was no surprise to her when she heard that once upon an age, many generations from the present, Ngorongoro, though autonomous, once swore fealty to the snake lords.

Bushiri was now performing cartwheels, whilst Boitumelo flexed his well-cut physique.

This was all perplexing to Nia. "What do they want?"

"They do this every time they get the chance. That is their way of showing that they are interested in one of us."

"Or maybe all of us," Jani chortled. "The ancestors know they can afford it."

Wealthy or not, Nia thought one of them had a head too big, and another's face she reckoned looked like a puff adder's. Furthermore, their display was a strange concept to her. In her understanding, the way a boy expressed his desire for a girl was by an emissary. "I see. Are you interested?"

Eniola laughed. "My heart belongs to another. He is so handsome. Fufu . . . is it okay if I call you Fufu? You should see him. Looks are very important to me, but he is also kind and fierce and a very important man in the village. I am well prepared for marriage. It's what I have always dreamed of. I can't wait. I just hope he sees that I love him."

"Well, good luck on that," offered Nia.

"Thank you," Eniola replied politely. "In some tribes, when a man wants a woman, he kidnaps her. Why can't I be kidnapped?"

"I'm sure your time will come soon."

"If the ancestors are good. Only they know how much I have prayed. How much I have sacrificed. Every day I wake up and pray. Before lunch and before I sleep."

"And who is that?" pointed Nia, not far from where the group of boys performed woo. He sat on a rock and peered into the wild, clutching his spear tightly as one does a lover.

"Oh, him. That's Hokoyo. No one knows where he's from. He came to Ngorongoro some seasons back. He doesn't say much. All he does is sharpen that spear of his, and prepare for some crazy war only he sees. You should stay well clear of him. There is something in those eyes of his—I can't quite put my finger on it." She shook her head and turned back to Nia. "Anyway, how are you finding it in Ngorongoro so far?"

"Just fine, thank you."

"How delightful! If you need anything, please don't hesitate to ask."

"I won't."

"Great! Anyway, we should be heading back. Come on girls." Eniola burst into song as she balanced a pail of water on her head.

Nia did the same but as she spread her hands out wide, the bowl jiggled and came tumbling down, creating a big splash and wild laughter.

Eniola afforded herself a mild chuckle and then voiced, "Now, now, now girls. It's not her fault she wasn't blessed with elegance. Is it now, Fufu?"

In truth, most princesses were tutored from a very young age to balance objects on their heads peerlessly, but Nia had always skived those lessons, preferring to practice somersaults, cartwheels and spear work with Uncle Machupa's blade as he slept off his noontide libation. Before she could dry herself, everyone collapsed their knees and clapped their hands as Wafula appeared. Toni tugged at her skirts. "Oh," Nia pardoned, before she was in a nice little squat, mimicking the others as they clapped their hands.

On Wafula's head sat plaited hair adorned with colorful beads. On top of it was a monkey-skin cap with cock feathers hanging from it. His necklace was made of seeds of wild fruit. Around his wrists were a mangle of copper and leather bands. He even had a lackey following a few paces behind him, waiting on his beck and call. "Chafu, if I may have you for some moments?"

Eniola, whom had been smiling and pouting her lips was soon flabbergasted as she looked at Nia rather confused.

Nia was shoulder to shoulder with Wafula in no time. "Look at you—a big man in the village. Who would have thought? I am happy for you."

Wafula could do worse. Though it was a small village, it had circular compounds connected by well-defined streets, and the people seemed happy with their rustic way of life. "You shouldn't be. Back at Pyre Fortress, you and I would play kites and climb trees for fruit to pass time. Now I have to do this, I have to do that."

"It's part of growing up."

He sighed as images of his prelapsarian days overwhelmed him. "I guess so. I just wish it could be like it was."

"Well that will never happen."

"Anyway, I want to show you something."

They walked past the main village gates for several minutes until they reached an offshoot that led them past a small set of hills and thick shrub, until they were at the foot of a pond. She found it rather unremarkable. It seemed like an ordinary vlei, but upon further inspection, she noticed the waters were bubbling subtly.

"Our mystic says in ancient times, the Creator sent a bushfire of epic proportions—A bushfire that scorched the whole world. After you told me about the migas you encountered, I wondered to myself why such a normally shy deep dwelling creature would be so near the surface. The mystic says that is because the earth is warming up."

Nia looked down.

"What's wrong?"

"Do you know why mother and I ran away?"

Wafula shook his head.

"My father . . ." She didn't want to verbalize it. "The Sangoma convinced my father that the world as we know it is in peril, and that the only way to stop the doom, is by making right with the ancestors. He said, as men would spill their blood on the battlegrounds, women had to shed some too, through purification. I was supposed to be the first at the Flame Festival. Father said there was no better blood to appease the ancestors than that of a princess'."

Wafula reflected. The Flame Festival had come and gone, and another one was in the short horizon. "You are safe here. I will protect you, and die trying if I have to."

Nia looked at him, and she believed him. He still had the indefatigable zeal of his youth, which she had long lost. "Sure, you would." She put a finger on his cheek and rubbed it. "Let's not be so gloomy. Forget about this doomsday nonsense and let's do something fun."

Nia was laughing as she pulled out an arrow from the wooden plaque they had stuck on a tree, so tall it sailed into the sky. "You see, I told you I was better than you."

Wafula moaned as he slid out a quiver and raised his bow. He pulled back the arrow, aimed momentarily and let go.

"Not bad," commended Nia, nodding her head in appreciation before snatching back the bow. She fiddled with it, feeling the rigidity of the string and then closed her eyes, pulled, and let go. Her arrow landed right next to Wafula's.

"Not bad either," he admitted. "Is this what you spend your days doing?"

"I try to do this as often as I can. Usually early, before the cock crows."

"And your mother, she lets you do it? If I recall she never approved of you fighting . . . playing with me . . ." Their locking of eyes lingered more than usual, but Wafula interrupted it by producing two sticks. "Left or right?"

She inspected them carefully with one of her eyebrows raised and then snatched one, and without alert, Nia was dashing toward Wafula. He parried her attack, twisted and unleashed a jab. She dodged it, blocked the next assault on her right, left and leapt over the low strike. She grinned and backed off several paces. She lifted her stick and prepared herself—her legs wide apart and her weapon parallel to her eye as Ginger trotted to the scene and curled herself under the shade of a sprawling shea tree for a front row seat.

"The bushfire technique, I see . . . Well, some variation of it. It is clear to see you haven't been formally trained." Wafula arranged his feet to match hers and lifted his stick. "This," he exclaimed, "is a true bushfire stance." He attacked first, aiming for her face, but she blocked it, turned and with the motion, swung her foot around, which he dodged under, leaving her free for a sweep. She landed on her back, but as swift as a mongoose, she flipped up, and bent backward to evade Wafula's follow-up. Nia was upright in a matter of moments with several quick jabs on his chest that had Wafula's back scraping a tree trunk and his teeth, gnashing in pain. He came again and for every cylindrical stroke, left and right, right and left again, she matched with her double-handed grip as the beads on her skirt and half-top rattled, creating a song that matched the chirping of the birds. He kept at it until finally, her stick snapped. He licked his lips and went in for the kill. The princess turned and ran, but before Wafula had her in his grasp, she was running up the tree before she pushed away and soared high, landing behind him and tackled him to the ground.

They rolled around, back and forth over the leaves and fallen shea nuts, like two tangled snakes snapping at one another in a battle for supremacy until Nia had him pinioned between her thighs. She could see little constellations of stars on his upper cheeks, beside his nose. She felt a magnetic force, dragging her lips down toward his, until she could feel his warm breath on her face. She almost lowered her head even further but instead rose and offered him her sweaty hand. "I have to be getting home now."

"Me too."

"Same time, same place, say tomorrow?"

"If you dare."

When Nia finally arrived back at the village, Toni greeted her. Before Nia could tell her about her wonderful day with Wafula, giggles interrupted them. Not far from where they stood, gazing eyes beamed her way and with them, hands covering mouths. She could hear the words 'slut', 'whore', 'harlot', and other opprobrious names being muttered amongst the childish chortling as she approached. "How is it going, girls?"

Eniola did not reply. "So, where were you?"

"Oh, nowhere."

"Nowhere, huh? Did you not go off somewhere with my Wafula?"

Nia did not reply. "Wafula and I have been friends for as long as I can remember."

"Make sure it stays like that, Fufu!"

"Is that a threat?"

"All I am saying is if you know what's good for you, you better stay away from him. Are we understood?"

Chapter 31

The Apprentice

In order to commence my education in the art of mysticism, I had to perform a rite of passage. This entailed a series of tasks, many of them humiliating and physically punishing. I endured them with little fuss. In my consideration it was small penance if I was to gain the knowledge to produce fire from the palm of my hands. I was also required to confess my wrongdoings in thought and deed. It was a lengthy cross examination but after the ordeal was complete, I felt clean, unburdened, as the senior witchdoctor had hissed—reborn. After my initiation process was complete, my inauguration ceremony deep in a remote area in the Mukuvisi Woodlands, which could only be reached by canoe, attracted a number of the region's spirit mediums, some even coming from as far as Chipiko and even Ngorongoro. To their witness I swore to remain chaste and most importantly, to never reveal the secrets of our trade. When the drum roared announcing my acceptance as an apprentice, a goat was slaughtered, and celebrations commenced, a night filled with trance induced festivities.

When I woke up the next morning, my new life began. I shed my neat loincloth and replaced it with a shaggy apron of raggedy animal skins. I knew my journey was not going to be easy, but I relished it. I relished becoming a keeper of sacred knowledge, to learn the customs, history and mythology of the ancestors I would serve. This would give me the keys to the universe, its past, its present and most importantly, its future.

My orientation period entailed silently observing my master perform her duties. Yazuru's tasks largely consisted of aiding the ill, disgruntled and those that needed a bit of luck. When not tending to the village folk, I followed her on her journeys deep into the woods and her excursions to the top of the highest hills and most perilous cliffs in search of silence, herbs and the rarest eggs. She took me to places I had never seen, secret parts of the woodlands and hidden caves amongst the hills, all the while teaching the secrets of the vocation. "This profession is no joke, boy," she told me. "You will learn how hostile and violent some spirits can be. You will have to learn to distinguish between the different types of spirits and learn how to differentiate wickedness and spiritual affliction."

I nodded my head in apprehension. I was like a sponge. I took in everything she told me and the more I learnt, the more curious I grew.

"One cannot practice to become a spirit-medium," she told me as she stood at the top of a hill overlooking the plains. "It cannot be bequeathed like a title. We are selected by the spirit realm—as I truly believe you are—by our ancestors—the long dead who watch over us. Our work is the most important of all professions, even eclipsing that of a chief."

My vision had become clearer than ever, even eaglelike since I took apprenticeship with Yazuru, so in the distance I could spy Huni, Ilangabi and Lelakabe clearly, all separated by forestry, chains of hills and shoots from the Nhunundudu. "With our knowledge and connection to the spirit realm we hold the power of healing and control over natural disaster, earthquakes, hurricanes, floods, wildfires, drought and pestilence. Due to our efforts we have kept Mount Pyyros' anger at bay." Abruptly her neck twisted like someone had called her name from afar. "Listen closely." She cupped her ear. "Hear that? Those are the spirits. They live amongst us. For our societies to thrive, the realms of the spirits and the living must coexist in harmony. It is our duty to ensure that this harmony is maintained. Our ability to dance between the realms allows us to channel the dead. That is where we are going now. This farmer we are going to visit lost his beloved wife. He has been inconsolable, bordering on madness, and has stopped performing his duties. His wives have asked me to intervene, hoping I can organize a final meeting between him and his deceased wife, so that he may have closure and return to the crop fields."

I smiled inside. My primary motivation for joining the order was to learn how to produce fire from nothing, but then and there I decided that healing was my true calling—what the ancestors had sent me to perform. I wanted to ask my master if she could speak to my mother and father, but when I had decided to pursue the work of the spirits, I had consequently forsaken them. My fellow witchdoctors were my family now. They were now the people I sought for when I needed counsel or companionship. "So how does this work?"

"The bereaved family will give me a basketful of the deceased's earthly possessions—clothes, jewelry, an object she was attached to. Using the herbs and the ground hornbill eggs we obtained the other day I shall make a concoction, mix it with the possessions and then set the basket aflame. Only those with the gift and the knowledge can withstand possession from a spirit without going mad or at worst, dying instantly, so I shall allow the farmer's wife's spirit to possess me, and through me, they shall communicate."

I scratched my head in apparent apprehension.

"Don't worry. Just watch everything I do."

We travelled the land far past many villages that neighbored Molora. I remember the first time I saw a waterfall. Its raw power was astounding, exhilarating yet terrifying, the relentlessness of the gushing waters, the effervescing beneath. It made my heart flutter and ponder on the mystical sumptuousness of the Creator. The beauty of the occasion gave me the courage to ask, "Master, who is Ruwa?"

By the look on her face I could tell that she did not want to answer. "She was a witchdoctor. One of the finest spirit-mediums I have ever had the pleasure of meeting. Her connection to the spirits was so natural, and her desire to heal, so pure." She looked down in sadness. "She was your mother."

All I needed was confirmation, but in truth, I already knew, such was my prompt progress in the ways of the spirits. I could also see that she once loved her. I now realized why she had backed me when all the other witchdoctors had denied me.

"She went against the rules of our order and fell pregnant. By whom, I do not know, but she died bringing you into this world. For what it's worth, she loved you dearly. I could tell by the way she used to rub her belly. Her smile, I shall never forget." She stood up and looked ahead, far into the sunset, bold, red and gold. "We shall never speak on this again."

I turned my attention back to the torrents that exploded amongst the rocks beneath and followed the mist that rose, and there I saw it, up amongst the clouds, an arc of colors, proud and as pronounced as the rock cave paintings that my master had showed me. Yazuru looked my way and smiled for the first and last time in my memory and then left me alone with my mother to say goodbye.

Life was now better than anytime I could remember. I was doing what I loved, being around nature and learning its secrets. However, this bliss ended when my master was summoned to Molora. I began to tremble as soon as we entered the patient's quarters. As my master had taught me, witchdoctors were not supposed to have emotion, but I could not help but feel distraught as I saw Tawara, my protector, the orphan girl I grew to love, lying on the bed mat helpless, shivering with sweat all over her body. I cannot quite elucidate the despair I felt that day. Despite the vows I had made to my new brothers and sisters, I couldn't reconcile losing the only person I had ever loved. My guardian whom I would see no more, nor hear her sweet voice.

I wasn't at her funeral. Unlike the majority of the people unified under the flame of Mount Pyyros, the people of Molora still buried their dead, rather than the cremation rituals the rest of the kingdom practiced. I watched from afar high atop a hill. I couldn't bring myself to see her chucked into a hole. I was angry and consumed by a bitterness I failed to shake for the rest of my miserable life. My master was a witchdoctor. She could summon a ball of fire but was unable to rekindle my dear Tawara's dying embers. With a rolled fist high atop the hill as wind brushed over my headdress' feathers, I made a vow that I would never let anyone I loved suffer as Tawara did.

Later that night, whilst the whole village slumbered, I crept into the black and stealthed towards the village burial grounds. After looking around to make sure no one was in sight, I started digging. I dug long enough until finally, there she was, what once was my Tawara, my guardian, wrapped in an animal skin. Though her dark skin had gone pale, she still had that understated beauty she carried with defiance. I was disobeying the ancestors, but I cared not. I was prepared to pay for my abomination, however severe the penalty. I scooped her up gently and took her to an abandoned shack deep in the Mukuvisi Woodlands beyond the swamp where no one dared treading, and laid her down on a table that I had meticulously prepared.

Chapter 32

Revelations

Princess Nia ate her breakfast daintily, as if only to entertain her company, now and then brushing off the lilac leaves that nestled onto the table. In the distance, as the other girls swept the dust away from the thoroughfare and footpaths, she could feel eyes peering her way, watching like hawks soaring through a cloudless sky. She didn't pay it much mind though. She laughed and played with her hair as Wafula updated her on his new life as the Ngorongoro chief's personal attendant.

Chief Ilahle had taken to Wafula's sensibilities so much so they had built him a hut near the chief's private chambers. Wafula had become somewhat of a big brother to him—An older figure he could admire.

"I have to go now," apologized Nia. "I'm sure my mother needs me for something."

"Can I meet you later today? By the river?"

Nia could see that there was something Wafula was eager to say to her. She smiled. *How can I deny him?* She couldn't believe that the man standing in front of her was the same Wafula she would play kites with. "Sure."

Nia wrinkled her nose as she entered her lodgings. She looked around, turning things upside until she lifted her blanket to find a dead gerbil. She calmly turned, exited the hut, and there sitting with her posse not far away was Eniola, more pleased than her usual haughty self. When their eyes met, Eniola's face slowly turned, until her eyes were evil incarnate. Eniola raised a finger and motioned it slowly across her throat. One of her lackeys cackled like a goose. The others joined in as they skipped off, bouncing about and flashing their bottoms as they hooted and tooted.

Nia shook her head in disgust. She entered the hut, removed her jewelry and picked up the dead gerbil by its tail. She walked across the village thoroughfare until she arrived at a compound. Outside the kitchen-hut pounding sorghum was Eniola. She didn't notice Nia until the princess had cast the gerbil into the wooden mortar. Nia sprang for Eniola and gripped a good batch of her hair and began to slap her over and over again with the soft and then hard side of her hand. Eniola's lackeys were soon on the scene, but they were like a hare caught unawares by a cheetah hiding in the grass. Nia ripped off Eniola's beads from her neck until they were little balls rolling on the earth. She picked up the rabbits Eniola was preparing for skinning by the ears and walked off past the perplexed onlookers.

There was banging on the door later that afternoon. Zandile opened it to find Eniola's father, Boipelo, waiting impatiently. His clenched face turned when he caught the queen's fiery eyes, the type that subdued men, women and beast, thus, he set his to the floor. Behind him a few paces lurked Eniola.

"Good afternoon, Boipelo. What is the matter?"

"I heard troubling news when I returned from my crop fields. I looked upon my daughter and I could see that she was troubled. I asked her, the only daughter of my late first wife, what is the matter? She didn't want to say, but the truth finally emerged from her lips that she was beaten and robbed of her rabbits by your daughter."

Zandile turned to Nia with her eyebrows bridged. "Chafu, is this true?"

The princess bit her lip.

Zandile turned back to Boipelo. "I am very sorry for this. I do not know what is wrong with this one. I have taken her to every spiritual healer I can find but she never changes." She turned to Nia. "Chafu, apologize to Eniola."

"But she started it!"

"Girl, you will do as you are told, is that understood?"

"Yes, mother," Nia replied meekly. She stepped out of the shadows, tilted her head down and began, "Eniola, I am sorry that I hit you."

"And what else?"

"And that I took your rabbit. I promise to never do it again." She said the last words with her fingers crossed behind her back. *Chafu made that promise. Not Nia.*

"Good!" adjudicated Zandile. "Thank you Boipelo for notifying me of this. Chafu will be punished. May the flame guide you. Good day."

Boipelo turned and ushered his daughter back to his compound, but not before Eniola furtively stuck her tongue out toward Nia, sending the princess seething inside. When the door shut, she screamed, "I hate her, I hate her, I hate her!"

"Calm down, daughter," Zandile ordered. "Sit down and talk to your mother. Why did you beat her and take her rabbits?"

"She and her friends laid a dead gerbil in my bed."

"And you are sure about it?"

"Yes. She and her friends gloated when I found it. She's jealous, mother. Jealous because Wafula and I are friends."

"Now, now, now, child. You cannot go around beating everyone who does you wrong. You are a princess. You can't behave that way."

"But I don't want to be a princess. I never asked for it."

"Listen, Nia, a princess deals with these matters in other ways. You have what these people don't—power, influence and also a lot of cows. You can use all of those things given to you by your ancestors to get your revenge. Is that understood?" Nia nodded her head. "I understand that times have been hard. You've been through so much for your meager age, but you have to stay strong. You have to stay good. Revenge and anger, it only corrupts the heart. Don't end up like your father and mother. Alright?"

Nia grabbed a cloth that was lying on the table and placed it over her shoulders.

"Where are you going?"

"To meet Wafula."

Zandile shook her head and smiled. "Go meet him then! I will have to punish you later."

Wafula was waiting for her when she arrived by the riverbank. Trees formed an unbroken canopy above their heads and along the riverbed, providing much needed solace from the late afternoon sun. Perched birds chirped away from the branches as a cool breeze swept their way. Wafula reached into his bag and took out a wooden vase. Something compelled Nia to reach out for it as her eyes dilated. Wafula quickly snatched it away. "Just as I suspected."

"What are you talking about? Give me that. It's mine!" Nia reached for it, but he had one hand patting away her searching fingers and the other with the vase, stretched out of her reach. When she finally realized her ridiculousness, she calmed herself. "I just want to see it."

"I don't know if that is a good idea. That look and reaction, you had it that night. The night you and I snuck into the Fire Caves."

Nia's thoughts went back to a time that now seemed so far away, the meandering narrow pathways, chambers and cobwebs stuck in her hair. She recalled the beautiful illustrations they had discovered of the Ifirit and the flaming spear. A bolt of pain had gutted her at the moment she discovered the wooden vase. It was the night she first bled, blood that heralded her womanhood and eligibility for marriage—eligibility for the Sangoma's rusty blade. "What do you mean?"

"This might sound very strange and rather improbable, but I think this vase has powers. Wishing powers."

Nia laughed. "I think becoming a big man in this village has gotten to your head."

"Listen, Chafu. That night after you left me in the caves, I went home with the vase and had it next to me as I prayed. I prayed that my mother would find a husband with many cows and soon after that, my mother found a husband with many cows. The next time I prayed with the vase nearby, I asked the ancestors to bless me with a noble title one day. The next morning there was a knock on my door. It was Chief Mazviriri's guards. They led me to his chambers where little Ilahle sat next to him. There he made me the boy's page. When Chief Mazviriri passed away the following winter, Chief Ilahle made me his chief attendant."

"That is so stupid, Wafula. Why did you do that, pray for a noble title?"

He looked down. The leaves of the tree nearby blew slowly and the birds in the trees chirped. "So that one day I could marry you."

Nia was left open-mouthed. She didn't resist when Wafula's lips followed hers until they were united. It felt good. She had never kissed a boy before, but she felt she could do it more often—Especially *his* lips. Embarrassed by her passions she pushed him away.

"What's wrong?"

"Did you wish for that too?"

"It's what I have always wanted to do, as long as I can remember!"

"What I mean is, did you use your genie to fulfill your wish?"

"No. I promise. Chafu, when I realized what was going on, I did some research. I visited several griots and wise men around the kingdom. My journey was fruitless until I found a hermit deep in the swamplands. His knowledge is from a chain of a thousand generations. He told me that genies did once exist, in the age of the nyaminyami. The only thing is, they each only have three wishes."

Nia took her time to contemplate the revelations. "So, you suspect you have used up two?"

"Yes."

She shook her head. "You could have wished for anything, like peace amongst the kingdoms, an end to drought . . . an end to poverty and you wished for some cows and nobility?"

"Chafu, I didn't know I had a genie, not until after the second wish."

"If it is as you say, what are you going to do with the last wish?"

Wafula looked into the river. It was so clear one could see the smoothness of the rocks underneath. "I don't know."

"What do you know, Wafula?"

He turned his head back toward her and met her lips again. Not long after, Nia had her fingers digging the crack of his back. Suddenly he took back his lips. Nia's eyes remained closed, but when they opened, she had to look down and there knelt on a dropped knee was Wafula. In his hand was a short blade. She took out its twin, which he had given her the day he left Pyyros. It rippled as the sun's rays caressed its surface. "Chafu, I want you to be my wife."

Nia was whistling when she entered the hut she and Zandile had been given. The queen looked up and raised an eyebrow. "What's going on with you?"

"Nothing."

"Nia. I thought we had gone through this. You cannot lie to your mother."

"It's nothing . . . just . . ."

"You are in love, aren't you?" Zandile recognized that look. Sekai once had it too, after a banquet in Kwa'Jivu many seasons ago, when she had fallen in love with the queen's long-lost brother, Neo.

"Mother, no, I am not. Well, maybe," Nia finally smiled. "Wafula asked me to marry him."

"What?" Zandile had tried all she could to discourage their friendship from the time they were little toddlers, crawling around court discovering life. Farakaii's young face flashed before her—how handsome he was—the kindness he exuded and his dark penetrating eyes. "Well, what did you say?"

"I didn't give him an answer. I told him I needed time to think."

"I will not interfere here. The choice is yours and only yours. I will support you, whatever your answer is. Come, now. Let us pray for Asha's recovery."

After Nia had fallen asleep, Queen Zandile took a walk to the riverside. As her toes broke the water, she felt a presence behind her. "I have been praying for your recovery. Sometimes until my teeth bleed." Everyday Zandile had visited Asha as he slumbered and sang him a tune.

The Desert Snake was holding his flame-shaped *mbira*. He blew the dust off the oval casing and plucked a string. "Remember this one?" He plucked at it again, and then again until he had a soft melody. Zandile let her head lie on his shoulder as the tune weaved along, up and down like the hills and mountain ranges they had crossed, so beautiful she might have wept if the recent past hadn't hardened her heart.

"You saved my life," thanked Zandile. "And almost died doing it."

"I promised our lord I would get you home."

"You are a survivor. You've always been one."

"I'd say the same about you. I thought you were dead—the both of you, but something urged me on, the ancestors perhaps, but whose?" It was a full moon. He looked up at it and strained a smile. His near dance with death had taught him to appreciate things he had always taken for granted, the stars, the aromatic smell of the earth—the crickets that stridulated behind them. "Why didn't you leave me to die and run away?" A swirling wind breezed past and between them. "You should have. I am bound to take you back."

Zandile looked down as she sighed and then inquired on his state.

"I still have some trouble breathing and feel a little light in the head, but I should be well enough to resume our journey home to your husband when day breaks."

"That is not what I mean. What I mean is, what happened to you during your travels? On our journey from the Snake Pit I could sense that something had changed in you, like you are not the same Asha that I once knew."

He looked down. He wanted to tell her about Zara-Fe'yi, the slave girl he had freed—his daughter—but he couldn't bring himself to it.

"You used to confide in me," Zandile continued, now running her fingers through his hair. Some of it had grown back, but it wasn't the flowing voluptuous mane she had been accustomed to.

The Desert Snake looked into the night sky and then turned his eyes on her. "Whilst I was in Ashu looking for you, at a tavern, I overheard a group of young men talking. They said that a Prince Themba of the Akuwa was in Pyyros. I thought it a lie, but I heard the same bruited about at the Mukonikoni's and Huni's." He looked into the wild. "Finally, I get my chance at revenge."

Zandile was perplexed. "What has he done to you?"

"Nothing, but his father murdered my family. I made a vow I would kill him, but his seed will do . . . for a start."

Zandile looked at the Desert Snake and shook her head in pity. "Oh, Asha. Farakaii did not murder your family."

"Then who did?" The queen looked down and struggled for words, so the Northman gripped her tightly by the arm and shouted. "Who did it?"

"Maghedzi," she finally ceded as her voice began to tremble.

The Desert Snake's eyes widened in disbelief. He didn't believe her—he couldn't. "Lies," he spat.

Zandile lifted her head and met his eyes as tears began to form. "I'm sorry, Asha, but it is true."

The Desert Snake rose, unsheathed his shotel and set it about the tree nearby. When he was done, the thick tree balanced nervously and then fell with a thud, causing a cloud of leaves and dust. When the carnage had settled and the sandman had regained his composure, with barely concealed rage he turned his sword upon Zandile and demanded, "You knew all along?"

Zandile couldn't meet his eyes, a transpicuous, glaucous, pale yellow-green. She preferred to look into the current of the flowing waters as tears coursed down her cheeks. "Do it," she whispered. Asha's blade waited menacingly above her, the moon's light bouncing over it. "Do it," she commanded. "End my misery!"

The Northman's chest was heaving back and forth, and his teeth gnashed as he prepared to slash. He willed himself to do it, but he couldn't, like a supernatural force had afflicted him. After another attempt, his shoulders hunched and with tears now streaming down his cheeks he ceded, "You and he are no different. You deserve each other!" He slipped his sword back into its scabbard, crouched momentarily and then leaped into a tree nearby and disappeared into the night.

Chapter 33

The Woodland Fiend

What I did to Tawara that night was not a first, nor the last. You see, as an inquisitive little creature, when I was younger I often played with insects. I would catch a grasshopper or a beetle and clip its wings just to see what happened. I was enthralled by the metaphysical world and meant to explore it—all its wonders and secrets, however gross or stomach churning. I spent the whole night investigating the cause of her death, as I had determined I needed a cause if I wanted to find a solution, so maybe, in another lifetime, I could save her. I opened her chest with a knife and peered down at her entrails—her heart, liver, lungs, pancreas and spleen. I took one out at a time and under the torchlight examined them until I could hear the early morning birds chirp. I opened the top of her head and pulled out her brain and spent the whole day meticulously scrutinizing it, from its meandering roots and its gray, yellow shadows and even dissected it so I could learn more about its components. I kept her until I could no longer endure her decomposed state. I gave her one last kiss, put her parts into a sack and buried her deep in the woods under a jacaranda tree.

My mood and disposition changed drastically following this episode. As I mentioned, I was always a joy to be around with a broad smile and earnest warm eyes, but now I had transformed into something I did not recognize. My village was also changing. There had been an assassination attempt against the chief and he had responded by raising an army to attack the neighboring village, Huni, which he claimed was harboring the assassins. In response to this possible invasion, Ilangabi had seized all trade with Molora raising the price of millet and barley. Furthermore, a succession battle was brewing between the ailing and old chief's sons. All this political upheaval and the fear it had caused amongst the villagers worried me not. Healing is what I had decided to dedicate my life to, to the exploration of the human body. Nothing else mattered.

I took up my curiosities with my master and pressed him on the issue in an indirect manner, but Yazuru was from a long unbroken line of mystics stuck in their old rigid ways. I grew more frustrated as the seasons changed. I wanted to explore it all. When I thought of the moments after Tawara's passing, dander brewed in my heart when I recalled my master's reply, when I queried the cause of my protector's demise. "The will of the ancestors," she had told me. I repeated the words to myself manically as I lay on my bed mat and ground my teeth as I stared at the thatched ceiling until the cock crowed.

I began to resent my master despite myself, especially when another person died, shivering similarly to poor Tawara, sweaty and weak, groaning in pain. I decided he was holding me back. I was determined to learn the secrets of nature. I declared to the ancestors with a tightly rolled fist that I would usher in a new age of healing. Thus, later that night I stole into the village cemetery and took the fresh cadaver. Most people stayed away in fear of the ghosts and goblins we were told roamed the cemetery at night, but I wasn't troubled by such things. I was a young man possessed with the spirit of exploration, inflicted with empathy and the desire to end pain.

I made it a habit, stealing and dissecting every fresh corpse I could until I began to notice correlations, commonalities, amongst the cadavers and began the rudimentary understanding of the human body. I was never happier than when I was dissecting organs and comparing them, thus sadness and melancholy took a hold of me once more when the malevolent spirits of death had moved onto another village. Not a single mother's wail was heard for an entire season, and slowly, village folk smiles returned. I became desperate. I needed to continue my quest for knowledge.

One day as I was wandering around in the bush near a stream from the Nhunundudu, in the distance I spied one of my tormentors. He was the leader of the local bullies who lived to call us orphans names and terrorize us whatever chance they got. When I saw that he was alone, I made my way towards him. When he finally heard my footsteps, he turned around, and naturally, was shocked when I shoved him into the river. "Motherless," he shouted when his head popped out of the water. "Wait and see what will happen when I come out." He pushed towards the bank, but before he could haul himself out, I set my hand over his head and watched with sick glee as he kicked and desperately flailed his hands. When the waters calmed, I hid his body in the bush nearby and returned at night to transport the cadaver back to my secret laboratory.

Like a sick addiction, when the specimen was too rotten, and I had to dispose the body, I was left with an emptiness that spurred the feeling of despair and remorse for what I had done. I couldn't sleep at night and when I finally did, the boy's face visited my dreams. Only one thing could cure my wretchedness. I assumed the role of the ancestors and fashioned myself a mask that resembled the most harrowing of creatures and set myself upon the world, no better than an animal in the wild, preying on the weak, mostly the old, but my prized assets were the young. The Mukuvisi Woodlands was my favorite hunting grounds. I became so prolific that a rumor began to spread around the region that there was an ilombe, a giant snake with the head of a human abducting wanderers. They were not in the wrong. There was a monster, but that fiend was I. Who would have guessed that the little orphan boy with the sweet handsome face would bring such misery upon the world?

Despite the sorrowful cloud that had engulfed Molora, my heart remained obdurate, even more so when I felt my quest for the secrets of the body were stagnating. I had mastered the human anatomy, but now I needed to know how it worked. I had to find working, human bodies still breaming with life. So rather than killing, I captured my specimens, and with the knowledge I had gained from my apprenticeship, concocted an elixir that induced paralysis in my victims. Their bodies couldn't move, but I could see the pain in their eyes as I sawed off their limbs and opened their chest cavity. But knowledge was all that mattered. I had even forgotten Tawara and why I had originally pursued my cause.

My arrogance and the surety of my righteousness, as fiendish as it was, would eventually lead to my downfall. As I was about to saw open the chest of a live specimen I had acquired, I turned to find my master standing at the door entrance. I cannot quite describe the look on her face. It was beyond horror, disgust, and even fear. It brought a touch of sadness to me, to see the woman I had held such high esteem and awe for view me with absolute contempt. "Put that down," she cried.

In most situations like this, one finally is awoken to their heinous deeds and realizes the error of their way, but I remained cold. I was convinced though gruesome and villainous as my activities seemed, I was doing it for the greater good of mankind. "Master," I greeted cordially. "What brings you all the way here?"

Yazuru looked around as her eyes slowly flared in disbelief, all the bodies, some dead, others in paralysis, decapitated, organs and heads in jars. "What in Gyiku'o's name are you doing, child?"

"I am performing the ancestors work," I told her as I set my saw down casually back onto the board next to my fine healthy specimen and wiped my hands clean. "Something that you and your kind have neglected. You sit there and collect livestock, crops and shells from the poor and promise them things you lack the knowledge and connection to the spirits to perform. You are a disgrace." I spat that day. Something I never contrived to perform.

"You shall end this evil!" she barked at me, but nothing was going to halt my work. I had made too many strides, gained too much knowledge. I was convinced I was on the precipice of the cause of my beloved Tawara's death. My eyes widened when she opened her palm and summoned a ball of fire.

"You will not take my work away from me!"

"Then you leave me choice," she told me wistful.

She raised her hands into the air and launched the ball my way. I dipped my head and scrambled for my staff. She dashed towards me and our staffs met. "I should have listened to the other witchdoctors. I saw great potential in you, but you have allowed your rashness to learn cloud your judgment."

"No, master, I am the ancestors' instrument. Through me, there will be no more suffering."

"That's where you are wrong, my apprentice. YOU are the instrument of what you vowed to end. Don't force me to kill you."

"If I stop my work, then I would be as good as dead."

"Then so be it." She kicked me on my chest sending me crashing into my specimen and stepped back as fire raged behind her. She quickly reached into her cloths and brought forth a batch of herbs and swallowed them.

Immediately I could sense strength flow through her body, a power I could not contend. I shall not go into the details of our mighty battle, but our exchanges led us out into the woods. Our clash resembled a cataclysmic event with trees downed and vegetation eviscerated. Birds took to the skies and the creatures that lurked stayed hidden as the struggle raged on between master and apprentice until predictably she was standing above me with the largest ball of fire I had yet seen her summon. Witchdoctors are not supposed to have feelings, but I could see the pain in my master's eyes. I was ready to die. There was nothing left in this life for me. "Kill me," I told her. "End my wretchedness."

She lifted the ball above her head, but just before she obliterated me, something compelled her to halt. "You do not deserve the mercy of death." She extinguished the fireball, bent over me, and as she muttered some words, brushed her claws over my face. "Everywhere you go you shall be reviled," she cursed. She stood up and walked way. Her last words towards me we were short. "Never return," she told me, thus with my tail tucked between my legs, and with my laboratory and all the work I had accomplished engulfed in flames, I took one last look at my birthplace, where all my misery began, the Mukuvisi Woodlands, and followed the Nhunundudu until I reached a hamlet.

It was early when I arrived, with little children playing in the dusty pathways as peddlers opened their markets. As I walked down the thoroughfare, I could feel something strange with every passing step I made. When a group of children caught sight of me, their eyes widened and scrambled away into the alleyways. I stopped a man and asked for directions, but peculiarly, he began to shake, and then with a face white with fright, scurried into one of the huts nearby. I continued towards the food stall to put some food in my belly, but just before I arrived, I saw a mob storming towards me clutching hoes, sickles and pitchforks. I lifted my animal skins and scampered away as a hail of stones whistled past me.

When I was at a safe distance from the hamlet and anyone who meant me harm, I stopped by a pond to cool off and plot my next move. I dipped my hands into the water and let it wash over my head. When the ripples seized, and the water had calmed, I spied something peculiar in the reflection. It had ghostly pale skin, obscenely large protruding eyeballs and pasty saliva edged into the sides of its droopy lips. I rubbed my eyes, set myself on my knees for a better view and looked again. I sprang to my feet, grabbed a rock nearby and cast it furiously into my reflection causing an explosion of water that sailed down my head. I fell backwards and looked at the clouds above as lion-fig leaves blew towards the mountainscape until they were one with the ground hornbills that roamed the cloudless skies, and a solitary tear broke down my once beautiful eye.

Chapter 34

A Chick to a Cock

It was a festive afternoon at the Ngorongoro village center. Chief Ilahle sat childish as can be, clapping and bopping his headdress from side to side as the village fool played *mbira* and sang riddle. The little chief's headdress balanced uneasily, as the young paramount had yet to grow into it. It was a wonderful headdress that had been in his family for many generations, since the days when Ngorongoro swore fealty to the extinct Chiphalaphala, whom were once kings and used their might to wrestle Ngorongoro from the snake lords of the west's yoke. It had a knob that stuck out above the forehead and another edged out from the crown of the hat. It was mainly red, but little yellow, blue and white beads adorned it in a simple straight-line pattern, and a flame shape around the central knob. Two horns stuck out either side of the crown, pointing forward, imitating buffalo horns—a symbol that represented the wearer's authority. The village fool skipped his toes and fell to the floor and then hoisted himself up in comedic fashions to the cheer and laughter of the raucous crowd. Wafula, as always, was by the young chief's side, stone faced with spear in hand, a plain instrument compared to others, but vulgar nonetheless, with a short shaft, and wide blade.

Nia sat quietly to her mother's surprise with a modest comportment and calm Zandile had never seen prior. Dare she say it—the queen thought the girl didn't have it in her fiber. All Nia had been since she learnt to crawl was dirty knees, roguish demeanor and a brutish mouth. There was a call for refreshments amongst the men of title. Nia was about to rise, but

Eniola was up as quick as a rodent. She smiled slyly Nia's way and then smarmed towards the wooden pail filled with *whawha*, dipped a large bowl into it and went around refilling the men's calabashes, taking an unctuous moment when she got to Wafula. He nodded curtly, but his gaze was firmly set on Nia. The princess smiled bashfully and then quickly looked down.

After the calabashes had been refilled, Wafula's adopted father, Ife, rose, and with an open palm, banged hard on a drum. After he gained the crowd's attention, he began, "Now that the whole village is present and in good spirits, I have an announcement to make. My good friend here Boipelo and I have agreed to join our families. Thus, we have decided that this young man that has become my son, Wafula, is to marry Boipelo's daughter from his late first wife, Eniola." He let the applauses lave over him as his smile beamed.

Nia's face dropped, as did Wafula's as a hand gripped his arm and hauled him up until he and his newly betrothed's hands were united in the center of the congregation as the crowd's approval washed over them.

All of a sudden, a human tunnel opened as an emissary ran through the sitting crowd and fell in front of the chief panting heavily, his forehead and neck lined with sweat. The three parallel lines above his eyebrows showed he was from the neighboring tribe, Chipiko. "Chief Ilahle, an armed militia has attacked our village. Our walls are still intact, but only the ancestors know for how long. We need your help!"

Chief Ilahle sniffed back the mucus that had been dangling at the threshold of his nostrils. Like his father before him, the boy-chief carried on his person a carved ceremonial blade that he would lay across his knees as he ruled. He pressed it on the ground and helped himself up. "What should we do, Wafula?"

Wafula bit his lip and thought for a moment. "We help, that's what we will do. The Chipiko are a close people, and share the same ancestors."

"I will lead the battalion," boomed a voice from the back of the congregation. Hokoyo stood up, slim, ripped and clenched of jaw. It looked like his pectoral muscles were about to pop out of his stomach as he slowly walked toward the chief. There was silence as the crowd waited in anticipation until Chief Ilahle, with the wave of his hand, gave him permission. Without hesitation, Hokoyo cried, "Warriors, rise!"

Bushiri, Bomani, Idi and Boitumelo were the first up until a couple dozen or so followed. "At your service, commander!" they saluted. That perplexed Wafula, whose face was an amalgamation of confusion and surprise. Ngorongoro already had a commander of its regiment, Chief Ilahle's uncle, Uzuoka. He was mat-ridden with illness, so Wafula had expected to deputize in his absence.

"Go and prepare yourselves," commanded Hokoyo, with his blade pointed at the village gates. "We leave at once!"

Wafula entered Chief Ilahle's chambers as Tsungano, the chief's senior uncle, echoed Wafula's own sentiments, "You are still young, little chief," Tsungano patronized. "This is not a wise decision, giving Hokoyo command of your army!"

However, the young chief had made his mind up. "This is what Hokoyo was made for," Ilahle insisted. "He is truly his father's child. We cannot deny him for much longer. His time has come."

"I shall go with the battalion," declared Wafula.

"Your place is here. Next to me," replied the chief.

"I can't stay behind in the safety of our walls whilst Hokoyo and the others are fighting."

"Do not forget who raised your station, Wafula!"

It seemed the young chief had grown resolute overnight, but Wafula, much like the chief sat in front of him, had made up his mind. "I haven't forgotten, Chief Ilahe." Wafula snatched the pendant that heralded him as the chief's principle attendant, slammed it onto the floor contemptuously to the chief and onlooker's astonishments, and stormed off.

He was changing into his military attire when Nia walked into his private chambers. "What are you doing?"

"I'm going."

"But the chief, he said your place is by his side."

"My place is in front of the cavalry, not at home like a woman…" he paused and shook his head. "I'm sorry, Chafu, it's just…"

"If you are going. I am going too."

"You have no business there. You will get yourself killed."

"So be it."

"I will never forgive myself."

"You can't protect me forever. I am a grown woman, and, I can fight." She had bested him many times during their secret duels in the Ngorongoro veld.

After some contemplative moments, Wafula reached up to the spear resting on the wall, snatched it, and tossed it toward the princess in disguise. He rummaged a box near his mat and brought out a leather mask. "It's best you wear this, so no one knows it's you."

Chapter 35

The Last Dwarf

Prince Themba and his page, Pikoro, were on the third day of their journey when the Akuwa prince's blood eye caught the glimmer of a settlement up ahead in the distance, nestled in a valley hidden behind a cloud of fog. He dug his heels into his equine and directed it atop a small hill and looked out across the prairie, his eyes following thick fog that slowly crept toward the hamlet. He reached into his bag, pulled out his map, and surveyed it for some moments, screwing his mouth as he did. "I can't find the settlement on the map," he finally revealed. "But perhaps we can find something there to eat," he declared optimistically.

"Are you sure it is safe to go there?" Pikoro was apprehensive, scratching his head as he observed fog tendrils, fingerlike, clawing their way toward the hamlet.

"A man who has mounted a hippo does not fear the roar of the lion," replied the prince, solemnly looking ahead.

"You've mounted a hippopotamus?" Pikoro's mouth was agape in apparent amazement, so wide a fly almost found its way into his cavity.

Themba shook his head in annoyance, whistled, pulled back the reigns of his equine and thundered down the dew sodden grass toward the settlement as a thick dark cloud descended upon them.

An overwhelming sense of peril hit the prince and page when they arrived at the threshold of the hamlet. The main gate was unmanned, and the walls but a hedge even a dwarf could leap over. There were rows of sparse dilapidated haphazard huts on each side of the main pathway, and next to them, piles of rubbish, dross, fruit and rotting carcasses that attracted flies like moths to a flame. They followed it, as wary eyes looked their way. "Stay alert," the hippo prince warned. Such places were renowned for attracting blades for hire, cattle robbers and poachers.

The settlement thoroughfare was small and filled with the sick and destitute. There was little sign of commerce, a few food stalls, butcheries and vegetable peddlers. Some huts were roofless, with charred frames and splintered wood. A pair of dogs copulated by the side of the wide walkway, just a few paces away from a man spread across the floor, slumbering away an afternoon of hard drinking. A beggar came up to the prince but Themba shooed him away like a pesky fly. He looked around. He couldn't see anyone with any jewelry of any sort, just a miserable bunch of people idly staring at them as they moved past.

One of the vagabonds, a legless woman with sores around her mouth, leapt from the stool she sat, and began dragging herself across the thoroughfare. "Dhob," she cried at the prince desirously. "Yat! Please!" It took great effort, but she thrashed at the earth, her black nails digging at the mud, and willed herself to a few paces away from Themba. "Just a small bit, please! Just enough to get me by for the night. I do anything," she begged, as she clawed at Themba's cow-tails, one of her breasts dancing in full view. Themba wrestled himself free and upped his speed down the pathway away from the thoroughfare fiend, screwing his face in annoyance and unleashing a huge spitball on the side of the pathway for good measure. He had no time for the weak, and even if he did, he didn't have what she was looking for. He reached into his sack, took out a batch of the herbs prescribed by the Sangoma, shoved it into his mouth and exhaled.

His moment of relief was immediately halted when Pikoro's nasal delivery interrupted, "So, Prince Themba, when am I going to get my own spear?"

"When you become a warrior."

"How do I become one if I don't have a spear? You know what I shall call my blade? Bolo's Bane," the boy from Shambamuto beamed.

Themba rolled his eyes. If anyone was responsible for Bolo the reaver's fall, it was he. He had trained the people of Shambamuto to fight and helped prepare them for Bolo's attack, and it was he, not Pikoro, who was at the forefront of the insurgence, as he had been at the foot of Death Valley when he slayed the Ashu champion. Bolo's eyes and the twig that dangled from his mouth had never left Themba's consciousness, or his dreams. He remembered the shock in Bolo's eyes when Chief Kaya's blade came down into his shoulders and through his heart. Tsitsi had been shocked too, as was the messenger boy he had impaled. It was apparent by his lifeless glare as he lay spread out over the bloodstained jacaranda leaves. "There is more to being a warrior than spear," Themba finally spat.

"Like what? You have two now! Can't you give me one? Pleeeeeease," Pikoro's teeth gleamed.

Themba and his twin, Simba, had been so excited the first day they joined Comrade Chengetaii's tutelage, but they were unpleasantly surprised when the first stages involved chores around Hippo Valley. The veteran warrior had made the cadets clean up the city, as well as help the poor and ailing—to instill duty—service—to the people—to the weak. "For instance," Themba thought, "You don't even know how to make a proper fire." Themba had been flabbergasted one late afternoon, not long after they had set off from Pyre Fortress, to find a dead fire after he had secured a couple of rabbits for supper. "What would you do if you were alone in the wild?"

"I would eat fruit."

The prince shook his head and rolled his eyes. *The boy is foolish indeed* and he still had that fatuous smile on his face. As game was becoming more and more scarce, so was fruit. Most times, Themba would be loathed to return home carrying nothing but rabbits, but they were a long way away from home and the lush hunting grounds he was accustomed to. "That is why you are not a warrior. A soldier listens to his master's instruction." He thought of his uncle, Comrade Chengetaii, who had always had a demeaning and condescending tone toward him. Themba now knew that the captain had only good intentions. He had made him a formidable warrior, a savior of some sorts, Umuzi—the Champion of Pyyros and Shambamuto. "Enough of your prattle. We are being followed."

"By whom? I don't see anyone."

"Just stay alert, okay?" Themba was tired. All the way from Pyre Fortress he had to explain the most rudimentary of concepts. "How do I do this, Prince Themba? How do I do that? He wouldn't have been surprised if the boy asked him how to empty his bowls. He shook his head and bit his tongue. The boy wasn't completely useless. He had after all acquired the information that Queen Zandile and Princess Nia had taken flight. "Your time will come when the time is right. You know, I trained with a stick for many seasons before I was even allowed to look at a spear." Smoke was rising from a shack. "That must be the eatery."

The door opened with a creak. Themba had to pinch his nostrils as they entered. There was the thick smell of sweat, mold and unwashed bodies even the smoke blowing from people's pipes couldn't mask. Layers of dust lined every inch of the room, cobwebs stuck in every corner, and ants marched across the grime-laden floor.

In a dark corner sat a hooded figure. Licorice scented smoke clouds rose from his spiraled pipe. "That is one of the men that has been following us," informed Themba behind his palm.

"Oh," stuttered Pikoro. "Who do you think he is?"

"I don't know. Maybe a spy sent by King Maghedzi or Chief-Treasurer Mutasa. Don't worry about him. Keep your head down. You don't want him to know we know he is following us."

"Whatever you say, master."

In the middle of the eatery on a large table sat several suspiciously armed men having their fills. Themba didn't mind. He had a weapon too—several, his trusty spear, which was now accompanied by his new glass blade, Torch, a bow made from rich darkwood, a knife that dangled by his waist, and a war club that rested in the crack of his back. He whistled and beckoned to be served. "Two large bowls of sorghum pap, nightshade and tenderloin. I want the silver skin trimmed off, as well as the gristle and fat. I want it nice and compact. You understand?"

"Sorry, we do not have that here."

The prince was used to the finest of cuts. "Okay then, bring us the best of whatever you have. Oh, and two calabashes of *doro*. Our equines outside need to be cleaned and fed too." Themba brought out a head of shells, which the innkeeper snatched.

After weighing the shells in his palm, the innkeeper leaned closer to the prince and in a low tone warned, "Those men are thieves—killers. They are members of the Matsotsi. You'd do good to eat quickly and leave. Don't say I didn't warn you." With that the innkeeper slipped away to perform his tasks.

"So, what is our next move?" inquired Pikoro.

"The Sangoma says there are five instruments spread out across the kingdoms. These instruments are the key to us finding the nyaminyami." Themba pulled out five stones from his bag, all different colors, each representing a flute, mbira, marimba, hosho, harp and ngoma. He bade Pikoro to close his eyes and then jumbled the stones in his fist. When Pikoro plucked at his palm, Themba's blood eye lit up, matching the stone, crimson, ruby and scarlet.

With a new wind of excitement, Themba snatched his map from his bag and spread it over the table. Chuckling, he declared with the tip of his knife pressing over the map, "Here is where we are going! I hear some of the best musicians reside there. Perhaps we can get some clues that will help us in our search."

His enthusiasm was interrupted when the food finally came, a combination of rodent and half rotten vegetables. He was about to complain but his destiny lay await. He didn't have time to quibble. As he picked at the bowl, he felt a presence hovering above him. He looked up. The largest of the men the innkeeper had warned him about stood in front of him with a wide crooked grin that stretched from ear to ear. Themba could also smell him, a farrago of old *umqombothi* and night soil. "Good day," Themba greeted politely, with a big smile of his own beaming from his face. "How can I help you and your fine men?" Themba used his hands to convey his message. His arms felt much lighter, without the jewelry he was used to wearing—gold, silver, diamonds and sapphires. "Join us." He lifted his *umqombothi* and offered it.

All he understood from the man's seemingly agitated speech was a truculent, "Akuwa," and then with the back of the man's hand, Themba's calabash was rocking from side to side and decent beer seeping into the cracks of the stone floor.

The prince remained phlegmatic, with a supercilious smirk across his face. He rose from his stool, and in the best way he could, explained he didn't want any trouble.

"Your shells," Themba understood, "And no trouble."

He surveyed the eatery. The whole tavern was now looking his and Pikoro's way and some had risen from their benches and stools. His math counted seven enemies. "I need my shells," the prince insisted. He motioned his hand to his mouth. "To eat." *To save you, to save you all*, he muttered under his breath. He needed shells for their quotidian needs like food, shelter and any other trouble that would come his way. If need be, he meant to buy his way out of trouble, but it seemed this man wanted it all, which was made plain when the man pressed a thick finger onto the hippo-prince's chest.

"Me eat for you."

"It's okay. I can eat for myself. It is wise for you, if you go back to your table, sit down, drink, eat and be merry." Themba felt this could have been simplified if he mentioned he was a prince, but he wanted to keep a low profile. "I buy for you and your friends next round of *umqombothi. Kachasu* even," he winked. "I even drink with you." The prince looked around laughing lightly but reluctantly. "I have jokes and stories." After receiving a few more barbed insults, with sudden force, Themba had the bottom of his palm crashing the bridge of the thief's nose. He couldn't have hoped for a better strike, but he didn't have time to savor it. He twisted his waist, swirled around, and with the side of his heel, had an attacker flat on the ground. He had the next foe groaning in agony as he had his wrist bending backward, sending his knife flaying to the floor. A cup came flying the prince's way, but he did well to dodge it, and leapt for the oncoming brigand. Themba swept him to the ground and knocked him unconscious with the butt of his spear. He thought that would deter the rest, but unfortunately, this time, he was surrounded. "I don't want to fight," shouted the prince, but his words were drowned in the melee.

Pikoro's stick waved left and right, catching a Matsotsi in the face, but soon enough they were too close, too numerous. He dropped his stick and wrapped his arms around the closest body and found himself in an embrace that led them to the floor in a twisted stranglehold.

As the prince and page wrestled there was a sudden crack and then another as the hooded man had entered the melee on their behalf. He waved his spear around, but soon enough the Matsotsi came again. The hooded man's blade spun creating a gust of wind, then swung left and right at the oncoming onslaught equivalent to a swarm of bees. Soon Themba was on all fours spitting blood after a savage club to his chest. The prince's cheek felt the cold floor when an elbow crashed down on his back.

He strained to open an eye.

He found himself in a fishing boat, tugging at a fishing line until Pikoro's jacaranda shaded eyes gleamed at him, his tongue wild and mouth filled with razors—his sharp nails clawing at the canoe, rocking it from side to side. *You should have stayed in Shambamuto,* the prince whined, but his head turned when sudden screams, the tear of flesh and crunching of bone evoked his consciousness. One by one men dropped in agony and the ones who didn't, ran for their lives.

"Quickly, Prince Themba, this way," called a voice.

Somehow a calabash hadn't been touched by the ruckus. Themba grabbed it, took a long-hurried gulp, wiped off the froth from his moustache and hurried out, following Pikoro and the hooded stranger onto the settlement thoroughfare where they were met by a mob moving their way with pickaxes, hoes and sickles in hand.

"This way!" Their diminutive savior hollered. They sped past the stable boy, all the while fog creeping toward them like probing fingers. They launched onto their equines and galloped through the thick mist and into the surfeit of tall grass, laughing as stones and rotten fruit flew their way.

"Where did you learn how to fight?" Themba asked, when they finally halted atop a hill well away from the hamlet. "I have never seen a midget swing an axe so heavy," the prince praised, as he causally stroked his equine's side.

"I am not a midget. I am a dwarf."

"Oh." Themba was surprised. "I didn't know there was a difference." Despite that, Themba could see that the dwarf was strong, like a ratel, the way he held his two-handed axe with one hand, and the carnage the dwarf had caused at the eatery.

"My name is Jag'd, and this here, is Hondo. We overheard you were going on some sort of expedition. Let us join your team, Prince Themba of Akuwa."

"How do you know who I am?"

"I knew your ancestor, King Anesu. You are a spitting image of him."

Themba smiled inwardly. Many a man would lie to join the company of a prince of Akuwa. "The elders teach us, if you want to go quickly, go alone."

"And they also say," the dwarf replied, "If you want to go far, go together."

This dwarf has a point. Behind all the hunting techniques and war strategies Themba had learnt, he remembered the saying, *cross the river in a crowd and the crocodile won't devour you.* "How do I know that you are not false?"

"Ask Rwizi, if he is still alive. But if I had a guess, that tough old hippo still is. He was a man of great physical stamina and intellectual vigor. Feisty that one was and courageous. I was there with him on the journey to the top of the Sacred Hills to seek the council of the Sisters when Hippo Valley was torn apart by disparity and strife. My fellow dwarves, Mud'k and Mamdab'o died, leaving me alone as the last of my kind." He looked down and shook his head before returning to meet Themba's gaze with tears in his eyes. "I have never met a better man than your ancestor, King Anesu. His reign left a profound effect on Hippo Valley and the entire world! If you are half the man he is, I will serve you until my dying breath and beyond!"

"And what about you?" Themba inquired as he appraised the dwarf's accomplice. "What's your story?"

"I have none," answered Hondo, pulling back his hood, revealing a face Themba somewhat found familiar. He had a shaggy head of dark hair flecked with grey, and in a dark bronze face, a pair of keen hazel eyes with a roguish hint. Below them was a strong jaw decorated with a thin beard. "Jag'd and I have been wondering around the kingdoms finding whatever work we can." He wore his loincloth short, so that his knees and part of his thighs were exposed.

The dwarf dropped a knee. His bald head gleamed in the sun and his large ears tweaked. He had a heavy brow and a piggish nose. His black eyes were large and in them, Themba saw in him a stern officiousness. What he needed were docile men he could rely upon. When he would try to help his mother in the kitchen as a young calf, she would pat him on his curious little fingers and tell him, "One pot, one cook."

"As you have seen, I am as good as anyone with an axe," continued the dwarf. "Your expedition will require you to brave crags and rocky hills, correct? I'm familiar with those too. Our people are of the mountains." He paused and looked down mournfully. "Once were. I'm quite handy at metal work as well and . . ." the dwarf stroked his beard in thought. "Oh, I can sing too."

It was a long journey they were about to embark on, to several locations across the kingdoms. A sweet voice could lessen the burden and the dwarf had experience in such expeditions. Themba turned to Hondo. "And you? What are you good at?"

"Fighting," he replied matter-of-factly as he dropped a knee. "It's all I'm good for actually. I'm also quite good at making fires. I gather you've had a problem with that on your travels."

"Why would you want to join me? We are likely to die."

"For the adventure," replied Hondo.

"Yes," agreed Jag'd. "Adventure, but most importantly, I made a vow to serve King Anesu for the remainder of my days."

Themba looked upon the dwarf wearily for some moments, and then at Hondo. He took out his skin and took a sip, his eyes still suspiciously gazing upon the couple and the spear stuck in the earth, tight in Hondo's grasp. "*Masimbi* steel?"

"You are familiar with it?" replied Hondo.

"I am. But I have something much better." Themba slid out Torch, twisted her between his fingers and offered her. "A gift …"

"…For taking off the Ashu champion's head," finished Jag'd, handing the spear back, after a good and thorough inspection.

"You heard?" asked the prince.

"We saw it. We have been observing you since we spotted you marching with King Maghedzi and his Fireflies. How brave you were. Walking into Death Valley alone and defeating the Ashu champion."

"I only work through the ancestors."

"And may you continue to do so, Prince Themba of Akuwa!"

"Can any of you play any instruments?"

"Several," replied Jag'd.

Themba extended his hand and helped the dwarf rise, broad hands, about twice the prince's and hairy, as were his legs and chest. "Do you drink?"

"I was wondering when you were going to ask."

Chapter 36

Distributaries

Princess Nia and Wafula canoed toward Chipiko, side by side, as the wind brushed their faces. *This is what I was made for!* Nia felt an exhilaration she had never felt prior, even more so than when her father let her hold his shiny black spear. That night was the first and last time she saw a semblance of a smile on the king's face as she waved it around and pretended she was slaying a horde of marauding tokoloshe. Now she was doing battle for real.

Hokoyo stood at the front of the head vessel, the largest canoe of the flotilla of canoes screaming encouragement. "Row," he bellowed. "Faster," he screamed as spittle fell over his lips, wide and full. He had divided the rescue brigade into two battalions, one led by himself that would canoe down the Ngorongoro tributary, and strike from the unmanned Chipiko river bank, whilst the other, led by Boitumelo, would attack by land.

There was smoke rising from the village when they arrived, just as the Chipiko village gates fell. A small child wandered around aimlessly crying for its parents as smoke, arrows and the cacophonous sound of terror dominated the village thoroughfare. Soon the child was scooped up by a man and taken away as it kicked and wriggled. One man fell to a painted woman who moved faster than anyone Nia had seen. Beside her was a man, clad in green, who stopped a man dead in his tracks with the wave of his hand before his spear cut through the man's stomach. Next, the green-clad man spun like a whirlwind, drawing in the attackers headed his way, cutting them into mince.

He beckoned for his accomplices, pointed his barbarous spear and commanded, "Free the livestock! Free the children! Kill the rest!"

Nia couldn't believe her eyes when Hokoyo vaulted out of the canoe and onto the riverbank. He landed with his cow-tails billowing behind him. He seemed to be able to fly for some moments, soaring well over his own height, performing a roll and then unsheathing his spear. The attackers drew back at his feral sight, with his concave cheeks that sharpened his jawline crowned with a deep ample cleft. They were clutching swords, spears, clubs and axes, but despite that, fear shone through their eyes, so much so, one of them let his spear slip and darted off into the carnage. "He is a beast. He is no man!"

The rest finally summoned enough pluck and attacked, but the masked Nia, Wafula and the remainder of the naval contingent were soon by Hokoyo's side.

"Attack," Hokoyo screamed with ravenous animality. "Kill them, kill them all!" Left and right Hokoyo laid about, cleaving off the first man's leg at the knee and slicing through the stomach of the second. The third buried his spear into Hokoyo's shield, convex and elliptical. Hokoyo slammed it into the attacker's face, knocked him off his feet, and slew him as he tried to rise again. "Who is your leader?" he barked, but there was no response, just lifeless eyes staring at him. He turned and grabbed a woman by the neck and hoisted her over his head. "Who is your leader?" She didn't answer so he pressed harder. "Who is he?"

"Ba…tu…saii," she croaked before her throat snapped.

Meanwhile, Wafula was struggling to wrench his spear free from a rib cage. As he finally managed to, he felt a stinging pain in his left shoulder, so he spun and shoved his spear through the attacker's face. The woman swayed momentarily until Wafula jerked the steel free and sent the corpse staggering loose-limbed across the red soil. As Hokoyo gave him an acknowledging nod,

Wafula heard the remainder of the Ngorongoro forces cackle and scream as they stormed through the fallen Chipiko gates.

Boitumelo and Bashiri were the first through, howling like rabid dogs on a blood trail. Bomani was not far behind them, ducking an arrow before sending an axe spinning through the air to catch a man in the chest. He rolled under an attack and retrieved the axe. Blood erupted from his victim's torso creating a shower in which he basked. He shrieked in ecstasy, and then charged for the next victim, but that shortly ended when an arrow flew through his neck.

Wafula shook his head sympathetically, and dashed toward the village thoroughfare. Livestock thundered their hooves, trapped in their enclosure, barking and hooting from the mayhem all around, and Hokoyo was the chief architect. *He makes violence a dance*, Wafula gasped, as the bullish warrior slay one man after the next, parrying attacks lazily like it was all a boring game to him. *He is one but fights like a regiment!*

Hokoyo would have slain another, but he felt a stabbing pain on his side. He looked down and smiled at the sight of his blood. "Well struck," he commended, before spinning and taking the foolish assailant's head off clean. He wiped the blood off the axe with his skimpy loincloth that exposed his huge thighs, twisted his head about and searched for his next victim, eyebrows bridged like an ox. "There you are," he snarled. He darted across the thoroughfare, back toward the riverbank, pushing bodies out of his way. "You!" Hokoyo called across the carnage. "Are you the leader of this battalion?"

After pulling out his spear from a corpse, the man turned toward Hokoyo and casually answered, "What if I am?" His cotton wraparound was spotted with blood and gore.

"Then you are a dead man, Ba—tu—saii!" With bridged eyebrows, Hokoyo bulled toward him.

Batusai leapt to meet him, spinning his spear over his head and then stabbing from behind his neck. Hokoyo performed a roll-dodge and retaliated with a shield-bash, creating a cyclone that sent Batusai backward in a gale of wind. He gave him no respite. He was on him immediately after, this time with a low attack, which Batusai deflected off his spear shaft. Hokoyo came again, this time high, but Batusai swerved away from it like he could stop time, and repeated that feat left, right, and right again.

Hokoyo was perplexed. He had never dueled anyone quite so fast and could sense a supernatural power emanating from his every stroke—his every movement. He recollected himself and paced around formulating an alternative strategy.

Batusai, perhaps sensing weakness, came charging with his spear, but Hokoyo blocked it, kicked him in the chest, sending Batusai back-first into a tree trunk. Violet, lilac and mauve tinged leaves fell softly over Batusai as Hokoyo raised his spear and put all his weight behind his strike. Like a crab spider, Batusai spun away just in time to watch Hokoyo's spearhead crash through the tree bark.

Batusai was now back on the offensive, slashing sideways, but he only found a shadow. "The antelope can never outrun the cheetah," barked Hokoyo, catching Batusai at the throat with a bloody fist and hoisting him into the air.

"Yes, that is true, but an antelope can turn sharply at the last moment!" With that, Hokoyo felt a bolt of force on his chest that hoisted him backward and into the bloodstained waters.

On the Chipiko thoroughfare Nia cut through flesh and bone. After striking down an opponent, she stopped and surveyed the carnage. She could feel warm blood trickling down her fingers, but nothing could faze her, not after all she had been through, fleeing one city to the next, evading land and water creatures. *No longer have I the emotion of fear . . . There is nothing anyone can do to me. There isn't any pain I haven't known.* The sound of a baby crying interrupted her thoughts. She followed it into a hut.

She raised her spear immediately when she entered, but stopped mid-cast when she discovered a girl, about her age, with the baby cradled in her arms. "Put that child down," commanded Nia. "Slowly."

The girl did as she was told, erecting herself with her arms spread out wide.

"What are you doing here?"

"I am performing our Mother's work. You should too."

"You came here, to these people's home to destroy their community and abduct their livelihoods and young."

"We are setting them free."

Nia could see there was no way she would convince the girl otherwise. It was apparent by the stubbornness in her eyes, eyes that were old and storied amongst her smooth childish facial features. Nia shook her head in pity. "How did you end up with these people?"

"Men came to our village with spears, demanding all unmarried women to travel to Pyyros where we would be purified at the Flame Festival. My father helped me escape and died for his troubles. During my flight, I met a man, the Mufundisi. He changed my life."

Nia slipped off her mask, revealing her face. Bomani's stricken body came into her thoughts, and the carnage the attackers had caused, the burning huts and little children that cried out for their parents. The cut on her shoulder was burning too. She lifted her spear and released. She didn't know why she missed from such a short range. She had become so accurate she could take down a bird in full flight. The girl darted toward the exit, leaving the baby crying on the granite floor. "North of the fever trees. You will find freedom there."

When Nia returned outside, Batusai was screaming, "Sound the retreat! Withdraw to the rallying point!" Trumpets followed his instruction as the attackers clutched on whatever they could as they made a break for the village gate.

followed the Ngorongoro battalion as they pushed the attackers out. When they had disappeared into the bush, she ran to Wafula who stood by the village threshold panting, blooded up with a swollen eye. She reached for his side. "We have to take care of that."

"I'll be fine. We need to make sure everyone is okay." They had secured the village, but at a great price—burnt huts, abducted children and stolen livestock. "I think he's still alive." Wafula ran to an injured man's side and surveyed his wounds. "He looks like he won't make it!" He barked for the healer who was hard at work tending to the other survivors. The unfortunate ones were laid across the thoroughfare for family members to identify.

Later the Ngorongoro contingent prepared to return home. Wafula turned to Nia. "You see, Chafu? We make a great team. We always have."

Nia could not disagree, from when they were little nuisances devising different ways to amuse themselves, from flying kites, climbing trees and rocks, to discovering ancient ruins. "That's true."

"I hope you are not upset with me. I had nothing to do with the marriage arrangement with Eniola. I do not love her."

"I know."

"I am going to tell my father I do not want to marry her."

Nia looked down. "About your proposal. I'm sorry, but I can't. I mean, I think I love you…I do…but…" She stroked his chest lightly up and down and played for a few moments with his necklace which was now bloodied. "…But I'm not ready. My destiny lies elsewhere. I hope you don't hate me."

Wafula looked down, trying his hardest to keep his face, but after some moments, he raised it and declared cheekily, "You wouldn't make a good wife anyway. I will wait for you, though. You are worth it. One day you will want to settle down."

She looked up and smiled. "I have to go. Don't follow me. Promise me."

Wafula nodded. "What should I tell your mother?"

"This is what my mother wanted for me." She smiled. "Use your last wish wisely."

"I will, Princess Nia."

Chapter 37

Estuaries

Mount Pyyros rumbled as the Sangoma hang on for dear life high up on Mount Pyyros' mountainside. His life had flashed before his eyes and taken him back to where his story began, in the somber shades of the Mukuvisi Woodlands. Now returned to the present, he glanced down and saw the bubbling lava that was menacing up the Guardian of the Lost City's throat, so he shuffled along, felt for a grove above, and hauled himself up as crumbles of rock fell over his headdress. His eyes followed the debris and watched as they sank into the burning void, just like his trusty mystical staff he was never without. "Why did I take those precious stones," he regretted. The Guardian had warned them. It was too late now, he shook his head, prayed for forgiveness so he might be welcomed into the spirit realm, and wondered how he would be remembered—as the most talented spirit-medium of his time? a muporofita whose life was to heal? Or would he be remembered as he truly was? The woodland fiend of Molora? A grave-defiler and thief?

Life appeared above him. He willed himself for one last push, but as his fingers latched onto the final edge he saw King Maghedzi glaring down at him, his thick eyebrows bridged and flaring viciously, looking as sinister as the violent fumes that now decorated the Pyyros backdrop high up atop the volcanic mountain side. "Mambo!" the spirit-medium pled. "Give me a hand. I can't hold on for much longer!" His arms were getting tighter, weaker, well past their breaking point.

"The flute. Hand it over first."

The Sangoma did as he was bade. He threw his arm behind, unfastened the latch that secured the ancient artifact and hoisted it up towards the king who looked like a father reunited with a long-lost son when he wrapped his fingers around the instrument. "Mambo," the mage cried. "Raging Inferno, Eternal Flame, Bush Fire," he tried.

Maghedzi paid him no mind. After more pleas, finally the king looked down and sneered. His nose flared and then wrinkled as he raised his foot, and just as his sandal thundered down, Reza flew to the rescue tackling the king to the ground.

She cast her fangs at him as they locked in a ferocious struggle, like two lion cubs vying for pride supremacy, snapping viciously until she caught the king by the shoulder as they rolled back and forth over Mount Pyyros' shoulder. The king managed to set himself free and took out his dagger as Reza cackled frighteningly as the king's blood dripped from her snout. They paced around each other until the hyena attacked, but Maghedzi did a quick spin and sliced at the side of the beast, grinning as he felt muscle tear. The hyena groaned as she looked to her wounds, her bushy black tail flapping wildly as chunky beads of saliva dragged from her mouth. She dug her paws into the dirt and leapt towards the awaiting king who rolled out of the way just before Reza's teeth took another pound of his flesh. She cackled and lunged once more with a ferocious barrage but Maghedzi was the master of several forms of the Bush Fire stance. He shifted left and right and back, dancing his way from Reza's bite stronger than any creature the Creator had devised. She retreated, cackled and then came again, but this time, the king shifted to the side and sunk his dagger deep into the hyena's back. He held it there for a good while, Reza's whines but music to him, twisting and turning the blade, deeper when he thought of his renegade wife and daughter. He had searched the whole kingdom and beyond, and had even destroyed Ido in that pursuit. His only hope now was the Desert Snake.

Satisfied, he staggered off the hyena and dragged his feet towards the Guardian's mouth to finish the job, but when he arrived, there was no Sangoma in sight. He picked up the flute sitting amongst the spree and set it to his lips. He took a long deep breath, but before he exhaled, the flute rolled from his fingers as a steering pain engulfed his upper thigh. He turned, furious, like a hippo over a camp fire and searched the area as he grabbed the arrow with both hands, gnashed his teeth and heaved. The next arrow sent him staggering backwards until he was hanging unsteadily over the lava behind him. He felt hands upon him that snatched him away from the welcoming lava beneath and tossed him to safety as the Guardian looked down at him. Maghedzi willed himself back onto a knee and looked up, bewildered, gasping as a blur clad in crisp white became whole.

"I did as you commanded me—as always," his adopted son, Asha, the Desert Snake began, as he threw the mangled carcass of the boar-croc, ngiri'mamba, in front of the king. He casually stroked his hair, now back to its full voluptuous glory and continued, savoring the look of horror that had twisted Maghedzi's face into a monstrosity, once the king saw Kuluma's olive-green armor-scaled coat riddled with holes. "I found your wife and daughter. However, when I was bringing them back to you, as you bade, your queen told me some things. She told me you had been deceiving me my whole life. When I heard that Prince Themba of the Akuwa was in Pyyros, I got excited. I thought, finally, my chance for revenge had come, after all these years of patience and prayer. I told Zandile all about it, and she told me that I was mistaken. Words cannot express the heart-sickening dejection I experienced at the moment." His luminous eyes darkened like a predator on its prey. "It wasn't Farakaii that massacred my family, it was you. Admit it."

Maghedzi denied all the charges, but soon he began to reason, and invoked the ancestors short of begging, when the

Northman told him that he once desired King Farakaii's children's heads.

"You wouldn't. I raised you amongst my flock, like a son."

"No, you bred me to be your henchman."

The king looked around at nothing. He was no longer on Mount Pyyros' slopes overlooking his kingdom, but above the Great Divide. He could feel the silky soft sand and ground below yield as the golden flecks fell over his sandals, but this sand was far from golden. It was dark and bloody with severed human limbs around him. "What do you want?" he finally said. "Cows? Gold? Land? I'll give you whatever you want!"

"What I want is my family back."

"You can have that. I can help you return to your people."

"I thought they were all dead."

"Not all of them."

"The passage is sealed."

"There is a way, and I can show you how. I have the final piece to the riddle. The flute . . ." Maghedzi searched the area, but it was gone. So was the hyena, Reza. "The Heart Stone . . ." he began rummaging in his bag for the gem. "Its true power was revealed to me in the Lost City of the Volcans. That is where I just came from! It is the key to crossing the Great Divide and uniting the kingdoms against the coming Evil that means to annihilate us." Panic-stricken, he turned the bag upside down and emptied the contents. He started patting himself all over, frantic, looking for the lithic, but it was nowhere to be found. His grizzly voice wilted when he finally realized. "It's that wizard...the Sangoma...he...he..." His shoulders sank, and his arms, once full of mite, fell loosely down his side. "... stole it from me." The king shook his head as he gritted his massive jaws and took one last wistful look down at his dominion, Pyyros, with all its districts, the neighboring villages, the winding hills and the vast grasslands where his cattle fed—the kingdom he had steered through the Great Dry and rescued from anonymity.

"That is where you are wrong, father. YOU are the Evil."

Resigned to his fate, Maghedzi tilted his head to the side and stretched his neck. "Do it then! As I taught you! Clean and swift," he barked.

The Desert Snake turned his head when he heard an echoing cry in the distant sky that filled him with the most uncomfortable of dispositions. He followed it, squinting from the sun's rays, and as he did, his mouth dropped when he saw a ball of fire weaving a tail of black smoke towards the elysian tapis of the amber dyed horizon. When the anomaly was one with sun, he returned his attention to the man who had raised him—a wounded man, not the same warrior king he watched conquer village after next leaving soot and ash in his wake as he expanded the Piripiri dominion—the man who had taught him everything he knew— how to fight, how to spite—how to never forgive a slight. "That won't be necessary," Asha finally declared. "Your end will neither be swift, nor clean." He slid out Zaza-Feyi from her scabbard and blew the dust away from her pommel he had now fashioned into his late daughter's image, a long face with dimples that appeared when she laughed. He brushed her braided hair and lingered over her wide staring eyes that smiled at him as her side, pale and grey rippled and shimmered. He calmly wrapped his hands tightly around her hold, pulled her back, and with the blurred images of his slain blood smiling from the firmament, slit his eyes and set his family free.

Curtis lives in Sweden. He got an itch to write early in his life and pursued these activities through comic books and short stories. It all came together with the release of his first published book, "The Rites of Passage: Red Jacaranda Leaves". Curtis holds a teaching degree, a Bachelor's in Political Science, and a Master's in International Relations.

***